BUCK YOU

BUCK COWBOYS (#2)

ELLE THORPE

WWW.ELLETHORPE.COM

#3

For Thomas,

As you get older, remember that it's okay to be the nice guy. Not every girl wants a bad boy. Some girls want a Dominic.

PROLOGUE

I knew pain. There'd been spills off my bike when I was a kid. Or the time I broke my arm after I jumped off the barn roof. And there'd definitely been injuries from being stupid enough to climb onto the back of a bull and try to ride him for eight seconds.

But those had been few and far between. And oddly minor, for how dangerous the sport I loved was.

I heard what the fans said about me on the circuit. That I somehow drew 'easy' bulls because my dad was Kai 'Frost' Hunt, four times WBRA champion. But anyone with half a brain and a lick of bull riding knowledge knew nobody wanted an easy bull, anyway. Nobody wanted one who didn't kick or spin or try his damn best to get you off his back. You wanted the bulls that had you digging your heels in, every muscle in your body working to keep you on so you didn't end up mincemeat beneath his hooves. Those were the bulls that got you big scores. Those were the bulls that won you championship buckles.

But that left the whispers of the other riders. Those hurt more than the fans, and they were none too subtle.

She doesn't belong here. This ain't no girly competition.

The judges go easy on her because she's a woman.

The judges score her higher because she's Frost's daughter.

Nobody ever said it to my face, but I heard it all anyway. I heard it in the way they frowned, or in their annoyed hat toss when my score rocketed up the leaderboard. I heard it in the way I wasn't just one of the guys, who liked to drink beer at the bar after work, like I was back home.

Their rejection was a different sort of pain altogether, but one I'd dealt with my entire life and could no longer afford to care about. I'd had to learn to lock it up, and shove it deep inside, where it was barely even a pinprick.

Because I was going to be the first woman on the WBRA circuit.

I was going to win the whole damn thing, take home the check, and add a shiny championship belt buckle to my collection. No matter what it took.

Until I wasn't.

Until I was thrown off that bull at the Masonville Invitational, landed awkwardly, and heard the pop of my shoulder dislocating.

Until the acute agony of muscle tearing ripped through me.

Until the bull's hooves slammed down and shattered the bone so bad it pierced through my skin.

A new pain like nothing I'd ever experienced before splintered through my entire body. It radiated from my shoulder in a blinding rush that took out all other senses.

I lost the screaming of the crowd and the smell of the dirt beneath my broken body. My mouth filled with blood, but I didn't taste it. When my vision flickered, it was almost a welcome relief.

I needed to get up and run. I needed to get out from

beneath the bull's hooves that pounded into my flesh, vicious and unforgiving.

But the worst of the pain came from my head, and the knowledge that with one ride, my career was over before it had even truly begun.

Nobody came back from this sort of injury.

So when the darkness tried to take me, I let it.

Because there was no pain worse than that.

1

Dominic

Maria Kaur. 44 Eastbridge Ave.

My gaze traced the letters of her name, running silently over each line and curve. Eastbridge Ave wasn't that far from here. Just on the other side of town. That couldn't be right.

You sure? I typed back.

Wouldn't have told you if I wasn't.

"Dom!"

I snapped my head up at my father's shout and guiltily shoved my phone back in my pocket. "Yeah? What's up?"

"You just gonna stand there texting your girlfriends or do you want to come and actually do some work? You know that thing I pay you to do?"

I jogged across the yard to our barn where Dad had lined up buckets of feed for the animals. I got busy scooping pellets from a bag and distributing it evenly, just like I'd done a million other times over the years. "Sorry," I muttered, feeling like a naughty kid who'd tried to shirk his responsibilities. "Won't happen again."

My dad shot a glance at me. "Why do you look like

you've seen a ghost? It wasn't that big a deal. I'm just bustin' your balls. This place will be yours soon enough, and then you can set whatever hours you want. You're almost never late, anyway."

I nodded distractedly. I could only remember a handful of times, ever, that I'd been even two minutes late for work. It wasn't in my nature. My dad expected me to be here at six each morning, so I was here at five 'til. Unlike my two younger brothers, who were still probably in bed and would roll up for work at whatever time they deemed it worthy.

Ah, to be a selfish teenager. It must have been nice.

Like I could talk. I shot another glance at my father, and my chest panged with what I'd done. I was just as selfish as my brothers. In a much worse way. Nobody's life would change dramatically if they were thirty minutes late to work every second day.

But what I'd done could change everything. Not just for me, but for my parents...and for the woman I didn't know, but whose address now burned a hole in my phone.

Maria Kaur. 44 Eastbridge Ave.

Was Kaur a married name? Or would that have been my surname if she'd decided to keep me? Pain ricocheted through my chest, until I realized my dad was staring at me, waiting for me to say something.

"Sorry, what?" I tried to focus on him.

"I was just saying I talked to Frost last night."

"Summer's dad? How is she?" I was suddenly a whole lot more interested than I had been a minute ago. Like a man dying in the desert, I lapped up information about Summer Hunt as if it were water.

I always had. I hadn't heard from her in almost a year, not since the night of her accident, but it hadn't stopped me thinking about her. Constantly. Even though that wasn't my right.

Dad picked up a handful of feed, letting it run through his fingers and back into the bucket. "Physically? She's not riding anymore. I know that much. Sounds like she's given up trying. She's moving to the city."

I dropped my shovel, cringing as it clattered to the ground. "You're kidding? She was talking about it last time I was out there, but it's been over a year. I just assumed she'd changed her mind." And by changed her mind, I meant come to her senses. Summer Hunt was as country as I was. I couldn't picture her living in a city any more than I could picture myself renting an apartment in New York and suddenly wearing suits instead of jeans.

I shuddered at the thought of a stuffy, white, button-down shirt and an ugly patterned tie that would choke me.

Dad picked up my shovel and handed it back to me. "Apparently not. Frost is cut up about it. Disappointed she won't make the pros now but stressed out of his head about finding someone to take her job, too. His other daughters aren't interested. Neither of them ride."

"She's always done a lot out there. Big shoes to fill."

Dad and I both went back to work in companionable silence, distributing feed buckets to each of our bulls, and I used the manual work to push Summer and her future plans out of my head. Like I'd had to do so many other times, I reminded myself she wasn't my concern. She'd made that pretty clear with her radio silence.

It was better if I just concentrated on my own fuckin' business. And my business was these bulls. We had cattle out in fenced-off fields at the back of our property, but it was summer, and they'd be just fine munching on the grass until it started getting cold again. Unlike our buckers, who needed constant specialized feed and vitamins to keep them in prime condition for rodeos. A sick bull didn't kick. And no cowboy wanted to ride an animal that just stood there in the ring like a limp biscuit.

Dad and I split up with me silently vowing to put everything else out of my head and do the job I was paid to do, but every pen I went to, my phone buzzed in my pocket, reminding me of what I'd started. I tried to ignore it, but eventually, curiosity got the better of me.

Checking to make sure my dad wasn't around, I pulled the phone out. Julian's messages lit it up and I scanned over each of them, until one caught my eye.

Dude, I'm sitting out the front of her house and I think she has a family. A husband. Maybe a couple of kids? I think you have a whole family over here you have no idea about. You want me to look into it some more?

My throat closed up. *No.*

No? What are you going to do, then?

I watched my dad from across the yard. He was a good guy, and I was so lucky to have been raised by him. He'd taught me everything I knew about bulls and riding and ranching. Despite the fact I wasn't his biological child, and my two younger brothers were, it was me he wanted to pass the ranch on to when he retired, just like his father had passed it on to him.

He had no idea I'd opened a can of worms by searching for my birth parents.

Now, there was only one way to close it. I had to know. It had been eating away at the corners of my mind for the best part of a decade. I had to make it stop before it drove me completely insane.

Don't do anything. I'm going over there. I need to talk to her.

After feeding my father some sort of bullshit excuse about needing to run into town for supplies, I drove my truck across our little country town and turned down Eastbridge Avenue with my heart hammering. The properties at this end of town weren't like ours. My family lived in an older-style farmhouse that had been renovated from the original my great-grandfather had built a hundred years ago. I'd moved out to one of the newer cabins on the property once I'd turned eighteen and needed some space, but the hundreds of acres of land that surrounded the dwellings were all ours.

Here, the properties were smaller. Subdivides from what was once a property like ours, probably sold off during a year where the rain didn't come as expected, or cattle prices bottomed out. When those things happened, you could either tough it out to hope for a better go next year. Or you could sell up to a developer, who would turn your property into a suburban neighborhood, just like the one I drove through now.

I parked my truck out the front of a modest-sized house, with a neatly tended yard, and just gaped at it.

If things had been different, this was where I might have grown up. Without a horse or a cow in sight.

I could barely comprehend that thought. Who the hell was I without bull riding and farmwork? I'd always thought those things were in my blood, my soul. But staring up at my birth mother's house, I realized they weren't.

They were just things taught to me.

My soul didn't know the dirt and hard work and sunrise starts.

Right now, my soul didn't know anything.

"Get out of the fuckin' car, Dom," I muttered to myself. Dad would be expecting me back soon. But nerves and excitement had me gripping the steering wheel too tight, my fingernails pressing into the leather cover.

The front door opened, and a small dark-haired woman strode out into the early morning sunshine, blissfully unaware that I was about to throw a curveball in what seemed like a pretty nice life. She jiggled the handle once, making sure the door was locked, and then hoisted a purse strap over her shoulder.

My entire body locked up, frozen at the sight of her face. She was younger than I'd expected. She didn't really appear all that much older than me, though the adoption records had said she was seventeen when I'd been born, which meant she was in her forties now.

She opened her car door, and I hurtled out of mine, running a few steps across her lawn.

She looked up and flinched.

Couldn't blame her. I was a big guy, a complete stranger, running at her at full speed. I was probably lucky she hadn't maced me.

"Sorry." I dug my heels into the grass to stop myself. "I didn't mean to startle you."

Her eyes were the same deep brown mine were. Her skin the same tanned olive. "Can I help you with something?"

I had no idea why her casually polite words took me by surprise. What had I been expecting? Some sort of mother-child bond that immediately spelled out who I was, without even introducing myself?

Like it was ID, I pulled a business card from my wallet and passed it to her. "Uh, my name is Dominic West. I was adopted twenty-four years ago."

I didn't have to say any more. Maria's eyes widened, the

card and her purse slipping from her shoulder, crashing to the ground, and spilling the contents everywhere.

I lurched forward to help, kneeling to collect a tube of mascara that had tried to roll down the driveway.

Maria crouched to frantically shove things back into her purse, muttering something. When I held out the mascara, she snatched the little tube from my fingers.

Nausea swirled in my stomach, mixing the nerves and excitement all together. On autopilot, I held my hand out for her to shake. It's what I'd been taught as a child when meeting someone new, and it was so ingrained in me now that I did it without thinking, despite the less-than-warm vibes this woman was putting out there. I tried to smile, but it was wobbly.

She glanced down at my hand, then back at the house again. Her frown deepened, lining her forehead with creases. "You can't be here."

Like it was suddenly made of cement, I dropped my hand and shoved it into my pocket. She was right. I'd gone about this all wrong, but I just knew I wouldn't have come at all if I'd stopped to truly think about it. "I know, I'm sorry. Maybe we could meet somewhere, to talk? I can come into town on my lunch break..."

Maria shook her head, fingers clutching for the door handle again. It took her two tries to get it open. "No, I mean you can't be here at all. I don't know what you want from me, but I have a family now. A life. And they don't know anything about you. Or your...please. Just leave."

I blinked. "I know this is out of the blue, but maybe—"

She held a hand up. "Stop. There's no maybe. She told me you had a good home, with good people. Isn't that enough?"

She? I just stared at her, with no idea how to answer that.

Her words rang true. I had the best family I could have ever hoped for. My parents loved me fiercely, and I'd never wanted for anything.

But that didn't stop there being a part of me who needed more. Something inside me had never felt quite whole, and that wasn't something my parents or my brothers or my friends could fix.

"No, it's not enough," I said truthfully.

Irritation flashed in her eyes as she slid behind the wheel. "Well, it's all I have to give. It was all I had then, and it's all I have now. You need to leave."

"No, I—"

"Leave before I call the police."

I gaped at her, checking her expression to be sure she was for real.

She was. There was a dead seriousness in her eyes, and she clutched her cell phone like she'd use it as a weapon if she had to.

Pure, unbridled pain like I'd never felt before shattered through my chest, stealing my breath. This wasn't how this was supposed to go. She was supposed to be happy to see me. She was supposed to stare up at me in wonder, and then smile and maybe wrap her arms around me, and say I was the image of my grandfather as a young man. She was supposed to take my hand, and introduce me to her family, and make coffee so we could talk and catch up on the twenty-four years we'd been apart.

I'd never once let myself consider her complete and utter rejection. Those weren't the sort of dreams adopted kids had. It was always the fairy-tale reunion, where your birth parents had just been waiting for you to reach out so they could welcome you back into their lives.

Maria slammed the door in my face and zoomed out of

the driveway like she couldn't get away from me quick enough.

She didn't look back.

For the tiniest of seconds, I considered going to her front door, banging my fist against the wood, and outing her to her entire family.

For the tiniest of seconds, the thought of imploding her life, just like mine had been, gave me satisfaction.

But I couldn't do it.

I wasn't the guy who did things to hurt others purely out of spite.

I'd just wanted to know her. I'd just wanted a minute of her time to heal the part of me that had always wondered.

I guess I'd gotten it. I knew now. For better or worse, I knew.

I trudged back to the truck with a stifling pressure crushing down on me. It wrapped itself around me, squeezing my chest until I couldn't breathe. I stared at the house I could have grown up in if only she'd wanted me. I sat there, while minutes turned into an hour, feeling more and more claustrophobic as the time slipped by, and still I couldn't bring myself to drive away.

This morning would haunt me. Her scathing rejection would play over and over in my mind, and just when I thought I had forgotten it, I'd be reminded every time I drove past her house on my way out of town.

The look in her eyes as she'd threatened to call the police would break me if I didn't do something.

I pulled out my phone and found the number for my dad's friend, Frost. Georgia was two hours ahead of us, so there was no chance the man wouldn't already be awake, despite the early hour here.

He answered on the first ring. "Dominic? Everything okay?"

No. Everything is shit. I don't want to be in this tiny town where I might run into the woman who birthed me yet can't stand the sight of me. I don't want to drive past the school and know that I have biological siblings inside it who I'll never get to know. And I don't want to go home because my parents know me better than anyone, and they'll see it in my eyes. I'll have to tell them what I've done. I'll have to tell my mother, that despite her giving me everything, I was selfish enough to want more. I'll have to watch something in her eyes die, with the knowledge that I needed more than she could give.

I closed my eyes and leaned my head on the window. "I need to get out of Wyoming for a while. I heard you've got a job opening."

2

"So, do I need to tell you what happened out there?"

Despite the fact Preston Innes was almost a foot taller than me, I had no qualms about berating him when his form sucked. And the ride I'd just witnessed had been about as graceful as a hippo doing a pirouette.

"Yeah, I know." He brushed dirt off the ass of his jeans.

I fought the urge to roll my eyes. "Did you even bother using your core? Those abs of yours just for show, or do they actually work?"

Lennon, my youngest sister, nudged me with her elbow, her eyes wide and horrified. "Summer!"

"What?" I laughed. "If he wants to ride with no shirt on because he's a show pony, then I'm going to give him shit about it."

Preston grinned, but Lennon obviously didn't share my amusement. She'd gone bright red and shuffled off without saying goodbye.

I wasn't surprised. My sisters weren't really into the rodeo scene, and by default, the family business. They weren't used to the daily banter I had with the guys I trained. Especially ones like Preston, who'd been here for years. Normally I had a few of the guys out here to practice as well, but Preston had a big competition coming up, so he'd paid for some extra one-on-one time. Which was just about up. "One last ride," I called. "And this time, make a goddamn effort."

His overconfident swagger had me rolling my eyes. The guy wasn't half as good as he thought he was. But I still liked him. He reminded me of myself. I'd probably been just like him, back in the 'before' as I liked to call my pre-injury days.

A dust cloud at the main entrance kicked up, and when it cleared, Austin's silver BMW picked its way over the ruts and gullies, going about three miles an hour in an attempt to not scratch the paint.

Preston had shooed the bull into the chute, and I'd helped him with his ropes before Austin even got out of his car. He was only just approaching as I climbed over the fence and yanked open the gate.

The bull exploded out of the chute, with Preston sitting high on his back, core actually engaged this time.

"Babe! Come look at this email!"

I waved a hand distractedly in Austin's direction, trying to keep my focus on what Preston was doing. He really just needed to —

"Summer! I need to talk to you."

Irritation spiked through me like an electrified cattle prod.

The bull spun to the left, sending Preston off his back and into the dirt.

I sprinted out into the arena, shouting at the bull, grabbing his attention to steer him away from his rider. If there was only two of us out here, the person not on the back of the bull did all the jobs. Helped with ropes, pulled the gate, and acted as the safety crew. It was rarely a problem with these bulls well used to bucking off their rider, then immediately heading for the exit gate where their food and water waited for them.

But that didn't mean I could be anything but one hundred percent on my game. I was responsible for my students while they were under my guidance. Austin knew that. So the fact he was still talking at me, distracting me from my work, and putting one of my riders at risk, ground my nerves. I'd told him a million times that I couldn't talk when I was at work.

With the bull safely in his pen, I focused back on Preston, who was still sitting in the dirt.

"Better?" he asked, grinning up at me.

I held a hand out and pulled him to his feet. "Yeah, better."

Preston's gaze strayed to Austin. "Your ball and chain seems kinda pissed. You gotta go?"

I didn't want to discuss my personal life with one of the guys I trained. I liked Preston, we were probably even friends, outside our student-coach relationship. But that didn't mean I wanted to talk about my personal life with him. "Your time is up anyway. Just put the gear in the barn, okay?"

He saluted me, like the smart-ass he was, and strode off toward the seating outside the ring.

I finally turned my attention to Austin.

He was watching Preston walk away, his eyes narrowed. Then he scowled at me. "Why are you coaching so late? And where is everyone else?"

He reeked of jealousy, which was just ridiculous. My job was working with young guys. It was just the way it was. But even after all these years together, Austin still made snippy comments about it.

I ignored him, like I always did. I'd learned years ago that it was better to distract Austin than try to explain that I loved him, and the fact I worked with other men was really irrelevant. "What did you want to show me?"

He thrust his phone in my direction. It was one of those yuppie kinds that was almost big enough to be classified as a laptop. I stabbed the screen to light it up.

It was an open email from a big accounting firm in the city.

Austin didn't even wait for me to read it. "I've got a second interview! It says they really liked what I brought to the table and want to discuss things further. I've got an interview next week. Do you want to come with me this time?"

I tried to rack my brain for an excuse. "Ah, no. I don't think so. I'll probably have to work."

Austin's frown reappeared. "Your dad owns this place. Take a day off and come with me. We can look at apartments while we're there. Maybe even go out for dinner and see a show. Stay in a fancy hotel..."

I knew most women would probably jump at that sort of invitation. But I had no interest in seeing a show or eating food that had been blended down to some sort of pulp and slathered across a plate to be artistic. What was wrong with a good old steak and fries from the bar?

I kissed his cheek apologetically. "It's just that Preston has a big ride next weekend, so we have a lot of extra training sessions coming up. Next time? I swear."

Austin put his phone in the pocket of his dress shirt with a sigh. "Sum, I'm going to get this job. You realize that, right?

This second interview is really just a formality. Which means—"

"We're moving. I know. You already told everyone." It came out more forceful than I intended. But I wished he'd stop bringing it up. I knew he was trying to get me excited about the move—the move I'd agreed to—but I just couldn't. I supposed I should at least be happy that we wouldn't be moving there without a job between us.

But I hated the idea of leaving this place. I hated the idea of the polluted city air and high-rise buildings instead of open fields. I didn't want to go. But Austin did. And he'd spent years sacrificing his career while I tried to get to the pros and then recovered from surgery. It was his turn. I had to be fair. Even if the thought of moving made me want to throw myself in the dirt and hug the fence post until I was forcibly removed.

"Anyway, I just wanted to stop by and tell you to start getting moving boxes organized. But now I've got to go prepare." Austin jingled his keys. "I'll swing by tomorrow after work, okay?"

I nodded and watched him get in his car and drive off. He hadn't even asked how my day was. Or kissed me goodbye. Now that I thought about it, I couldn't remember the last time either of us had even bothered.

I hadn't missed it.

The thought was depressing. I sank down into the dirt and ran my fingers through the soil. We'd turned the lights on so we could see, but beyond that, darkness engulfed the ranch. And all around me quiet invaded. I closed my eyes. This is what I would miss. Every day I spent in the city, working at a job I hated—because I *would* hate dressing in a suit every day and sitting behind a desk shuffling papers—

I'd be dreaming about coming back here and sitting in this dirt.

"What are you doing?" Preston called.

I blinked open an eye. "You still here?"

"Yeah, got distracted talking to some of the horses in the barn."

I would have laughed, but I did the same thing on occasion.

"Penny for your thoughts?"

I couldn't give him that. I couldn't tell him that I might only have a few weeks left here as his coach.

Only a few weeks where the chance to ride again would be right there at my fingertips.

I bit my lip as that old, familiar desire rose inside me. The one that I'd been ignoring for a year now, because my injuries whispered they were too severe, too permanent to try again.

If I didn't try again now, that would be it. It would be really over. Really *truly* over, because there wouldn't be a bull and a bucking chute right outside my door.

I pushed to my feet and looked Preston dead in the eye. "Can you stay an extra ten minutes?"

He shrugged. "Sure. Got nothing better to do."

"Get some ropes. And a bull."

He eyed me. "I thought we were done."

Nerves shot around my stomach like rabid dogs released from a cage, and I was suddenly certain I would vomit. But I forced the words out of my mouth anyway. "You are. I'm not."

His eyes widened. Preston knew exactly how long it had been since I'd gotten on the back of a bull. But he didn't say anything. Just ran off to do as I asked.

I sucked in a few deep breaths and climbed to the top of

the bucking chutes on legs that wobbled. I shrugged a few times, watching while Preston got a bull into the chute and put a rope around him.

I eyed the bull he'd chosen. "Thanks for going easy on me," I drawled, voice dripping with sarcasm. He'd picked out Grave Digger, one of the meanest bulls we had.

He tightened a rope. "If I'd picked an easier bull, you would have sent me back, we both know that."

He was right. If I was going to ride again, I didn't want to do it on some baby bull barely strong enough to hold my weight.

He handed me the ropes, and I got settled over Grave Digger's back. He kicked the stall, just to show me how unimpressed he was that he'd been dragged out again after being put back in his pen.

"You sure this is a good idea?" Preston asked.

"No. But I'm gonna do it anyway."

"Figured as much." He climbed down and took up his spot by the gate, wrapping the gate rope around his hand once to give him a better grip.

Seconds felt as long as a week, while nervous sweat beaded at my temples.

"You ready?"

"Just pull the fucking gate, Preston," I griped.

For once, he did as he was told.

Grave Digger stormed out, kicking his hind legs and turning straight into a right-hand spin.

Muscle memory kicked in.

It didn't matter that I'd been out for a year. I'd ridden this bull so many times, I knew him almost as well as I knew Austin. I raised my left hand in the air, partially for balance, partially because it was an automatic disqualification if you touched the bull.

That was all it took for it to come unraveled.

Pain splintered through my left side before I could even get my hand over shoulder height.

Along with it came the fear. Complete and utter terror that it was going to happen again.

I couldn't do that sort of pain more than once. I wouldn't survive it.

I yanked my hand from the ropes and dismounted, landing on my feet and sprinting for the safety of the fences. Babying my bad arm, I grabbed the fence with my right hand, using my legs to haul me up and out of the reach of Grave Digger's horns.

My heart thumped erratically, adrenaline coursing through my veins but not having its usual effect of pumping me up.

Tonight, all it did was make me nauseous.

I retched over the side of the fence, nothing coming up, but I couldn't seem to stop.

Preston didn't say a word. He didn't try to comfort me or tell me it was all going to be okay. He just waited until I turned around, took one look at my face, and lowered his head. "I'll put him back and clean up. You go. I'll see you tomorrow."

Heat flamed in my cheeks, and stupid, angry tears pricked at the backs of my eyes. Goddamn it! What the fuck had I been thinking? I knew I didn't have the strength in that arm to ride anymore. Even after a year of physical therapy, I'd been told time and time again that it was just never going to be the same.

I'd nodded and accepted my medical team's diagnosis.

But somewhere deep inside me, I'd held out hope.

A hope I'd just killed by trying to be the same girl I used to be.

She was dead. And she needed to find new dreams. A new life. In a new town, far away from this place and the memories of who she used to be.

I found my phone on one of the seats and brought up my text messages to Austin, stabbing at the screen with jerky, angry motions that belied the message I typed out.

Good luck with your interview, babe. I hope you get it.

3

Dominic

Planes were not made for anyone taller than about five foot six. That was the realization I came to as I tried to fit my six-foot, four-inch body into a seat that was obviously made for the vertically challenged. My knees pressed into the back of the seat in front of me, and I twisted awkwardly, trying to get comfortable.

I now understood why my father had always insisted on making the painfully slow road trip from Wyoming to Georgia instead of flying. Over twenty hours on the road was less torture than turning myself into a human pretzel in an attempt to avoid banging my elbows on the tray.

A woman sat beside me and watched me struggle for a moment. She was short, probably only about five foot, with a tiny sleeping baby strapped to her chest. "If it helps, you can take up some of my legroom."

"Oh no," I assured her automatically. "I'll be fine."

She smiled. "I know it sounds like I'm just offering to be polite, but truthfully, I'm trying to butter you up." She pointed at the little one tucked against her. "Karli is probably going to wake up and scream this plane down at some point in the next three hours. If I've built some goodwill with you, maybe you won't be so annoyed when that inevitably happens."

I peered at the baby's tiny smushy face. The kid couldn't be more than a couple of weeks old, and was so peaceful, her dark eyelashes fanning out across her pale cheeks. "I can't imagine anything that angelic-looking making any sort of disturbance."

The woman grimaced. "Well, now you've done it. You've put it out there in the universe, and I guarantee she's going to try to prove you wrong. So please, take some legroom, and remember that it was you who uttered the incantation to rain hell down on us." But she said it with a smile and smoothed back her daughter's wispy blonde hair in a touch that reeked of love and devotion. "I've just adopted her, so we're still kind of feeling our way around each other. I'm hoping that once I get her home and settled, we'll have time to build a bond."

A pang echoed through my chest. Just days ago, a comment like that wouldn't have bothered me at all. I probably would have launched into the tale of how I was adopted, too, and how great a life I had.

But now, any talk of adoption had my palms sweating. I smiled stiffly at the woman and turned to look out the window, even though all there was to see was tarmac and luggage handlers throwing suitcases into the belly of a plane on the opposite runway.

Guilt ricocheted around my body when I remembered my mom's face as I told them I was leaving. I couldn't explain the real reason why I'd taken a job so similar to the one they were offering me on their ranch, but across the other side of the country. I'd made up some bullshit excuse about needing to make my own path and do some traveling before I settled down.

I didn't mention that I'd found my biological family.

I'd learned young, that anytime I brought up my birth parents, mom's eyes glazed over, like a little part of her was dying, even though she tried to be supportive. My dad suddenly stared down at his cereal, intent on getting that very last cornflake out of the milk, chasing it around his bowl with his spoon. My younger brothers asked questions, and Mom tried her best to answer them, but it was never lost on me how much it hurt her to do so.

So I'd stopped asking and gone behind their backs to find the answers I needed.

Now I was here, on a plane to Georgia, because I was running away from the fact I'd been rejected all over again. I couldn't even tell my family for fear of someone else hurting even half as much as I did right now. They'd get over the upset of me moving. That was minor in comparison to admitting they weren't enough for me. There was FaceTime, and they'd come visit.

My parents had two biological sons. The farm should go to one of them. They'd see that, once I was out of the picture.

At least that's what I'd told myself as my old man had held me tight at the airport and told me to come back soon.

It's what I'd had to say over and over again in my head as tears had slid down my mother's cheeks.

I was an ungrateful asshole. I wished I'd never opened the can of worms. But it was too late now.

I really hoped the little girl bundled up in her new mama's arms didn't turn out to be such a jerk. I hoped she had the sense to know what a good thing she had, and not be forever wondering who she was and where she came from. Or why she'd been given away like she didn't matter.

I hoped she didn't get to twenty-four, only to realize all these things and royally implode her life like I'd just done.

I stared out at the scenery. We'd taken off at some point and I hadn't even noticed, but I was glad for it.

Each mile we traveled took me farther from the fact I'd just devastated the people who cared most about me.

Evidently, the *only* people who cared about me.

The airport in Atlanta was packed and full of families and friends reuniting with hugs and tears.

But Kai 'Frost' Hunt was not one for such displays of emotion. He leaned against a concrete pillar, his ever-present wide-brimmed hat dangling from his fingers. He'd earned the nickname Frost when he'd toured with the WBRA, because he rarely smiled and was always fully concentrated on his rides.

Nothing had changed in the decades since. The man saved all his smiles for his wife and three daughters.

Though I did get a nod, which was practically a hug in his book. He held a hand out, and I shook it, shouldering my backpack.

He eyed it warily. "That all you brought? Thought you were staying indefinitely."

"I am." I didn't want to explain how I'd brought nothing more than the bare necessities with me. I hadn't wanted any memories of home. I'd left everything behind in my cabin. It would all still be there whenever I managed to return to face my parents and explain why I'd so abruptly run off to join the circus. Or join a bull riding school, as the case was.

Kai raised a shoulder in indifference, and I was glad for his lack of patience with small talk. That would do me well. Because I didn't want to talk at all. Small talk, big talk, nothin'.

I just wanted to get out in the dirt and whip some bull riders into shape. Maybe have a ride or two myself.

I knew Kai could appreciate that.

We walked through the airport side by side in silence, but it was companionable sort of quiet. It wasn't until I'd thrown my backpack into Kai's truck and pulled myself into the passenger seat that curiosity got the better of me. "How's Summer?"

Kai sighed without looking in my direction. "You want the brutal honesty, or the canned response I give people who ain't family?"

My heart gave an uneven thump. Here was another person who considered me family. A good, hardworking man, who had worldwide titles to his name and a successful business that he'd built from nothing. So why did I concentrate on the one set of parental figures who didn't consider me worthy of being a worm in their garden, let alone a member of their family? They shouldn't have mattered.

They did.

But also, fuck them. They didn't get to control my life with their continual rejections. So I pushed all that aside and focused back on Kai. "Brutal honesty."

"I barely recognize her. She's not the same girl she was before..."

Before her accident.

I'd been there that night in Masonville. She'd gone down hard, her shout of pain drowning out the rest of the crowd. I'd jumped the damn barrier without even thinking about it and sprinted across the dirt. The bull fighters had gotten the bull's attention by that point and moved him on, but there was nobody by Summer's side as she lay screaming in the dirt, her arm bent up at the wrong angle, bones sticking through the skin.

I don't even think she'd been aware of my presence, she was in so much pain.

That was the last time I'd gotten to see her. Her jackass boyfriend had finally caught up and pushed me aside. He'd been the one to hold her hand while she passed out. He'd been the one who got to ride in the ambulance with her. We'd all gone to the hospital and sat nervously in the waiting room while she was in surgery, and Austin had stared me down the entire time like the whole thing had been my fault.

She'd come through the surgery but had refused all visitors but him and her family. I'd hung around the ranch for a few more days, hoping she'd change her mind, but she hadn't. And I'd been needed at home, so I'd made the slow drive back, feeling like shit.

It was only then that I'd let myself realize that the entire reason I'd been in Georgia was for her. She'd been my teenage crush. The one girl I could never get out of my head, even though she'd never looked at me as anything but a friend.

Her rejection was just another in a long list of them.

And none of it mattered now. This time, I was here for me.

Kai's truck trundled over the grate and past the huge sign declaring this property to be Hunts' Bull Riding School. I'd driven through these gates many a time over the years growing up, but never with the knowledge that this property was now my home.

Unless I fucked it up and got myself fired.

But that wasn't going to happen. I might not be able to work on my family's ranch right now, but I knew nothing else. Ranch life was the only one I was qualified for, but more than that, it was the only one I wanted. I wasn't cut out for anything else.

Typical of Kai, he bypassed the main house and drove straight out to the back, parking by the training rings.

"It was only a three-hour trip. You're good to start now, right?"

Too bad if I wasn't. Kai wasn't the sort of guy you said no to.

But he was right. I was ready to work. The more work the better. I wanted to bury myself in so much work it would take me weeks or maybe even months to dig myself out. And maybe by then, I wouldn't feel like I'd just lost a piece of me.

I pushed open my door and breathed in the fresh country air. It settled deep in my lungs, calming my nerves.

"Dominic!"

I closed my eyes for the tiniest of moments as Summer's shout sank deep inside me, worming its way back to the place it had left off.

Which was suspiciously close to my heart.

Shit.

I plastered on a smile and strode across the dirt to meet her.

God, she was as beautiful as I remembered. Her hair was a little longer, flowing down her back from beneath her hat. She smiled widely at me, pearly white teeth sparkling from behind her full pink lips.

Lips I'd dreamed of kissing on more than one occasion.

I eyed the sling hanging from around her neck. It had been a year since she'd been injured, and she was still bandaged up?

To my surprise, she stepped straight in and put her good arm around me, her cheek pressing to my chest.

"It's so good to see you. I meant to call." She pulled away and gestured to her arm. "I've been busy."

"Yeah, of course," I said lamely. I didn't really think I'd crossed her mind at all in the time since I'd seen her last, but her hug right now had been genuine, and I couldn't blame her. She'd gone through a lot.

I was just grateful to be here now, and back in her presence.

She grabbed my hand and pulled me toward the small set of bleacher-style seats, chipped and faded by the relentless Georgia sun and years of exposure. "Come say hi to Austin. You remember him?"

"Uh, yeah. Your boyfriend, right?"

A stupid part of me held my breath and hoped she'd correct me.

But she just nodded.

They were still together, then. Of course they were. He'd been talking of moving to the city the last time I'd been here. Obviously, that was who she was moving with.

I'd been prepared for this. What I wasn't prepared for was the intense anger that engulfed me when I looked Austin's way.

Austin hadn't changed a bit. If Summer hadn't been standing right next to me with her arm all banged up, I would have assumed no time had passed since the last time the three of us had been together.

Austin's gaze slid from my face, down my arm and to Summer's fingers wrapped around mine.

As if she'd only just realized we were still holding hands, she dropped mine like it was hot.

Austin didn't even bother saying hello. His annoyance rolled off him in waves, and he turned to Summer, like I wasn't even there. "What's he doing here?"

Summer's eyes narrowed. "Don't be so rude."

He moved to Summer's side possessively, stepping between us like I was something she need protection from.

Irritation rolled up my spine.

Summer stepped away, frustration flashing in her eyes. "He's allowed to surprise visit anytime he wants."

It almost made me grin. Austin still didn't know her. He never had. He'd never made the effort to read her signs. Not like I did. I'd always been hyperaware of her, ever since we'd come out here with my family when I was eighteen and I'd first set eyes on her all grown-up.

But then her words sank in. Surprise? Visit? "Didn't your dad tell you I was coming?"

Kai cleared his throat from behind me, and I shot a glance over my shoulder.

He shoved his hands in his pockets, pink flushing the pale white of his cheeks. "Uh, about that..." He reluctantly swiveled to face Summer as if he was suddenly a little frightened of her. "Dominic isn't here to visit. He's staying."

Her eyes widened, as did her grin. "Seriously? You're moving here?"

Her excitement zipped through me, my heart rate speeding up. She was excited about me being here? Fuck. I suddenly realized what an idiot I'd been. When she hadn't wanted to see anyone after her accident, I'd taken it personally. I'd let Austin telling me to leave get in my head, and I now I felt like a fool.

I grinned. "Yeah, well, somebody has to fill your shoes when you're gone."

Kai groaned.

I shot him a look of confusion, but he had his gaze trained on his eldest daughter. "Summer—"

She held up a hand, her gaze flashing first at her father, but then it darkened, landing on me.

She might be a foot shorter than I was, but never had an expression withered me on the spot the way Summer's did. I was entirely surprised to find that I didn't immediately catch fire and turn to ash.

"You're here to take my job?"

"Uh." The truth was, yes. I was here to replace her. But she was leaving. So why did that even bother her so much?

I had no time to ask.

Summer was too busy glaring at her father. "You brought him here to take my place without even telling me?"

He threw up his hands in frustration. "This is why I didn't tell you! Because I knew how you'd react. Summer, what the hell am I supposed to do when you're gone? You're moving to the city. You can't run the ranch from a shoebox apartment in a high-rise."

"Not yet, I'm not! We haven't set an official moving date."

"Right, and frankly, I hope you never do. But it's all Austin talks about. So I have to assume that you really are going—"

"Oh, we're going," Austin piped up. "No need to worry about that."

Kai glared at him.

I suddenly realized where Summer got hers from. She was the spitting image of her father when he was angry.

Kai kept going like Austin hadn't even spoken. "I can't have my business falling to pieces when you leave. I need someone to come in now, so you can teach them the ropes and smoothly hand over your position. When Dom called and asked about it—"

"You what?" Summer yelled at me.

"Whoa. I—"

But Summer wasn't having any of it. "You can't just walk in here and steal my job right out from under my nose, Dom! I thought we were friends!"

"We are!" I protested, even though we weren't really. At least not lately. We hadn't spoken since her injury. She'd wanted to be left alone, so I had. And evidently, once she'd felt better, she hadn't thought to call me.

Her fiery gaze bounced between me and her old man.

"Summer," Kai tried again, softer this time. "This is just business."

She raised an eyebrow. "Just business? Oh really? And here I was, thinking we were family."

She stormed off before Kai or I could get another word in, with Austin trailing after her, wrapping his arm around her shoulders possessively.

Kai scrubbed a hand through his short hair then put his hat back on. "Well, that went better than expected."

My eyes practically bulged out of my head. "Better than expected?"

"Well, neither of us got kicked in the balls. So that's something."

4

"Unbelievable!" I yelled, slamming my way into the main house, with Austin trailing me. "Seriously, what is wrong with the two of them?"

I glared at Austin like he should know. But he just flopped down on the couch and picked up the TV remote. I watched him for a moment, gobsmacked he didn't have a word to say about what had just happened. Where was the attentive boyfriend from just a minute ago?

My mother came out of the kitchen, wiping her hands on a towel, and frowned at me. "Want to tell me exactly what's going in here?"

"Did you know?" I demanded. "That Dad hired Dominic West to take my position? Of all people!"

She frowned. "He mentioned something to me this morning before he left to go to the airport. I think it all happened very quickly. But what's wrong with that? You're leaving. You can't expect your father to shoulder everything by himself. He did that for years until you were old enough to take a full-time job here, and it nearly sent him to an early grave. We're trying to ease him out of the business, not lump him right back into the middle of it. You know that."

I cringed. I remembered exactly how hard Dad had worked before we'd hired Hallie as lead hand, and I'd taken on a lot of the training responsibilities. Not to mention the paperwork and business accounting. It was bad enough I'd spent a year shirking my responsibilities when I was training for the pros. Which had turned out to be a massive waste of everyone's time anyway. Ever since my injury, I'd doubled down here at the ranch, making sure the place ran like clockwork.

I knew Dad would need help when I left, but this felt like a shove out the door. And he expected me to just happily train Dominic to take my spot? How the hell was I supposed to do that? He'd never worked here a day in his life. He had no idea how the place ran, or even what all the bulls' names were. "Why Dominic? Why not Hallie? Or Nate?"

Hallie had worked on the ranch for years, and her boyfriend, Nate, had come home from the WBRA tour last year. They'd both be more than qualified to run this place.

Mom looked at me like I'd grown another head. "Hallie's an amazing lead hand, but she doesn't know how to ride. That's not something you can learn just by watching on the sidelines, otherwise I could have picked up that job years ago. God knows I've watched you and your father ride enough bulls to last an eternity.

"And Nate doesn't want the job. Your father asked him months ago, when your physical therapy was complete and you and Austin started talking about moving to the city again. He and Hallie are weeks away from opening the B&B, so he's got his hands full there. There's going to be more work than ever once that's a huge success and Hallie leaves to run it." She folded her arms across her chest. "I really don't think it's Dominic that's causing this sort of reaction from you."

Her gaze flickered to Austin, her frown deepening.

I clammed up. I was a grown woman, and Austin was my partner. We'd been together since our senior prom, five years ago. I knew that some people in my life didn't exactly approve of him. Hallie and my parents being the main objectors. But I loved him. He'd stood by me when I'd had my accident and delayed his own plans so I could complete my therapy at my home. We had history. Memories. Those things counted for something in my book.

I glanced over at him. He was handsome, with his medium-brown hair and blue eyes. He was smart and witty. I liked his ambition. It was one of the things that had drawn me to him in the first place. He had big dreams and was determined to make them happen.

The problem was that his dreams were to become a top-notch accountant, at a big firm in the city. He was limited here, filling his time with keeping the books for local farms and the diner. Not exactly the big multi-million-dollar businesses he dreamed of working with. Those just didn't exist out here, in a town with a population barely big enough to record.

No, our plan had always been that if I didn't make the pros, we'd move to the city so he could chase his dream.

I hadn't made the pros.

So it was his turn. I owed him that. I'd promised. And I wasn't about to start breaking promises now. I sat beside him, and he put his arm around my shoulder. "There's no problem," I confirmed to my mother. "I was just taken by surprise."

"Well, good then. Because I already started planning a

welcome party for Dominic. You'll be there, right? Tonight, at the B&B. I already talked to Hallie about it."

"A welcome party?" Austin scoffed. "Seriously? What for? It's not like the guy has any friends here."

I elbowed him sharply and tried to cover his rudeness. "That's the point." I nodded at my mother. "We'll be there."

It had been a few weeks since I'd last been to the B&B that Hallie and Nate were restoring. I stopped to admire the fresh coat of gleaming white paint on the front door, and the newly installed brass knocker. I didn't dare use it, for fear of chipping the perfect paint, and anyway, this was my best friend's house. I never knocked.

I led the way inside, my fingers clutched around Austin's. "Hello?" I called out in the foyer, wondering where everyone was.

Austin gazed around at the polished floorboards and the gorgeous sweeping staircase that led up to the second story, where most of the guest rooms were. The bottom floor was a large open space that Hallie had filled with comfortable-looking couches, shelves full of books, and even a small bar in one corner.

"Oh wow," I breathed, taking it all in. "I haven't seen it furnished. I love it."

Austin wrinkled his nose, tugging me in the direction of the bar. "They're never going to make their money back on this place, you know. They've completely overcapitalized."

"Thanks for your opinion, Austin," Hallie said from behind us, voice dripping with sarcasm.

I cringed, hating she'd heard him say that.

He didn't seem at all bothered, though. "What sort of

alcohol do you have?" He disappeared behind the bar, searching for his drink of choice.

I linked my arm through Hallie's and steered her away. "Sorry," I mumbled. "Ignore him. He's been in a mood all day. This place is amazing, and it's going to make you a fortune once you open it to the public."

Hallie shook off the storm cloud Austin's comments had brought in and smiled brightly at me. "I really hope so. Because Austin is right. We have sunk a lot of money into this place. But we love it."

"As do I. He doesn't know what he's talking about."

The thing was, Austin did know what he was talking about when it came to money and finances. He had a keen interest in real estate to boot, so he was qualified to have an opinion. Which was exactly why he felt no qualms over Hallie hearing him say they'd spent too much money on the place. To him, it was a fact. And facts weren't something to get upset over. His brain was very analytical, with little room for emotion.

I needed to change the subject. "Thanks for hosting the party. It's actually nice to be off the ranch for once."

Hallie frowned at me. "You need to get out more. You work too hard."

I did, but I loved it. Not as much as I'd once loved bull riding, but teaching was the next best thing. I'd miss it terribly once we moved to the city. I faked a smile for my best friend because I didn't want her worrying about me. I'd given the people I loved enough to worry about over the past year, and I didn't want to add more to it because I hated the idea of moving away from home. I was a grown woman. I couldn't live on my parents' ranch forever. "I won't be working hard anymore, now that Dominic is here."

"Speaking of..." Hallie darted a glance over my shoulder.

I followed her gaze.

Dominic stood in the doorway, blocking the last of the fading afternoon light outside. I'd never seen him dressed as smart casual as he was right now, with black denim jeans, ripped at the knees, white sneakers, and T-shirt. In fact, I was pretty sure this was the first time I'd ever seen the man without boots on his feet and a hat on his head. His dark hair was combed and styled, and my gaze fell to the tattoo that snaked its way an inch up the side of his neck, the rest hidden beneath his T-shirt. I strained to see it better but couldn't make out the design.

Nate, Hallie's boyfriend, walked over to greet him, slapping him on the shoulder, the two of them launching straight into easy conversation, even though they'd only met a couple of times last year.

"Holy hell," Hallie whispered, her grip tightening on me. "I'd forgotten how insanely hot he is."

I laughed, "Don't let Nate hear you say that."

She shrugged. "Nate isn't the jealous type. He knows who I'm going home with at the end of the night. Austin, however, is looking like he wants to throw a drink in Dom's face right about now."

I glanced over to the bar and did a double take at Austin's expression. Hallie was right. There was pure hate in the curl of his lips and the narrowing of his already small eyes.

I shifted uncomfortably. "I better go see what his problem is. He's upset."

But Hallie dug her fingernails into my arm. "If he's upset because Dom walked into the room, that's on him. How are you going to work with Dominic if Austin is going to be throwing shade like that?"

"Austin will be at work most of the time. He has nothing to worry about."

Hallie huffed out a sigh that lifted her bangs. "I know that. You're the most reliable, steadfast, trustworthy woman on the face of the planet. Much to your own detriment."

I blinked. "What does that mean?"

She sighed. "Nothing. Your loyalty is a beautiful thing. I just worry that sometimes some people take advantage of it." She tugged my arm. "Let's go say hello to Dom. We're being rude."

I swallowed thickly. Standing over here eyeballing him wasn't half as rude as I'd been earlier. I trailed Hallie over to her boyfriend's side, who immediately wrapped his arm around her shoulder.

Dom glanced my way. "Hey, again."

I peeped up at him. "Hi."

The awkward silence between us was tangible.

Hallie cleared her throat. "Wow, well, this is uncomfortable. I'm going to pretend there's something I need to do in the kitchen now."

Nate grimaced. "Yeah, I'm going to pretend to help."

I shot both of them a dirty look as they took off in the direction of the kitchen. Great friends they were.

Dominic touched my arm, and I jerked back as if he'd electrocuted me.

"Whoa. Listen, I just wanted to say I'm sorry about before."

I gaped at him. "You're sorry?"

He grabbed the back of his neck. "I didn't mean to steal your job. I wouldn't have just waltzed in the way I did if your dad had told me you didn't know I was coming."

My dad entering through the front door behind Dom's back caught my attention. He raised an eyebrow, noticing me with Dominic, and a small smile lifted the corner of his mouth.

Irritation spiked in my blood. I clutched Dom's arm and pulled him away around a corner, not needing to see my father's smirk at that very moment.

Dom followed, until we were alone in the hall.

"It's not you who needs to apologize," I explained. "I was totally out of line. I'm sorry. It won't happen again."

He shrugged. "I don't want you to feel like I blindsided you. I would have let you know I was coming, but we haven't really talked since last year."

I bit my lip. That was my fault. I'd just been so lost to my own misery, I'd completely shut myself off from everyone apart from my immediate family. And Austin. *Shit.* He was going to be having a conniption about me disappearing into a quiet hallway, alone with another guy. "Let's just call it even, okay? The ranch isn't really that big a place when you're working there every day. And training you will be a whole lot easier if we aren't pissed off with each other."

He tilted his head. "So, we're friends again?"

"Sure."

Someone cleared their throat. "Summer."

I spun on my heel.

Austin watched from the other end of the hall, his expression unreadable. "Everyone is wondering where the guest of honor is. It's getting pretty full out there, and your mother said something about making a speech."

Guilt punched me in the gut, even though I hadn't been doing anything wrong. I plastered on a bright smile and went to his side, tucking an arm around his waist. His responses since Dominic's return had me a little uneasy. I didn't want him to feel like I was hiding anything.

Without looking back, I followed Austin out to the main

room. He was right. In the space of minutes, it seemed like half the town had arrived. It didn't matter that this had been a last-minute event. Parties were the lifeblood of this town, and nobody was going to miss a chance to ogle the new guy and check out the brand-new B&B while they were at it.

I caught Hallie's eye from across the room, and she mouthed, "Wow" at me.

I gave her an excited thumbs-up. Even though the B&B wasn't quite ready for guests, this was kind of a trial run for Hallie and Nate, and a chance to show off all their hard work.

There was a tinny clinking of a fork against a wine glass, and Austin pulled me to the front of the crowd, where my parents stood.

The room quieted, everybody turning their attention in Mom's direction.

She smiled widely. "A big thank you to all of you for coming out tonight to welcome Dominic back to town. Or to have a gander at Hallie and Nate's beautiful restoration. I'm sure you all know which camp you fall into."

There was a titter of laughter.

"Dominic, come up here."

I craned over my shoulder and immediately spotted Dom towering above the rest of the crowd. He was several inches taller than most, so he wasn't hard to pick out. He smiled his way around people, who patted him on the arm as he passed, until he stood by my mother's side.

"Kai and I have been taking steps back from the ranch over the last few months. And since our beautiful eldest daughter has decided to run off to the bright lights of the city, Dominic will be replacing her as our general manager."

I stiffened involuntarily and quickly untangled my

fingers from Austin's, not wanting him to notice my reaction to the reminder I was leaving.

He clapped politely, but I just couldn't. I stared down at my palms, trying to force them to come together like everybody else's were, but my body refused to obey. I didn't want to applaud the fact I was leaving. Or that my parents had found someone to replace me so easily.

Subconsciously, I'd been relying on the fact there weren't many people as qualified as I was to run Hunts' Bull Riding School and Ranch.

I hadn't counted on Dominic West walking back into our lives and making it all too easy for me to pack my bags and go. I'd been delaying for months, claiming the ranch as my reason for avoiding the house hunting trips to the city that Austin kept going on.

I already knew Dominic practically ran his dad's place. I had no idea why he'd decided to give that up, but that wasn't my business. And the man knew how to ride a bull. His dad had toured on the WBRA circuit right beside my dad. Anything I'd learned from my old man, Dominic would have also learned from his.

When I looked up, Dominic was watching me curiously. My gaze collided with his, and for the tiniest of moments, his expression stole my breath.

"Excuse me," Austin called, stepping forward. "There's something I'd like to say, too."

I widened my eyes. "Austin," I hissed quietly, but he didn't stop.

Dad eyed him, a frown on his face.

"It's true, Summer and I have been planning this move to the city for years. But as most of you know, her tragic accident last summer put a halt to that plan. And instead we stayed here, in our hometown, so Summer could complete her physical therapy. I'm not going to deny, it's been a difficult time for us." He held a hand out to me, and when I took it, he pulled me around to face the crowd with him.

Heat flooded my cheeks. This was awkward, standing between Dom and Austin, with my parents behind me, and a roomful of people watching us. This was not my idea of a good time. If I was on the back of a bull in front of a crowd of thousands, I had no problems. But up here, with a group of people I knew staring at me, I felt incredibly exposed. I shifted in my sling, a stab of pain spearing through my shoulder.

Austin turned to me, stealing my attention. He took a piece of paper from his pocket and glanced down at it. "Your injuries were bad. They made you so sad. But together we walked the storm. And now your smile makes me warm."

I squinted at him in confusion and whispered, "Are you deliberately talking in rhyme?"

He ignored me like I hadn't said anything.

There was a snort of laughter from somewhere behind me, and I suspected it came from my father. I shot him a filthy look.

Austin didn't seem to notice. He just kept reading his weird poetry. "We're starting a new life. One that will be rife. With things that you love. Like little gray doves."

Doves? What the fuck? I hated birds, didn't he know that? Ever since a rooster had attacked me when I was seven, I'd refused to even collect the eggs from the chickens Mom kept at the ranch. By association, I hated all feathered creatures.

"Austin," I murmured, growing increasingly uncomfortable. "What are you doing?"

He held his finger up to shush me. "We've been together a long time. Now it's our turn to hear the bells chime."

A ripple of excitement rolled through the crowd. I'm pretty sure one of my sisters squealed.

A cold sweat broke out across the back of my neck.

Then Austin dropped down on one knee. "Summer, you're my life. Now be my wife."

The oohs and aahs from the crowd turned into a cheer as Austin retrieved a little square box from his pocket and held it up to me.

On a bed of white satin sat an impressively sized diamond, imbedded in a band of white gold.

I stared at it for the longest moment while I tried to process his words. Sure, we'd talked about moving to the city. And we had been together for five years. But we'd never talked about marriage. I had no idea he'd even been thinking about it.

I blinked and lifted my head to see a roomful of people staring at me. My sisters. Some friends from school. I spotted Austin's parents in the middle of the crowd, happy tears rolling down his mom's cheeks.

Beside me, Dom's entire body had gone stiff.

Austin cleared his throat. "Summer?"

I gazed down at the strained look on his face. He raised one eyebrow, and I realized I still hadn't said anything. I was just standing there like some sort of fish out of water with my mouth hanging open, gulping for air.

I let out a strangled laugh. "Oh, this is where I'm supposed to answer, right?"

The room tittered, but my palms were sweaty. Austin shot a panicked glance at the rest of the room and then back at me. His eyes widened, urging me on.

I had to answer him.

"Yes?" My voice came out tiny and squeaky and as more of a question than a statement.

But then Austin was on his feet, swooping me into a spinning hug that nearly took out Dominic and my parents, while he pumped one fist in the air. The cheers that filled the room were earsplitting.

When he finally put me down, he took up my hand, sliding the ring on to my finger.

Over his shoulder I caught sight of Dom watching us, his expression unreadable. But that was better than the expressions on my parents' faces, who appeared downright disappointed.

I swallowed hard. This was what I wanted, right? This was the natural progression of things. This shouldn't have been as surprising and out of the blue as it felt. I shouldn't have felt like a bull caged into a corner, with no way out except to charge right though.

So when Austin kissed me, I put all those doubts aside and kissed my fiancé back.

The party became a whirlwind of congratulations and people grabbing my hand to look at my ring. Austin grinned through it all, his arm tight around my shoulder as he towed me around the room, accepting everyone's well-wishes.

The minute we got in the car, though, alone for the first time all night, his fingers clenched around the steering wheel. "What the fuck was that?"

The smile fell off my face at the acid in his tone. "What do you mean?"

He glared at me as he started the engine and jerked the gearshift into drive. He planted his foot on the accelerator, and we flew out onto the main road at an alarming pace that set off warning sirens in my head.

"You know exactly what I mean," he hissed. "I asked you to marry me in front of everyone we know, and you humiliated me!"

I blinked. "Humiliated you?" I narrowed my eyes and shifted forward in my seat, the belt yanking at my shoulder.

It was only then that I realized his eyes were slightly unfocused. "How much have you had to drink?"

I frantically tried to do the math in my head. I'd seen him with a glass in his hand for most of the night, but it had never been full. Austin always drove when we went out because he hated me driving his car. And it suited me since I didn't like his car anyway. I didn't want to be constantly worried I was going to get a scratch on his paint. That car had cost him more money than he could really afford, despite the fact it was secondhand, and he acted like it was plated in gold. But he never had more than one drink, so the fact he always wanted to drive had never been a problem between the two of us.

But it was a problem right now. Because although I might not have seen him refilling his glass, he definitely wasn't sober. "Pull over."

He acted like he hadn't even heard me. Just stared straight out through the windshield into the dark night beyond. "I got down on my knee and asked you to be my wife. It took you too long to answer. So yeah, Summer. You humiliated me."

I gaped at him. "You took me by surprise! That was supposed to be a party for Dominic and —"

His laughter was so bitter. "So now you don't like the way I proposed?"

I cringed. "No! I never said that. It was fine."

"It was beautiful. I wrote you a poem, for fuck's sake!" He jerked the wheel sharply.

I clutched the door handle to keep myself from slamming into the window.

"Maybe you would have preferred if it were Dominic down on one knee? Maybe you would have actually answered him within five minutes of him getting down in front of you?"

His jealousy was etched into the hard lines of his lips and the narrowing of his eyes. He reeked of it so bad, I was surprised there wasn't a literal smell.

Everything in me wanted to scream at him that Dominic had nothing to do with what had happened tonight, or my delay in answering his proposal. He hadn't even crossed my mind. That momentary pause, where I'd been lost for words, had nothing to do with anyone but me and Austin, and who we were as a couple.

He'd blindsided me and put me on the spot in a public way where I had no choice but to do what he wanted.

But I couldn't say any of that for fear of upsetting him further. I had no idea what to say to get him to stop and let me drive. All I could do was try to keep him calm, so he used whatever clear-headed function he did have left to keep us on the road and get us safely home.

I didn't want to die tonight, with his shiny, impractical car wrapped around a pole.

I tentatively put a hand on his arm. "Hey, I'm sorry. I love you. That's all that matters, right? I was just surprised. We've never talked about marriage, so I wasn't expecting it. That's all. I can't wait to be your wife."

A little of the stiffness eased out of his shoulders, and he kept the car steady. So I kept talking, doing everything I could to make sure I made it home safe tonight.

"We can have the ceremony in the city if you like. There'll be more options there. Once we move, maybe I can take a few weeks before looking for a job and start making some plans. And we can go to Hawaii on our honeymoon. You've always talked about wanting to go there."

We had never gone because I was always in training. I knew how much Austin had given up for me over the years. The old familiar guilt swamped me. I owed him this. This life that he wanted.

That didn't mean I wasn't mad as a hornet over the shit he'd pulled tonight, though.

He took my hand and squeezed it just a little too hard. "That's what I was thinking. There's this great hotel, right on the beach, and with the wage increase I'll get at the new firm, we'll be able to splurge and buy first-class tickets. You may not even need to get a job at all, you know?"

I forced a smile. What the hell was I going to do in the city if I didn't get a job? Be his trophy wife and play tennis at some country club? That thought sat like a stone in my belly.

Hallie had said to me once that Austin just wanted me barefoot and pregnant. I'd blown off the idea, because kids weren't even on my radar, and I assumed they weren't on Austin's either. We'd never talked about them.

There was a lot we'd never talked about, I realized now.

I held Austin's hand the rest of the way back to my home, with the knowledge playing over and over in my head that he'd willingly put my life in danger tonight, and I'd been completely powerless to stop it.

The minute we drove beneath the ancient wooden sign that declared this Hunts' Bull Riding School and Ranch, Austin hit the brakes, dropping down to first gear to avoid flicking gravel up.

He'd slowed down so he didn't scratch his car, but he wouldn't when I'd asked him to out of fear?

I unclicked my seat belt and opened the door.

"What are you doing!" he yelped, stomping on the brakes.

My fingers clenched around the doorframe, and I hauled myself out onto the driveway, legs still trembling slightly. "This is far enough. I'll walk the rest of the way. See you tomorrow."

"I was going to stay—"

"You should stay. You should park that car on the grass and then make yourself comfy in it. Because you're drunk, and you shouldn't be driving anywhere. But you sure as hell aren't sleeping next to me tonight." I slammed the door shut and walked off into the darkness without waiting to see whether he did or not.

5

Dominic

A surprise 'welcome to town' party hadn't been high on my list of things I wanted to do on my first night in my new home. Watching Summer get engaged in the middle made it probably the most uncomfortable first day on a new job ever.

I'd ground my teeth as she'd accepted his proposal and fought every instinct in my body that had wanted to reach over and yank her from his arms.

Just because I couldn't stand the guy, or the fact I thought they were a completely mismatched couple, didn't give me the right to do anything to rain on their parade. So I'd stepped back and watched the crowd swarm around them, offering their congratulations and well-wishes to the now happily engaged couple. Summer's younger sisters grabbed her hand, and she showed off a Texas-sized rock with a giggly grin.

Austin obviously wasn't short of cash then, even if he was only working in this small town. I probably couldn't even imagine the sort of money he'd make once he and Summer moved to the big smoke.

I spent the rest of the party hanging out with Nate and Hallie, who'd I met the last time I'd stayed at the Hunts' place, and they'd introduced me around. By the end of the night, I felt like I'd met half the town, and had managed to avoid Summer and Austin in the process.

There'd be no avoiding her come Monday morning, when she was due to start showing me the way she and her dad ran things out here. But the awkwardness was a short-term thing. A month or two, and then she'd be gone, so I needed to bring my A game, and show Kai that I was qualified for this job, all the way over here, on the other side of the country. Far away from my family, who were probably still confused as hell as to what I was doing. And far away from my birth mother. It was the way it had to be for now. Maybe one day I could go back and not feel the same hurt and shock and betrayal I'd felt at her rejection. But right now, Wyoming felt too small, and I couldn't be there.

So now I had to make a new life. At least until I could cope better with the old one.

I caught a lift home with Kai and Addie, and they dropped me at the door to my cabin, not unlike the one I'd had on my parents' property back home.

Addie had her window down and reached through it to stop me as I passed the passenger side on my way to my new home. "Sorry about tonight," she said softly.

I shook my head on autopilot. "Why? It was a great party."

It wasn't a lie. Nate and Hallie's B&B was amazing and had gotten a huge tick of approval from the town. The food had been delicious. And I'd gotten to meet people who had all welcomed me and talked about bull riding, and ranching, and all the other things I loved. In all those respects, tonight had been a raging success.

The only thing that hadn't gone down so well was Austin's proposal. That twit, with his rhyming bullshit. My nose crinkled just at the thought of it. Surely, she hadn't thought that romantic?

Addie squeezed my arm. "I honestly didn't know Austin was planning to hijack your party and pop the question. Sorry he stole your thunder."

I grinned at her. "Never much liked the thunder anyway. So he can have it. I'm happy for them."

"About as happy as we are, by the look of it," Kai mumbled from behind the steering wheel.

"Hey?" I wondered if I'd heard him wrong.

But Addie slapped his arm, thwacking her knuckles across his biceps. "Stop it."

When she turned back to me, she was all smiles. "I put some towels in your cabin for you, and a bag of groceries in case you get the munchies before you can get to the store. If you need anything else, just let me know."

"You didn't have to do that," I insisted, hating she'd put herself out for me. I made a mental note to replace all the food she'd given me when I went to the store tomorrow.

"Happy to. And you're welcome to come to the main house for Sunday night dinner as well."

"Oh no," I insisted. "I know that's your family night." I remembered from years of visiting them.

"What do you think you are?" Kai asked. "Your dad is my brother in every way but blood. And blood don't mean shit. You'll be there."

"Yes, sir," I said automatically.

He chuckled. "Good. Night, then."

The two of them drove away, leaving me in the silence and near complete blackness of the night. I ran my fingers over the jagged ridges of my key, but it was beautiful outside, and I didn't want to go inside just yet. Unpacking could wait until tomorrow.

I settled myself on the tiny front porch of my cabin, sitting on the rough wood steps, since there were no chairs. I'd get one when I went to town. It would be nice to sit out here in the summer evenings and drink a beer.

The sound of footsteps on the gravel road interrupted the silence, but I didn't think much of it. There were quite a few cabins around me. I hadn't yet gotten to meet any of the inhabitants, but I knew from previous trips that they mostly housed wannabe cowboys who came from all over to train out here with Summer and her dad.

It wasn't until the footsteps grew closer that I realized who they belonged to. "Summer?"

She stopped, whipping around and peering through the darkness in my direction. "Jesus, Dom. You scared the hell out of me. Lucky I wasn't carrying my rifle."

I raised an eyebrow. "You hunt?"

She wandered in my direction and leaned on the banister that edged the steps. "No, but that doesn't mean I don't know how to use one. Sometimes it's just a necessary part of country life."

I knew what she meant. I'd had to put down animals from time to time, that were too far gone to save. I never liked it, but leaving them suffering wasn't an option either. "Well, just so you know, I'll probably be around here a bit now, so if you ever do have your rifle in hand, I'll endeavor to give you more warning before I say hi. Perhaps a whistle? Or I could try smoke signals?"

The corner of her mouth flickered up, but it died quickly.

Fair enough. My jokes were lame. "What are you doing

out here? Shouldn't you and Austin be off celebrating your engagement?"

She sank down on the steps beside me. "You'd think, wouldn't you?"

"But you're not, because..."

She sighed. "We had a fight."

I hated that a tiny, assholey part of me was a little bit happy about that. I gave it a swift kick in the ass and sent it flying, because I didn't want to be that guy. "You wanna talk about it?"

"Honestly? No. I'd rather talk about literally anything else."

"Anything?"

"Anything."

"How's your arm."

"Except that."

I nudged her with my elbow. "Come on, tell me. You're still wearing that sling."

She lifted it, as if checking she could. "It's still useless. I hate the stupid thing. I wish they'd just amputated it."

I balked at that. "Come on, you don't mean that."

"Don't I? This stupid thing is the entire reason I can't ride anymore."

"Are you left-handed?" Most bull riders used their dominant hand to grip the ropes.

She shook her head. "No, right-handed."

I frowned. "So what's the problem then?"

She took her arm out of the sling and tried to lift it. She didn't get far, before she dropped it back down. "Can't hold it up. If I can't hold it up, I get disqualified."

I shifted on the step, leaning back against the rail, so I could face her. She didn't look my way, though, just toed the dirt with her boot, avoiding my gaze.

"Who says you have to hold it up?"

That got her to face me. "Have you forgotten the rules of bull riding? You touch the bull with your free hand, you're out."

"Yeah, but there's no rule that says you have to hold it up. If you were sitting on a bull right now, instead of on a step, is your arm anywhere near the bull?"

"Well, no. But it's in a sling."

"So wear your sling when you ride."

She snorted on a laugh. "I can't do that!"

"Says who? Show me where it says in the rule book that you can't compete with a sling on? And even if you do manage to find that, where does it say you can't just strap that arm to your chest? You said you wished they'd amputated it. If they had, would the WBRA say you couldn't ride because you only had one arm? I'd love to see them try. There'd be an outcry about discrimination."

She blinked. "I wouldn't have the balance without it."

I shrugged. "Fine. Valid point. But maybe you'd find a way. If you tried."

She clammed up at that.

"Does your silence right now mean you haven't tried at all?"

"What are you, my father?" she mumbled.

I could only imagine how many times Frost had probably lectured her about getting back on and giving it another shot. He was the sort of guy who never gave up. Never let anything stand in his way. "The Summer I knew wouldn't have let an injury stop her."

"Yeah, well, that Summer is dead and buried. This Summer is moving to the city with her boyfriend."

"Fiancé," I corrected.

"Mmm. Right."

I hated that she didn't sound excited about it. I stood, knowing I wasn't going to get through to her tonight. "I'll leave you to your extreme excitement over your pending nuptials then, shall I?"

"I am excited," she insisted.

"And that's why you're sitting out here with me, instead of having hot sex with the man who just asked you to marry him?"

"Dom!"

I sniggered at the fact I'd embarrassed her. "I'm going to bed. I suggest you find some enthusiasm for doing the same."

I slipped inside and shut the door before she could say anything.

Something was seriously not right between Summer and her fiancé. I just hoped she realized that before she did something stupid, like actually marry the guy.

6

I wasn't the sort of person who slept in. Even on my days off, I was up at dawn, pulling on clothes and boots and heading outside to check on my animals. But the morning after Dominic's 'welcome to town' party, I stayed in bed until eight.

Nobody bothered me. They probably all thought I was in here with Austin, celebrating our newly engaged status. But I was very much alone. I had no idea where Austin had slept, and I was angry enough that I didn't care.

But I couldn't stay in bed forever, so eventually I hauled myself out from beneath my sheets and dragged on some clothes.

Callie and Lennon, my twin sisters, both sat at the kitchen table, absently scrolling on their phones, neither of them even glancing up as I entered. It suited me. I wasn't in the mood for chitchat. I was in the mood for food, though, so I pulled a box of Froot Loops from the cupboard and poured myself a bowl. Austin always gave me a hard time about liking them in my twenties, saying he couldn't take me seriously when I was eating them, so my breakfast choice was a bit of a screw you, since I was still angry with him.

I jerked the refrigerator door open, and grabbed the milk, but paused before shutting it. "Why is the fridge so empty? There was a whole shelf of beer in here yesterday."

Callie and Lennon shot a look at each other, then put their heads back down. It was a twin thing they did regularly, communicating without actually saying anything out loud. It had bugged me when we were younger, that the two of them always seemed to be able to read each other's minds, leaving me on the outside. But I'd grown used to it. And frankly, I didn't want anyone else to be quite as in my head as the two of them were. It was kind of creepy.

"What?" I demanded, sloshing milk into my bowl.

Lennon stopped playing with her phone. "You should probably go outside if you truly want the answer to that."

A rising annoyance ticked a muscle in my eye. I abandoned my uneaten breakfast and strode out into the morning sun. It shined bright at this time of day and was low enough that I had to shield my eyes from the glare.

Something glinted in the grass at the far end of the house, and I hurried in that direction, stooping to pick the foreign object up.

I ran my hand over the glossy dark-brown bottle and picked at the label. Mom would have a coronary if she found out someone was just dropping empty beer bottles around her house.

I groaned when I realized who that someone was.

I followed the trail of empty bottles, scooping each one from the grass, practically growling with every step.

Austin's car was still parked haphazardly off to one side of the driveway. The back door open, his feet sticking out.

He was missing a shoe. That was the first thing I noticed. He only had one shoe, and he looked freaking ridiculous.

I gripped the doorframe and surveyed the interior of his car with my molars grinding. Austin was passed out, spread across the back seat in a mess of limbs. He'd unbuttoned half his shirt, the tails sloppy and untucked from his dress pants. More empty bottles littered the floor.

I wrinkled my nose in disgust. He reeked worse than a brewery. I shoved at his leg with my foot, but he didn't budge. If he hadn't been snoring, I might well have assumed he was dead. Right then, I wasn't sure I would have cared. I kicked him harder. "Austin!"

He started, jerking upright. His bloodshot gaze focused on me, and then he flopped back down, covering his eyes with his arm. "What, Summer? It's too bright. Go away and let me sleep."

"What, Summer? Really? Did you enjoy your little party for one last night? I can't believe you stole all the beer from my parents' refrigerator and drank yourself into oblivion!"

"You're the one who said I shouldn't drive home."

"So you didn't kill yourself, or worse, somebody else! Not so you could binge drink on my front lawn!"

The rumble of one of our ranch trucks on the driveway had me jerking back. I'd been so busy yelling at Austin I hadn't even heard it approaching until it was practically right on top of me. It stopped beside me, and I peered through the window, squinting to see who was behind the wheel, praying it wasn't my dad. He already wasn't Austin's biggest fan, and seeing him passed out in his car after drinking all his beer wasn't going to do Austin any favors.

The window dropped, and Dominic leaned out. "What's going on?" He glanced between me and Austin with concern, before focusing on me. "You okay?"

I was just grateful he wasn't my father. I threw my hands up in the air. "He's hungover. Or still drunk? I've no idea."

Austin's snores permeated the air again.

Dominic frowned. "Wait, he drove like this last night? What the hell, Summer? Why did you get in the car with him?"

"I didn't know!" I protested, "And he wasn't *this* drunk last night. He added to it after we argued, and I told him to sleep it off in his car." Hot, angry tears pricked the backs of my eyes. This was so mortifying. I hadn't seen Dom in over twelve months, and in the space of less than twenty-four hours, Austin had embarrassed me multiple times.

"I know what you must be thinking," I said to Dom, heat flushing my cheeks.

Dom studied me quietly for a moment, and I just waited for him to start lecturing me on what a dickhead Austin was, just like Hallie had done time and time again. Or maybe he'd just frown disapprovingly, like my dad did every time Austin ran his mouth.

But Dom's eyes were kind. "So you'll know I'm thinking about going into town then? I need breakfast and some things at the store."

I sighed a little in relief. I just couldn't deal with another lecture this morning. I'd already laid in bed all night, staring at the ceiling, lecturing myself for even getting in the car with Austin in the first place. I shouldn't have just assumed he was sober. I shouldn't have trusted him.

"Do you want to come?"

I blinked. "Me?"

Dom's lips morphed into a grin, showing off his white teeth. "Yeah, you. I don't think Austin is up for any sort of traveling right now."

I cast an eye over my fiancé again. "I should probably try to move him inside."

Dom shrugged. "Ain't nothing going to hurt him where he is. We'll leave the car door open for fresh air. He'll still be there when we get back, judging by the number of empties." His gaze flickered over my face. "Come on, get in."

I didn't want to deal with the mess that Austin had made. I might have been his fiancée, but I wasn't his mother. I dumped the beer bottles I'd picked up in his car. Let him lie there until my dad found him. He could try to worm his way out of that one himself. I was more than happy to be well away from the ranch when that happened. I doubted Dad would be happy that he didn't have a single beer left, because his future son-in-law couldn't control himself.

Plus, I really did like the sound of a proper breakfast. My Froot Loops were probably a soggy mess by now.

I ran around to the passenger seat and jumped in beside Dom. "I know a great place. Best pancakes in the world. Let's go."

The main strip in town was always busiest on Saturday mornings. The street bustled with cars and trucks, and we had to drive well past Ruth-Ann's Diner in order to get a parking spot. But the morning was bright and warm, and Dom and I strolled side by side with me showing him where the grocery store and pharmacy were and stopping every five feet so someone could stop me and congratulate me on my engagement again.

Once we got within eyesight of Ruth-Ann's cute pink-and-yellow-striped umbrellas that sat above her outdoor seating, I pointed them out to Dom. "It's just that place down there. You'll love it. Even if you go there for dinner sometime, I highly recommend ordering from the all-day breakfast menu."

I'd been walking eagerly, my stomach growling, but I slowed my pace when I noticed we were in front of the bridal shop. In the window, a stunning white satin gown hung from a headless mannequin. The bodice sparkled with hundreds or maybe even thousands of delicate glass beads and flared into a skirt that was the width of the large window.

Before I even realized what I was doing, I'd completely stopped.

Dom cleared his throat. "Uh, if you want to go in, you can. I can wait out here for you."

I blinked, startled out of my daydream. "Huh? Oh no. That's the last thing I want to do."

Dom cocked his head to one side, staring at the dress behind the glass. "Why not? It's pretty. You'd be beautiful in it."

I glanced over at him, smiling at the pink in his cheeks. "That's nice of you to say. But that dress is not me. Not even a little bit." I screwed my nose up at it. It was a perfectly nice dress. But it did nothing for me. I got none of the thrill other women talked of when shopping for wedding dresses. It definitely didn't scream, "Try me on and love me."

More like it whispered, "Run the hell away and don't turn back."

But I knew that was just residual Austin anger talking.

I wandered to the door and peered in through the glass panel. There were three other wedding dresses in view, but I was as meh about those as I was about anchovies in my Caesar salad. "I just can't imagine myself wearing any of these." I started walking again, eager to get away from the reminder of Austin and what had happened last night.

Dom jogged a few steps to catch up with me, then fell into an easy gait at my side. "Okay, fair enough. You don't like the traditional puffy white meringue-type dresses. So wear black. Or green."

"Can I wear my jeans?"

He laughed and eyed the pair I was wearing. "Maybe a washed pair?"

I swatted him with the back of my hand. "Get lost, these are clean!" Though when I looked down, I saw what he did. These jeans were ancient and had seen everything from the dirt of our training arenas, to blood from injuries, to cowshit. They weren't exactly pristine, even if they were straight out of the dryer. "Fine, a new pair. But you know what I mean. I don't want dresses and ballrooms."

Dom shrugged. "Who says you have to?"

I clammed up, but Dominic was quicker than that. "Austin wants a big wedding?"

We reached the café, and he pulled a chair out for me. I glanced at him in surprise, but he was just waiting for me to sit.

I realized then that Austin had never pulled a chair out for me. And I hadn't noticed because I'd never needed a man to do that.

But that didn't mean it wasn't nice that Dom had gone and done it like it was an everyday occurrence and not at all an odd thing to do for a friend.

I answered Dom's question as he got himself settled opposite me. "To be fair, we've never spoken about it. So I don't know for sure. But knowing him? He'll book a grand ballroom in some swanky hotel in the city, and invite everyone we've ever met, and probably a few dozen we haven't. It'll turn into some sort of networking opportunity for him."

Dom screwed up his nose then widened his eyes, like he'd only realized he'd been grimacing after the fact. "Sorry. My face isn't as tactful as my mouth. I'm sure a hotel wedding will be nice."

I laughed. "I think I agree with your face. It sounds awful."

He fingered the edges of the laminated menu without actually looking at it. "Okay, fine, so you don't want a typical wedding. What do you want?"

"To get married at the ranch," I said without even stopping for a breath. "There's a creek down in the back pasture, that's shaded by the trees. We'd have to shoo all the cows out of course, but it'd be the perfect spot to get married." I grinned. "And my stained jeans would probably fit right in with the cow pies."

"Nothing like the smell of shit to start married life off right."

I picked up a menu and busied myself, pretending to read it, even though I already knew exactly what I wanted, because I ordered the same thing every time we came here. Austin and I already hadn't exactly started off this new direction in our lives all that well, considering we weren't even speaking to each other the morning after our engagement. Dom's offhand comment about shit and married life jabbed at me uncomfortably. "Okay, enough talk about my wedding. What about you? Married anyone in the last twelve months?"

His eyes twinkled with amusement. "Oh yeah, been married several times since I last visited."

"Didn't like any of them enough to bring them out here with you, though?" I teased.

"Nah, thought I'd leave my options open for wifey number four." He winked.

I balled up a napkin and threw it at him. "Seriously, though. Girlfriend?"

"Nope."

"Why not?"

He shrugged, studying me. "Nobody caught my eye."

His gaze lingered on me just a fraction of a second too long, and I grabbed a menu, suddenly feeling the tiniest bit weird.

Last year when Dominic had visited, Hallie had teased me mercilessly about Dom having a crush on me. I'd completely brushed her comments off as ridiculous.

But something in that fraction of a second made me think that maybe she hadn't been completely off the mark.

Which was awkward, because I was with Austin, and I was never going to be the girl who cheated. It was highly unlikely he had a crush, anyway. He was just a bit of a flirt. Preston was, too, and that had never been an issue. We messed around and had a good time, but at the end of the day, we were friends.

I loved Austin.

At least I did when he wasn't being an asshole.

Which wasn't all that often lately.

When Ruth-Ann's teenage granddaughter came to take our orders, I was grateful for the distraction. I ordered the pancake stack, and despite my urging for Dom to do the same, he ordered a bacon and egg sandwich with a side of hash browns.

Our waitress left, so to fill the silence, I asked the one thing I'd been wondering ever since he'd arrived. "So, why are you here?"

He immediately looked down at the table, avoiding my gaze. "Needed a job. Your dad had one available."

"Bullshit."

His head jerked up at that, and he raised an eyebrow. "Blunt, aren't you?"

I shrugged. "I just call it like I see it. And don't tell me your dad doesn't want you working out at his place."

He sighed. "I forget that you know more about me than most people do."

I blinked in surprise. That was a little bit sad. Yeah, we were friends. We had some shared childhood memories from the times our families had made trips out to see each other. But we didn't see each other regularly. Hell, we hadn't even spoken since my accident, and I hadn't really noticed.

I was a bitch. I wished now I'd taken the time to call him. "Did you have a fight with your dad?"

He shook his head hard. "No, nothing like that. My dad is the best. My mom too. They're devastated I'm here." He gazed toward the kitchen like he was hoping our food might arrive and save him from finishing his story. But there was no sign of our waitress.

He sighed. "Did you know I'm adopted?"

I shrugged, racking my brain, searching for a vague idea of a memory from long ago. "Yeah, maybe. I think I heard our parents talking once when we were kids, but then I promptly forgot about it. You kind of look like your parents. You all have the same coloring."

"Yeah, everyone says that. It's just a coincidence, though. They adopted me when I was a baby."

"So you don't remember any of it?"

"Nope. But they told me young. So I feel like I've always known." He tapped his fingers on the table. "I feel really shitty about how I left. They've done everything for me. Never treated me as anything less than their son."

"Come on, spill the beans. What did you do? Wreck their car? Lose their prize bull?"

His lips widened into a smile. "No, nothing that disastrous. I wouldn't even be standing here right now if I'd lost Bucking Billy."

I sniggered. "Did you pick that name?"

"Shut up, what's your best bull called?"

"Grave Digger."

He chuckled. "Dark."

Our conversation was interrupted by the arrival of our waitress, and we both spent a few minutes in silence, digging into our food. As usual, my pancakes were amazing, thick and fluffy and dripping with syrup, just how I liked them. But as I chewed, I didn't stop thinking about the reason Dominic had effectively run away from home, even though he was twenty-four.

"Did something happen with your adoptive parents?"

He chewed and swallowed. "Was kinda hoping the food had made you forget about that. Yeah, something happened. Me. I had a friend who's good with computers find my birth parents. Well, my mom at least. And she lives not far from my place."

"Wow," I murmured, putting my fork down. "That's huge, Dom. Are you going to try to meet her?"

He grimaced, pain morphing his features.

It hit me in the gut. "Shit, I'm sorry. We don't have to talk about this. I can go back to teasing you about your four wives."

The lame joke broke a little of the tension that had cropped up between us, and Dom stabbed at his hash browns with a small smile. "No, it's fine. I just haven't told anyone yet because I feel like such a dumbass. I went to her house, the morning before I came here. She doesn't want to know me."

I swore underneath my breath. "Are you sure? Maybe she was just surprised and got a little tongue-tied."

"She threatened to call the cops."

"Yikes. Okay. Her loss then, right?"

Dom took another bite of his food and chewed slowly, mulling that over. "I want to believe that. I do. I wish I could be angry at her. But I'm not. I'm just..."

"Burying your head in the sand?"

"Yeah, maybe. Is that bad?"

"Normally, I'd say yes, but I think you're completely allowed to handle this in any way that you need to. If you need to take some time away and put a bit of space between you and Wyoming, then you're allowed to."

He looked so sad, and so broken, that I added, "I for one am glad you're here, even if I wasn't exactly one-hundred-percent welcoming yesterday."

He glanced at me in surprise, and I realized my words could have been easily construed as something more than the way I'd meant them. It was true, I was glad he was here. But this breakfast had also made me keenly aware that I needed to set firm boundaries with Dom. I didn't want to lead him on in any way.

"I really need a friend right now," I said softly. Because it was the truth. Hallie was always busy lately, either with Nate or work or the B&B. I couldn't blame her. Those things were all important, and things were really starting to take off for her. But it felt like her life was moving on without me. I had Preston, but he wasn't the sort of guy you could have a serious conversation with. He was all fun and games, and pranks and practical jokes.

Dom was more than that. Dom and I were similar in a lot of ways, both being the eldest child of pro bull riders. He got what it was like growing up with a father in the spotlight. And how that spotlight then shined on you and every move you made, big or small, good or bad.

He watched me over his meal, his gaze suddenly morphing into something that sent a tingle down my spine.

"Is that all you need from me, Summer? Just friendship?"

My stomach sank, and I played dumb, stalling for time. "What do you mean?"

He eyed me, indecision and longing flickering across his features. "I promised myself I wouldn't say anything, but fuck it. I swear, it's the only time I'm going to ask. Does he make you happy? If you tell me you're happy, then that's all I need."

"I'm happy with Austin," I confirmed quickly.

A little voice in the back of my head called me a liar.

But then Dom nodded, and the smolder was gone from his expression. He went straight back into his normal, friendly, smiley self. "Okay. Good, then. Because I could use a friend, too."

I smiled awkwardly. "So we're on the same page?"

He waved a hand around in the air like the last few minutes hadn't even happened. "Yeah, we're good. Should we get going, though? I need to get groceries still."

I put my hands on the tabletop and pushed myself up. "Let's do it." I followed him out of the diner, wondering how he'd gone from friend zone, to fire in his eyes, and back to friend zone in the space of minutes.

My head reeled.

And not in a good way.

7

Austin's car was gone by the time Dominic and I got back the ranch, and I was glad for it. I spent the rest of the day watching old rides from before my injury, something I'd always done if I was upset or annoyed and needed to refocus. Concentrating on my form and working out what I could have done better was something my dad had taught me, and it normally put me in an almost meditative state.

Only today, it had the opposite effect. I'd watched until I was angrier than I'd started, and then given up, flopping back on my bed to stare at the ceiling aimlessly while my brain ran a million miles an hour. Every now and then I glanced at my phone, but every time I did, it was still blank.

By late Saturday night, I gave up, realizing it was going to have to be me who was the bigger person. I grabbed my car keys from the table by the front door and drove myself over to Austin's parents' place. This would be the only good thing about moving to the city. It was well and truly time for the both of us to get out of our parents' houses.

I knocked on the door and tried to smile at Mrs.

Maxwell. Her smile turned into a grin as she recognized me, and she threw her arms around my shoulders, squeezing me tight.

When she pulled back, she was blushing. "Sorry! I'm just still so excited for the two of you. We're going to have so much fun planning this wedding. Austin said you were hiring a wedding planner in the city, but honestly, Summer. There's no need. I can help."

I blinked. Right, so Austin obviously hadn't told his mother about the argument we'd had. And what the hell was he talking about with a wedding planner? I didn't want some stranger forcing flower arches and synchronized dances on me. The thought alone sent a shudder through me. Along with a healthy dose of annoyance.

But none of that was Mrs. Maxwell's fault. I returned her embrace and mumbled something about having plenty of time to sort out the details.

She agreed and sent me on my way down the hallway to Austin's bedroom. The door was closed, and normally I would have just waltzed in. But my anger made me feel far away from him. Detached somehow. I just kept thinking over and over that he'd put my life in danger last night, and he hadn't even cared enough to pick up the phone and apologize.

So I knocked. Like we were strangers who barely knew each other. Not like a couple who had been together for years and had gotten engaged last night.

"Ma, I told you. I don't want any dinner. I've got a headache," Austin snapped from behind the door.

I narrowed my eyes. "Not your mother." I nearly added, "And don't be so fucking rude," but I didn't.

The door opened, and I came face-to-face with my fiancé.

"You look better than last time I saw you," I said by way of greeting, letting myself into his bedroom and dropping down on his bed.

He sat beside me, the mattress dipping beneath his weight. "I'm glad you're here, I was just about to call you."

A little spark of hope lit up my chest. "Oh?" Maybe I'd jumped the gun and come too early. Austin was good at holding grudges, but he normally came around eventually. Maybe if I'd waited another night, he would have been the one sitting on my bed right now.

It didn't matter. All that mattered was getting the two of us back on track.

His eyes glinted, a huge smile stretching across his face. "I got it!"

I frowned. "Got what?"

He rolled his eyes like I was completely ridiculous for not having any idea what he was talking about. "The job! The one in the city. They called me a few hours ago and offered me the position. It's everything I've ever wanted. Double the pay I'm at now. My own office and secretary. Just wait until you see it, Summer. They showed me when I was there the other day. It's not huge but it has glass windows that overlook the city, and we're on the fifteenth floor so it's a pretty awesome view."

My stomach plummeted, but I forced a smile. "That's amazing. I can't wait."

He grabbed my hand, hauling me to my feet, and dragged me over to his computer. "And I have a surprise for you. Close your eyes."

"I don't want to. I hate surprises."

"You'll like this one, I promise." He nudged me toward his desk chair, and when I sat, he came in behind me, covering my eyes with his left hand and leaning around me to work the computer with his right. There was a tapping of keys, and a clicking of the mouse, and then he moved his hand away. "Ta-da," he said quietly.

I squinted at the screen. It was a real estate website, with photos of the interior of an apartment on display. "What's this? Another apartment for rent?"

"For sale. Well, actually, it's not for sale anymore. It's ours."

My mouth fell open. "Say what?"

He laughed like I was a stand-up comedian. "I've been waiting all day for that reaction. I bought it! For us. Made them an offer a few hours ago and they accepted."

I was sure if my eyes got any wider they might explode. "I haven't even seen it and you bought it?" My words came out only slightly hysterical. Which belied the way I really felt. Because on the inside, I was completely flipping out.

Austin leaned in close to kiss my cheek, and I had to fight the urge to move away from him.

He didn't seem to notice. "I looked at this place when I was in there for my interview. It's perfect. Two bedrooms, which we'll need when we have kids. And it's almost brand-new, super modern and sleek. It's so gorgeous. I knew you wouldn't have time to come into the city to see it, so I just went ahead and did it. I'm going back to the city this weekend, so I'll see it again, and get measurements so you can start shopping for furniture. You love it, right?"

I started to tell him exactly what I thought of it. That it was nothing like what I wanted at all. Modern and sleek lines wasn't really my thing. Call me a creature of habit, but I liked the lived-in furniture at my parents' place. I liked that things squeaked with age and were worn and comfortable. I was the big wooden dining room table sort of girl, not the flashy glass-topped thing that only seated two people. I wanted to be able to have my entire family over for dinner, and for us all to sit around and laugh and joke and to be able to put my feet up on the coffee table if I wanted to. I couldn't do any of that in the apartment Austin had chosen without even consulting me. We'd be lucky to fit in a dining room table at all, judging by the photos. A panicky heat bloomed beneath my skin, and my chest went tight. I edged out of Austin's embrace, trying to get some air. He was crowding me, and it was all too much.

He still hadn't even apologized for last night.

But when I dragged my gaze up to meet his, something shook me.

His pure excitement.

Suddenly, he was the boy I'd fallen in love with as a teenager. The one I'd stayed up all night with on our first date while we shared our big dreams. It had all seemed so exciting back then, with our entire lives ahead of us.

I'd been brought back down to earth after my accident and reminded that dreams didn't come true. Not for everyone. Not for me. I wasn't the lucky few.

But Austin was. This was his dream right here. The one he'd told me all about as we'd sat outside under the stars, as seventeen-year-old kids.

So I forced a smile, put my arms around him, and told him I loved the apartment. That I loved him. And that I was going to love our life in the city.

But in that moment, I wasn't sure that any of them were true.

8

Dominic

I didn't see Summer again for the rest of the weekend. I heard via Lennon that she was spending it at Austin's place, and despite the fact I'd told Summer I was fine with just being friends, I'd still groaned internally at the thought of her forgiving him so easily for the stunt he'd pulled the other night.

But what Summer did, and more precisely, who she forgave wasn't my business. So it was probably a good thing she was away from the ranch for a while. It gave me time to remind my facial expressions to quit being so obvious.

By Monday morning, I had a clear head once more. I reported to the shed they used as an office at five to nine, early as always.

I should have known Summer would beat me. She glanced up from a pile of paperwork when I knocked on the door. Her gaze drifted to a clock on the wall. "Hey, you're early."

"Always."

"Yeah, me, too." She motioned to a seat across the desk

from her. "Do you want to push that around here and come sit by me? I'll show you how to do this invoicing."

I did as instructed, picking up a simple black metal chair and placing it beside Summer's padded, more comfortable-looking one. It squeaked beneath my weight as I sat.

She frowned at me. "I'll get Dad to pick up another chair when he goes to town. You can't be using that one all the time."

"No, no, it's fine. It will only be for a few weeks."

Summer turned her gaze back to the screen. "Right. Then you can have mine."

There it was again. The complete lack of excitement over the fact she was leaving.

Austin was going to break her by forcing her out of the country life. I could see it now, but I was helpless to stop it.

Not your business, I reminded myself.

She showed me a few things on the computer, but it was all pretty straightforward, and nothing I hadn't done before for my own family's ranch. "I think I have it. Can I have a go?"

"Sure."

We got out of our chairs to switch, and I edged around her in the cramped space, trying not to breathe in her intoxicating scent. But it was impossible. She had her hair down, an elastic around her wrist for when we'd later move to outside work, I presumed. The scent of her shampoo filled my senses. Her cutoff jeans were frayed at the edges and revealed her tanned, muscular thighs. It was almost a relief when she sat back down and they disappeared beneath the table once more.

Friends. Friends. Friends.

Friends did not check each other out the way I was. Or imagine what those legs might look like wrapped around...

Yeah, nope. Wasn't going there. She'd set boundaries, and I'd follow them.

Right up until she told me not to.

I really hoped at some point, she'd tell me not to.

The phone rang, and I jumped to answer it, because anything was better than thinking about someone who wasn't mine. It was only as I put my ear to the phone that I realized we hadn't even spoken about me taking over that role. "Hunts' Bull Riding School."

Summer watched me with a raised eyebrow.

"Sorry," I mouthed, while trying to listen to the guy on the other end. He mumbled through his request, and I asked him to hold for a moment.

I looked at the phone awkwardly, and Summer leaned across me to hit the mute button.

Fuck, her hair smelled good. Like vanilla and peaches. It sent my brain straight into thinking about what it would be like to lay with her at night and bury my face in her hair while we...

I huffed out a breath and tried to get my mind out of the gutter. "He's a guy from the WBRA. They've got a rodeo in Atlanta on Friday night."

She frowned. "What does he want?"

"Grave Digger."

"What?" Her eyes went wide. "Why?"

"One of the other owners pulled out. Family emergency. So they're scrambling for a replacement."

She thought about it for a moment, then shook her head. "No, tell him we don't do that."

I frowned. "Are you sure? It's the WBRA. They don't just ask anyone. Having a bull competing is almost as good as being up there yourself."

She rolled her eyes. "Doubtful. Nothing is like being up there yourself."

The door cracked back against the wall, and Frost strode into the office, cowboy hat perched on his head. "What all this about the WBRA?"

"They want Grave Digger for the Atlanta rodeo on Friday night," I told him.

Kai's eyebrows shot up. "No shit?"

"No shit. The guy is on the phone right now. Summer said no, though."

Frost motioned for the phone, and I handed it over.

He barked an introduction down the line, listened for a moment, then nodded. "Done. I'll send him down on Friday with my daughter and our new ranch manager." He hung up and tossed the phone back to me.

Summer squinted at him. "Since when do we hire out our bulls?"

Frost rubbed a hand over the back of his neck. "Been meaning to talk to you about that. I've been putting feelers out for a while."

"How long?"

"Ever since your accident."

Summer gaped at him. "What? Why?"

He sighed. "Because I wanted to give you something more than what you already have. I know teaching isn't enough for you. You don't get the rush you get from winning. I can't make you try to ride again, that's gotta come from you. But I've been there when one of Johnny's bulls have been named top bull of the year. It was one of the best nights of my life, and I know it was up there for your dad, too, right, Dom?"

I grinned. "Damn straight. We put a lot of work into those animals, breeding them to be the best kickers and spinners, then keeping them healthy and strong. You get a buckle for a championship winning bull, just like you do for riding one."

Summer didn't look convinced. She just folded her arms across her chest and leaned back in her chair, eyeing her father. "And you thought if I had a shiny new toy to play with, I might not move to the city?"

Frost didn't even try to deny it. "Yeah, that, too." He gave her one of his rare smiles. "Did it work?"

She sighed. "No. You know I have to go. Wouldn't you have gone for Mom?"

Frost's eyebrows pulled together. "I would have done anything for your mama. I still would. You know that."

"So why are you giving me a hard time then?"

Because Austin was a dick, and everyone seemed to be able to see it but her. Not that I could say that out loud, but I knew both Frost and I were thinking it.

"Because your mama would have never asked me to give up something so ingrained in my soul. She would have never asked me to be someone I'm not."

He brushed a hand over her hair in a fatherly gesture that reeked of him remembering her as a little girl, then left the room before Summer could even argue.

The door swung shut behind him, and Summer let out a growl of annoyance, throwing her pen so hard on the desk that it rebounded straight off and onto the carpet. "He always does this!"

I scooped the pen up and gingerly placed it back down on the table. "He just cares about you."

"He's trying to run my life."

I bit my lip, not sure whether I should say anything.

She threw her hands up in the air. "Jesus, Dom. Say whatever it is you're thinking. Your poker face sucks."

I cringed, but hey, she'd asked for it. And if I knew anything about Summer, it was that she didn't suffer fools. "I think he's just trying to stop you from making a mistake."

Our gazes clashed, and I wanted to say so much more. I wanted to say that *I* thought she was making a mistake. A colossal one.

But I couldn't.

She pushed to her feet and scraped her hair back into an elastic. "You know what? I don't even want to talk about it anymore. Let's go outside, this office is making me claustrophobic."

I stood and followed her. I didn't voice the thought that if the office here made her claustrophobic, that feeling was going to be a thousand times worse in the city.

9

Dominic

The week rolled on, and I learned Summer was a hard taskmaster. If I'd thought she was going to go easy on me because it was my first week on the job, then I would have been severely shocked. I wasn't averse to hard work. I wanted to do a good job here, that was the most important thing to me. I wanted Frost and Summer to respect me, and I was eager to show I wasn't green in either management or teaching.

But something seemed to have flipped a switch in Summer. She'd gone from being protective over her job, to dumping me in the deep end, and trying to pass the entire thing over to me in a matter of days.

I wasn't the sort to complain, so I just tried to keep up with her, all the while admiring her skill and the ease with which she ran this place. She was a natural leader and teacher, and the young guys all seem to like her. She knew how to joke around and have a good time, but she had their respect, so when she got serious, they listened.

Austin didn't come by once all week. I didn't miss him.

Friday morning, I had some cattle to bring in from one of the far pastures, and by the time I got back, Summer was waiting for me. "You ready to load this bull up and get outta here?"

"Yes, ma'am. Been looking forward to it all week."

Summer held the reins of my horse while I dismounted, patting the mare's sweaty neck. "You've never tried to load Grave Digger into a truck. You might change your mind once you see how fiery he gets."

I took the reins back, and our fingers touched in the process. I quickly moved them away, even though all I really wanted to do was hold her hand, just because I could. I'd meant what I'd said in the diner the other day. Despite the fact I knew she could do better than Austin, I respected her decisions. "He'll be fine. The fiery ones are normally the ones who do the best beneath stadium lights and with a crowd roaring. You wait and see."

"Hey, Dom!"

I spun around to see Preston hurrying out of the office, tugging his battered baseball cap back on his head. I liked the guy. He was a bit of a cocky show-off, but Summer was good at bringing him down a peg or two. And he did have the talent. Like Summer, he'd had to work hard, but it was there.

"I was just in the office looking for Frost," he explained.

Summer shook her head. "He's gone into town."

"Yeah, I figured when I couldn't find him. But hey, the phone was ringing while I was in there. Hope you don't mind, but I answered it."

From what I understood, Preston had been around this ranch for years, and was here so much he was like part of the furniture. Summer didn't seem at all bothered he'd answered the phone.

"Who was it?" she asked. "Dom and I are leaving soon, but I can return a call if it's urgent."

Preston shook his head. "Wasn't for you. It was Dom's brother."

I raised an eyebrow and pulled my phone from my pocket. It seemed weird that one of my brothers would call me at the ranch, instead of on my cell. There were no missed calls, but maybe I'd had no service and they couldn't get through. "Which one was it?"

"Felix."

Summer got in before I could. "Dom doesn't have a brother named Felix."

"Oh." Preston frowned. "Do you have a brother named something like Felix?"

"Theo and Spencer."

"Yeah, definitely wasn't one of those." He took a scrap piece of paper from his pocket and handed it to me. "He left a number to call him back on."

I glanced down at the piece of paper. My name was at the top, in Preston's barely legible handwriting, and beneath it was the name, Felix Kaur, with a string of numbers afterward.

Immediately I was jolted back to standing in that field at my parents' place and staring down at the text message with my birth mother's name. Maria Kaur. Felix Kaur.

"Is this a joke?" I snapped at Preston.

"Huh?"

Irritation pricked at the back of my skin. "Who told you I was adopted?" I turned to Summer. "You? Are you in on this, too?" I was all for practical jokes and having a bit of fun, but this wasn't funny.

But she shook her head. "I've never told anyone that. Not my story to tell."

Preston shoved his hands in his pockets. "I had no idea, man. I swear, all I did was pick up the phone and write down the message."

I crumpled the piece of paper and shoved it in my pocket while I tried to calm down. "Right. Yeah, okay, sorry for snapping. I just…I dunno. Thanks, Preston."

I led my horse toward the barn and handed it off to Hallie.

Summer followed me. "Hey, stop. Are you okay?"

Hallie shot us a curious look but moved the horse away to be taken care of, leaving me alone with Summer again. "I don't know. Kaur is my birth mother's surname."

Summer's eyes widened. "And this guy said he's your brother?"

I shrugged. The crumpled note in my pocket felt like it was on fire, spreading heat and a creeping sense of dread.

"What are you going to do?"

"Nothing," I said too quickly. "It's probably not true anyway."

Summer bit her lip, her disapproval in my decision evident. But at least it was a good distraction for me. Her white teeth, digging into that plump lower lip, drew my gaze, and it was near impossible to think of anything else when she looked at me like that.

It took everything in me not to reach over and pop her lip free, rub my thumb over the smooth skin, then follow it up with a kiss.

That would have been the best sort of distraction from the bomb that had just been dropped. But since kissing her wasn't an option, the next best thing was work.

"It doesn't matter," I told her. "I'll take care of it. Let's just get Grave Digger loaded and get out of here. We're going to be late."

Summer seemed like she wanted to argue, but I strode away before she could, and hoped she'd get the idea I didn't want to talk about it anymore.

A resounding crack of noise echoed through the cab of the truck, and Summer cringed, her fingers digging into the steering wheel a little tighter. "I told you he wasn't going to make this easy for us."

I turned around to peer though the peephole and found Grave Digger staring back at me with a 'I might kill you' glare.

"He's fine. He's just pissed off you took him away from his ladies. He'll forgive you once we get there and get him something delicious to eat."

We weren't far off the arena now, anyway. The open fields and small towns had already given way to more tightly packed suburban areas, and in the distance, the city buildings loomed into the sky.

Summer huffed out a sigh of displeasure when she saw them. "They're so ugly. And look at all the smog hanging around. It's like a dirty brown haze."

It wasn't really as bad as she was making out, but sure, the air wasn't as clear as what she was used to.

I changed the subject, not wanting to put her in a funk. It was bad enough that I'd been in one for most of the trip. It had been a pretty quiet journey, apart from the banging of Grave Digger in the back. "So where are we staying tonight? It will be easier to leave the truck at the arena and then just Uber to a hotel."

Summer pointed at the glove box. "Your paperwork is in

there. I printed out a confirmation slip for the room I booked for you."

I pulled it out and scanned over it. "You only booked one room?"

She glanced at me. "Don't worry, I'm not making you share with me. Austin is in the city for work. He always stays at the same hotel, and it's right by the arena, so I'll stay with him."

I busied myself with putting the paperwork back into the glove box because I didn't trust that my face wouldn't screw up in distaste at the thought of her staying with Austin. I'd had no idea he was coming, too, and it was a bit of a kick in the gut to find out I would have to put up with him at the rodeo tonight.

"It's good of him to come support you, with tonight being your first time as an owner." I was trying hard to be the bigger man, even if hanging out with Austin was about as much fun as getting teeth pulled.

"Oh, he's not coming to the rodeo."

"No?" I could barely contain my excitement.

"No, I figured we'll probably be backstage for a lot of it, right? Not much point in him coming just to sit in the stands and watch by himself. We only have two VIP passes. He's going to leave a room key at reception for me, and I'll meet him up there after the rodeo."

I ground my teeth to keep from blurting out that I would have sat in the stands by myself if she were my girl. I would have been there no matter what. Summer might have been trying to play tonight down, but this rodeo world was important to her. Austin had no interest in it.

"Yeah, I see your point. Just the two of us then, I guess."

"You, me, Grave Digger, and about seventy thousand screaming fans."

"Speaking of..." I pointed to a sign for the arena. "You ready for this? Because we're just about there."

She made the turn carefully, then glanced over at me. "Ready as I'm ever going to be."

10

I stared up at the huge building with a mixture of sadness and hopelessness. I really wanted to be excited for tonight. I knew Dom was, and I'd spent the whole drive quietly trying to pump myself up. Dom's family was big into raising bucking bulls. But that had never been a focus for my family. Dom's dad, Johnny, had been a good rider in his time, but he wasn't one of the greats like my dad was. Johnny had been happy to retire early and move into the other side of rodeos. But my dad had to be dragged from the back of a bull by his ear and forced onto a new path. He'd been one of the oldest guys on the tour when he'd finally conceded defeat after a knee injury that he just couldn't come back from.

Dom's whole life had never been about riding, not like mine had. He'd done the rounds of the local rodeos, and he was good. Better than most guys out there, but he'd never had the desire to take his career to pro level.

That was all my life had been about. From the minute I'd been old enough to get on the back of a sheep and try to ride it around a paddock, I'd wanted to win. I wanted more titles than my dad had. It was who I was. I was Kai Hunt's daughter through and through, and I was competitive to the bone.

It was incredibly hard to turn that off when it was all taken away.

I knew Dom and my dad were trying to give me something to fill the void. So for their sakes, I would try tonight. I would try to get excited about Grave Digger being the one out there in the spotlight, while I stood in the shadows.

I pulled my VIP pass lanyard over my head and forced a smile. I was at a rodeo, for crying out loud. This was one of my happy places, and at least I'd get to watch some good rides tonight. Then after that, I'd spend the night with Austin at the hotel. I'd barely gotten to speak to him all week, he'd been so busy with preparing for our move.

That move I still hadn't told anyone about.

Ugh.

Walking through the behind-the-scenes area of a WBRA event wasn't new to me. I'd never gotten to ride at this level myself, but I remembered coming back here with my dad when he'd still been competing. Dom seemed to know everyone. It felt like every second person stopped to shake his hand or ask how his dad was.

I nudged him. "You never told me how well-known your bulls are."

He made a face. "Hardly." But then another guy in a cowboy hat called out to him and waved us in his direction.

"See?" I asked, following along. "Peter Popularity. That's your new name."

He rolled his eyes and greeted the guy who'd called us over. It took me a second to realize I knew the man, too.

Dom shook his hand. "Brad, hey. How's it going? You know Summer Hunt, don't you?"

The older man's eyes widened from beneath his wide-brimmed hat. "Summer! Of course. How are you, sweetheart? Terrible injury you suffered."

I tried to smile at the head of the WBRA, though I didn't exactly love the reminder of my injury. "Yeah, it wasn't the best."

"Healed up now, though?"

I cleared my throat, trying to ease the uncomfortable lump that lodged itself there. The muscles I'd twinged trying to ride again had healed, and I was out of the sling, but I was never going to be completely healed. "Not exactly."

He frowned. "That's a shame. I was really hoping you'd be the first woman to make the team, what with being Kai's daughter and all. I've still got a soft spot for him, you know? Would make for a hell of a story. Much better for publicity than Millicent Young."

"Millicent Young?" The words flew out of my mouth, tasting kind of sour. "She's trying to make the team?"

"She's going to give the boys trying to qualify a run for their money, that's for sure."

A young man with a clipboard appeared and whispered something into Brad's ear before stepping away.

Brad turned back to us. "Excuse me, you two. There's always some sort of fire that needs putting out before the show starts, and it looks like I'm the only firefighter on duty. Real good to see the both of you. Say hi to your dads for me."

He disappeared into the crowd milling backstage, and Dom and I headed toward the pens to check on Grave Digger again.

Dom's arm brushed mine. "You haven't been keeping

tabs on the circuit? You seemed surprised that Millicent Young is competing."

"I haven't been able to watch it. It's too hard. But Millicent? She can barely sit on the back of a stationary bull, let alone ride one for eight seconds."

Dom chuckled. "I think we both know that's not exactly true."

I shoved my hands in my pockets grumpily. "Fine. She's good."

"But you're better."

Warmth flushed through me at his praise. The truth was, Millicent was extremely talented, and she worked just as hard as I once had. But I'd been damn determined to be the first woman in the WBRA. It pissed me off no end that she was going to get that title.

The first woman on the tour would make history. I had no doubt there'd be others who followed. But the first woman would pave the way. It would be her that little girls everywhere looked up to and tried to imitate.

Goddamn it. I'd almost forgotten how much I wanted it to be my name people talked about. Now here I was, trying to convince myself that *training* a champion bull would be enough for me.

Grave Digger was happier than a pig in shit when we found him in his pen, as were the other bulls that would be ridden tonight. These animals were a picture of health and vitality, and the security around them was huge. A prize-winning bull was worth hundreds of thousands of dollars, and I was still a bit shocked that Grave Digger had managed to make the cut. I recognized some of the other bulls and knew that Grave Digger couldn't perform half as well.

"So what do we do now?" I asked, eyeing the locker rooms. If I'd been competing, that's where I would have been, alone in the women's area probably, but pumping myself up and getting myself ready.

"We just wait. Nothing much else to do now. We've done our part, getting him here. Let's go find a good spot on the wings where we can watch."

"Oh."

Dom chuckled. "It's a much better view from backstage. You'll love it."

He was only partially right. The lights went down, and the pyrotechnics the WBRA were known for lit up the darkness of the arena. The crowd cheered, eager for the show to start. And they wasted no time, getting the first bulls ready, and sending riders out into the arena to do their best to get points on the board.

Dom let out a yell when Cody O'Brien scored an eighty-nine on the back of Crimson Hide. I clapped politely when Jordan Baker managed to one-up him with a ninety-point-two.

But all I really felt on the inside was jealousy. I watched Cody pump his left arm into the air with complete ease, and it ate me up inside.

They took it for granted, that they were young and any injury they suffered they could come back from. Nobody left this sport completely unscathed, but nobody assumed they'd be taken out before they even really had a chance to show what they could do.

When Grave Digger was loaded into the chute, I watched with a keener interest. He performed well, bucking and kicking, giving his cowboy a decent ride. The guy managed to stay on, too, and score an eighty-eight.

Dom put his arm around me and squeezed my shoulders. "Well, that was a pretty great start. Let's see what he's got for his second rider."

I winced at the stab of pain that rolled through my old injury. I suddenly wished I'd worn my sling, even though the doctors had told me I didn't need it.

Dom dropped his arm immediately. "Shit, sorry. Are you okay? I wasn't thinking..."

I brushed off his concern. "Of course."

"You aren't having a good time, though. Are you?"

I tried to smile, but I knew he'd see right through it. "No, not really. I want to love this side of the business like you do, but I just don't. I just want to be out there, competing, with the adrenaline rushing."

Dom nodded. "I get it."

"It's just hard to watch other people take my spot. It's not like I voluntarily gave it up, you know? It was taken from me before I was ready. I had goals. Things I needed to accomplish, and now I can't. And that just eats away at me, a little more every day. It's why I told Austin I'd move to the city. I've always known that if I didn't make the pros, nothing else would be enough for me. I love teaching, but it doesn't fill the gap. Neither will this. I need to move on. Find something entirely different to do with my life."

"In the city, though?" Dominic studied me, searching my expression. "Is that really where you want to be?"

"It can't be worse than watching other people fill my shoes and achieve the goals I'll never get to have again." I knew I sounded like I was having a pity party for one, and I hated it. But facts were facts.

Dom's gaze hardened, then moved from me to the middle of the arena. It was empty right now as the next rider prepared himself in the chute, so Dom stared at nothing but sawdust. I didn't miss the sudden tension in his shoulders, though.

His lips pulled into a tight line. "Fine, you want to go to

the city, then go. But don't do it without actually trying everything. How many times have you gotten back on that bull since you were injured?"

"Once," I admitted.

His eyes widened. "Are you serious? And you're giving it up because your first ride back wasn't perfect?"

Annoyance bristled down my spine. "You think I expected to be perfect? I wasn't even close! I'm giving it up because this injury is permanent, Dom! There's no amount of physical therapy that's going to fix it!"

"Says who?"

We'd both raised our voices, and people were starting to look in our direction. "Says my doctor."

Dom seemed to come to the same realization I had, that we were making a scene, so he lowered his voice. But his words were no less pissed off than his yelling had been. "Then you see another doctor. You don't just give up. The Summer I used to know would have never done that."

That got me in the gut and set a fire through my body. How dare he? He had no idea about all the hours I'd worked with a physical therapist, trying to get movement back in my arm. He had no idea about the pain it still caused. "Buck you, Dom. You don't know what you're talking about."

I stormed off, pushing my way through the crowd.

There was only a moment's pause before he ran to keep up with me. "Summer, stop. I'm sorry."

I shook him off. "I don't want your apologies."

He huffed out a sigh. "At least tell me where you're going?"

I had no idea, and I was too annoyed to talk about it. "Anywhere but here."

11

I stared blankly out the window at the city that would be my home in a matter of weeks. I barely saw the skyscrapers and cabs and the people out on the street, though. Guilt was too quick to rear its ugly head and taunt me about what a jerk I'd been to Dominic. He'd been nothing but a friend, both this last week, last year, and all the times he'd visited before that, and I'd been a complete and utter bitch to him tonight.

This had always been one of my problems. I was quick to anger, but I was also quick to get over it. I pulled my phone out and shot off a text message to Dom, apologizing for having a moment of insanity.

It was why I'd stayed away from the rodeo ever since my accident. Every time I'd tried, it just sent me into a funk that I could never seem to talk myself out of. I wanted to enjoy it again, but it had lost its magic for me.

It probably didn't really matter anymore, anyway. Austin hated the rodeo. Once we moved to the city, I doubted I'd have anything to do with bull riding. Sure, I'd ring my dad once a week on a Sunday, like a dutiful daughter, and I'd ask him how everything was going, but it would never be the same. It would never mean to me again, what it once had.

I tried to perk myself up with the thought of seeing my fiancé in a few minutes. I'd already let go of my anger over what he'd done last weekend, even though he hadn't apologized. We hadn't seen each other all week, and I didn't want to ruin another weekend being mad at him. This was supposed to be the most exciting time in my life. Getting engaged. Buying our own place, even though I still hadn't seen it. It was only Friday night. Maybe Dom could get Grave Digger home by himself tomorrow so I could stay here with Austin. I knew he was booked into the hotel until Sunday. Hopefully we could see the apartment and maybe even look at some wedding venues.

The cab dropped me in the valet parking at the front of the hotel, and I walked through revolving doors and into a huge, high-ceilinged reception area.

The man behind the desk greeted me with a polite smile. "Checking in?"

I put my phone down on the shiny marble, noting that there was a little number one in a red circle by my message app. I'd been so off in my head in the cab that I hadn't even noticed it come in. "Sort of," I replied, ignoring the message for now. "My fiancé already checked in. He said he'd leave a key for me. His name is Austin Maxwell."

The man's fingers raced across his keyboard, and then he pulled a white card from a drawer beneath the desk and handed it over to me.

"Room seven-one-nine. Just take the elevator to the seventh floor and turn left."

I thanked him quickly and pushed my oversized purse strap up on my shoulder. I hadn't really planned on staying more than one night, so I'd just thrown a change of clothes and underwear in there. I stabbed at the elevator buttons, and rode to the seventh floor, deciding that I could just go shopping in the morning. I needed new clothes anyway. I somehow didn't think that my wardrobe of worn jeans, T-shirts, and flannels was appropriate city fashion. I tried to tell myself that it would be fun to go buy a new wardrobe. But that would take some convincing.

I followed the numbered rooms along the corridor until I got to seven-one-nine. The card swiped silently, a little light to the left of the handle lit up green, and the lock clicked off.

But the room was dark and quiet, and I quickly realized he wasn't here. Disappointment seeped in that he wasn't waiting for me, but then I realized he wasn't expecting me for another two hours until after the rodeo finished. He'd said something about an early dinner with his new colleagues, so he was probably still there.

Not wanting to call him and interrupt their meal, I turned on a lamp and put my bag down. This room was fancier than the one I'd booked for Dom. It was set out like an apartment, with a living room and kitchen area, and a bedroom behind a closed door. I dug the toe of my boot into the plush softness of the carpet. It seemed like such a luxury. The ranch was all wooden floors, not even a rug in sight. It was easier to sweep and mop when you lived in the middle of a cattle ranch where muddy boots were the norm. But carpet was definitely one thing the city had up on the country.

A muffled noise came from the bedroom, and I flinched in fright, realizing I wasn't actually alone. Then felt stupid because it was obviously Austin, and he just hadn't heard me come in. I pushed open the bedroom door. "Hey, I didn't realize—"

A feminine squeal froze me to the spot. As did Austin's bare ass, the rumpled mess of bed sheets, long dark hair, and the red lacy bra discarded on the carpet at my feet.

Anger spurted inside me, spewing out of my mouth. "I didn't realize you were fucking someone else!"

"Summer!" Austin jumped off the woman, but that only made things worse.

That left her completely naked, her fake tits round and perky and twice the size of mine. She snatched up a sheet, but not before I caught sight of everything she had going on below, her legs widespread and glistening with the effects of what they'd been doing.

Shock punched through my gut, nausea rising and roiling until I was choking on it. But I couldn't move. Every muscle in my body froze up, locked solid, while I was forced to watch my fiancé rush toward the bathroom, pulling a condom off his still-hard dick.

His dick he'd just been fucking another woman with.

Hurt roared through me, but I stamped all over that, pushing it down, because there was no way, not in a million years, that I would let him see that this affected me.

Instead, I laughed. I let out a laugh that started from my throat but worked its way lower, through my chest until it rumbled through my entire body.

"What are you doing here?" Austin yelled from the bathroom.

"Oh, I don't know, I thought I was coming to see my fiancé. Did you forget? Should I have made an appointment with your secretary?" I glanced over at the woman who was trying to get her panties on so frantically that she'd managed to twist them up completely. "Maybe I can do that now? Is he free? Or should I come back at a more convenient time?" I raised my voice and shouted at the bathroom door again. "Like when you aren't dick deep in another woman?"

I bent down to pick up the woman's bra and tossed it in her direction.

"I'm so sorry," she muttered, putting it on. "I had no idea."

I flapped a hand around, not caring to hear her excuses. It wasn't her fault. I had no doubt in my mind that Austin wouldn't have once mentioned that he had a fiancée. It wasn't her responsibility to keep his dick in his pants. "Just go."

She struggled to grab the rest of her things and put them on as she pushed past me and hobbled to the door. I didn't watch her leave, but I was sure she was probably still only half dressed when she stumbled out into the hall.

Austin finally emerged from the bathroom and glanced over at the bed.

My blood boiled. "Sorry to disappoint you, but she's gone."

He folded his arms over his bare chest. All he'd bothered to put on was a towel, and that somehow made me angrier. He couldn't even be bothered putting on clothes and was standing there in front of me, his naked chest a reminder he'd just had another woman scratching her nails down his back. His pale skin was still flushed pink with the exertion of his effort.

Bile rose in my throat.

"You're early. I wasn't expecting you for a few more hours."

I gaped at him. "Is that your excuse? Yeah, Austin, I'm early because I was having a hard time being at a rodeo again. I thought coming to you might actually make me feel a little better. Wasn't I wrong about that?"

He pushed past me and strode out to the kitchenette.

I followed after him in complete an utter disbelief and watched while he took a glass from a cupboard and calmly filled it with water.

He didn't offer me one.

Lucky, because I would have thrown it in his face and then possibly hurled the empty glass at the wall. Or his head. "Are you seriously not even going to say anything?"

"Not until you calm down and stop being so dramatic."

I raised an eyebrow as hot, fiery fury rolled through me like the flames of Hell. My fingers bunched into fists, my knuckles cracking.

I'd never punched anyone in my life, but boy did this feel like a good night to start. "How's this for dramatic? You're dead to me. Thank fuck you went and did this before we got married, so I don't have to waste my time, or the ink from a cheap pen, signing divorce papers. You aren't worth it, and you can go to hell."

I grabbed my bag from the floor and stormed to the door.

He didn't follow. "When you're over your tantrum, we'll talk about this at home."

I swiveled slowly, stalking back until I stood in front of him. I tried to school my features into something calm and reasonable. Something rational that hid the rage protecting the tiny ball of devastation inside me.

He nodded, like I was a good fucking puppy.

The rage grew stronger, until it was a storm.

"Now, if you want to talk about this like adults—"

I didn't.

I swung my fist back and then rammed it straight into his cheekbone.

Something cracked, and I had no idea if it was my bone

or his, but his howl of pain was more satisfying than anything.

I didn't feel anything. I yanked my ring from my finger and hurled it at him.

"Summer!" he screamed, clutching his face.

But I was already on my way out the door. I let it slam behind me, closing out his cries.

Closing out an entire chapter of my life.

12

Dominic

On the tiny hotel TV screen, a shark sailed through the ocean, came up behind an unsuspecting orca, and sank his teeth into the whale's side. Blood filled the water, while the animals thrashed, foam frothing up in red-tinted bubbles.

I cringed at the vicious act, but it was oddly fascinating at the same time.

I needed to be more like that shark. I was so busy being the nice guy, always trying to make sure everyone liked me, that I'd somehow become the orca.

That realization didn't sit well with me.

Summer was off having a great time with her fiancé, after ditching me at the rodeo, leaving me completely alone to deal with Grave Digger. It was my job, fair enough, but it was still hers, too. She'd sent me an apology text, and I'd sent her one straight back, apologizing as well.

It was only then, when I'd gotten back to the hotel after making sure Grave Digger was okay in the temporary pen he'd been assigned, that I realized I'd apologized to Summer twice tonight, even though all I'd been trying to do was be a friend. I had my stupid feelings for her all mixed up in our professional relationship and didn't quite know what to do with them. I wanted to see her succeed. I could see that she wasn't happy and that she was hurting. Austin might not care. He might be happy to let her walk away from something that was a core piece of her. Summer was a bull rider, and even if he was willing to let her give that up without a fight, I wasn't.

So yeah, I pushed her. I wasn't coddling her, like he was. It might have ended in an argument, but someone had to say it.

"You're a fucking idiot, Dom," I muttered to the empty room. I'd come straight back here when the rodeo had finished. Why? A bunch of the riders and owners would have all been meeting up at a bar for drinks and to dissect each ride of the night. I would have been welcome there. Instead, I'd let my bad mood dictate my choices, and I'd come back to the hotel to sulk like a whiny fucking baby who hadn't gotten his own way.

I knew why. And it didn't have all that much to do with Summer in the end. I'd ditched the too-tight button-down shirt as I'd walked in the door, but I was still wearing the same jeans I'd worn all day. Shoved deep in the pocket was the balled-up piece of paper with Preston's messy scrawl, and the phone number for Felix Kaur.

My friend, Julian, had mentioned that my birth mother might have other kids. But there was no chance in hell she would have told them about me. She'd nearly called the cops on me for Christ's sake. I doubted she'd had a one-eighty change of mind as she drove away with a screech of tires, then gone home and told her perfect nuclear family all about the baby she'd abandoned.

I had two brothers. Theo and Spencer. I didn't need anymore.

But even I didn't believe that thought. I might have had two brothers who I loved, even if they were a pain in my ass from time to time. But part of me was starving for even the tiniest scrap of a clue as to who I was without my adoptive family. They were all I knew. They were truly all I needed. But there was still a part of me that yearned to know who I came from.

I couldn't silence it, no matter how far across the country I traveled. I'd tried to outrun it, but now that I'd gone down that road, I couldn't seem to cut it off. The road had wound its way back to me.

I couldn't just leave it.

I pulled out my phone and called Julian, flopping back on the bed among a cloud of fluffy white pillows while I waited for him to pick up.

"Bro," he yelled in my ear, without so much as a hello. "Where are you? Your dad said you up and moved to the other side of the country? Knee-jerk reaction, much?"

I stared at the ceiling. "Yeah, I know. Just needed a change of pace. Wyoming feels real small sometimes, you know?"

"Fair call. I'm pretty sure my neighbors know everything about me, right down to my underwear color and what sort of breakfast cereal I like. Nosy buggers. So what's up? I'm assuming you didn't just call for small-town chat?"

"Not really. You remember how you said I might have a brother? A biological brother, I mean?"

"You want to know about him now that you've had time to think it over?"

I nodded, even though he couldn't see me. "Please."

"Yeah, I saw him getting into a car with an older guy. Kid

looked a bit like you. Dark hair. Tanned skin. Tall probably, but he couldn't have been any older than twelve."

"Twelve?"

"Yeah, maybe ten? I don't know. Hard to tell with kids that age. Why?"

I shrugged. "Someone called the ranch I'm working at. Said his name was Felix and that he was my brother. Just wouldn't have expected that from a kid, you know? I thought he must have been older."

"Want me to research it some more?"

"You gonna get busted by the feds for breaking some sort of hacker laws to do it?"

"Nah, man. We good. Plenty I can find without getting arrested."

"Go at it then."

We hung up, and I tossed my phone across the bed. On the TV screen, the orca was dead, and the shark was enjoying his dinner. I groaned and stabbed a button on the remote to switch the channel.

The TV flickered for a second and then flashed up a warning about pay-per-view adult content. I squinted at it, realizing I'd stumbled on the porn channel.

I tapped my fingers over the remote, intending to flip to the next channel, but then I stopped. I was alone in a hotel room, with nobody to talk to, nothing to do, and nothing to watch, unless I was in the mood for another shark mauling.

Porn suddenly didn't sound like the worst idea.

I hit the 'okay' button, accepting the charges, and watched for a minute while the actress rode her partner, letting out over-the-top shrieks of 'pleasure' that nobody who'd ever really made a woman scream would believe.

A thumping knock came from the door, and like some fifteen-year-old kid who'd been caught with a *Playboy* and his hand down his pants, I grabbed the remote and hit the 'mute' button, glad my dinner hadn't arrived any later, or I might have been answering the door with a boner. And that would have been highly embarrassing for all parties concerned.

The hotel room wasn't big, just one room, with an en suite, so it only took me three steps to cross to the door, pulling out a few dollars for a tip.

I yanked the door open, ready to receive the meal I'd ordered.

"Hey, Dom."

The dollar bills slipped from my hand, and I fumbled to catch them. "Hey! What are you doing here?"

Summer stared up at me with those gorgeous brown eyes. "Long story. Can I come in?"

I pushed the door open wider, motioning for her to come inside. "Of course. Sorry, I would have put a shirt on but I thought you were room service." I closed the door as she moved past me and into the room. I checked to make sure it locked properly, then turned to face her.

She was staring at the TV screen with an amused smile on her face.

I suddenly remembered what I'd been watching and dove across the bed for the remote.

She let out a laugh. "Oh, please don't stop on my behalf."

We both widened our eyes at the idea of me doing *that* in front of her.

Her cheeks went pink. "Okay, well, I didn't think that word choice through, did I? Now we're as embarrassed as each other."

I chuckled. "I wasn't doing anything."

"Just preparing to?" Then she held up a hand. "You know what? Don't answer that. But do tell me if you want me to leave. I don't want to get in the way of your…alone time."

I rolled my eyes at her. "Piss off. I don't want you to leave. But I do want to know what you're doing here. Where's Austin? Shouldn't you be having your own 'alone time' with him right now?"

I immediately wished I hadn't said that, because it put the idea of her with someone else in my head, and that just wasn't something I wanted to think about.

She slumped down on the couch beneath the window. "Austin wasn't alone to have 'alone time' with."

She could have meant he was just with friends, but something about her expression said it was something more sinister than that. I couldn't stop my face giving away exactly what I thought of that.

"Yeah, that was my reaction when I had to watch him pull his cock out of some other woman's vagina. Good times!" Her laugh turned bitter. "*Buck* him. No, you know what? He deserves a proper swear word. *Fuck* him."

I went over to the couch and sat beside her. "Shit, Sum. I'm sorry."

"Why? It wasn't your fault my fiancé tripped and fell dick-first into another woman."

I hated the way she said it. So hard and matter-of-fact. It just made me all the more furious with Austin. What the hell had he been thinking? "Hey," I blurted out, grabbing her hand. "You're beautiful and smart and talented, and he's a moron who doesn't know what he had." I bit my lip as I realized I'd gone a little past the friendship line, but I couldn't bring myself to care. Every word was true. But I covered it anyway by turning it into a joke. "You want me to go kill him for you? I will."

She shrugged. "Don't bother. I punched him in the face. He's probably still crying over that."

I raised an eyebrow in surprise. "No shit?"

She let out a laugh. "Yeah, no shit. Frigging hurts now, too. My dad taught me a lot of stuff, but he's no fighter, and neither am I." She held her hand up, showing off an ugly red mark that would very likely be a nice shade of purple by morning. "Think it's broken?"

I studied it without touching her. "Nah, I think you're okay. I've had worse. I'll get you some ice, though."

I opened the mini fridge and pulled an ice cube tray from the tiny freezer section. I dumped the cubes into a hand towel and then went back to sit by her. She was staring at the porn again, but I didn't really think she was seeing it.

"Can I stay here tonight?" she asked, as I handed her the makeshift icepack. "The hotel is booked out." She threw me a smile. "I can take an exorbitantly long shower if you want to finish your 'movie.'"

"Of course you can stay. I'll take the couch."

But she shook her head hard. "No, this is your room, and I'm half your size. The couch is fine."

I studied her. "You seem to be taking this remarkably well."

She shrugged. "It is what it is."

I frowned. "It was a long-term relationship. And it just ended very abruptly." I realized as I said the words that she hadn't actually said it was over between the two of them. Maybe that's why she wasn't upset. *Fuck.* I hated the idea that this might not have been a deal breaker when she deserved so much better. "It did end, right?"

Her eyes widened. "What? Of course! There's no way I'd stay with him after that."

"Good."

We lapsed into silence, both of us just sitting beside each other on the couch, staring at the muted porn.

She elbowed me. "You think I'm beautiful, huh?"

I glanced over at her, and the corner of her mouth was lifted. I elbowed her back. "You're all right, I suppose."

She smiled, but then there was another knock on the door, and I got up again to take my dinner from the hotel attendant. I took it to the kitchen countertop, since there was no table, and motioned for Summer to join me. "Did you eat?"

She shook her head. "Was too busy breaking up."

"Come on then, this is huge, and I can't eat it all myself." It was a total lie, I could have easily demolished the entire burger and fries, but I wanted her to eat more than I cared to feed the rumble in my belly.

Summer wandered over and plucked a fry from my plate, nibbling on the end of it. We finished the food quickly, and then she disappeared into the bathroom. I turned off the porn and went back to shark documentaries while I waited for her.

After a while, the door opened, and she stuck her head out, steam billowing behind her. "Hey, Dom?" Her cheeks were pink, and judging from the awkward way she bit her lip, it was from embarrassment and not the warm water. "I just realized I have no pajamas."

I raised an eyebrow. "You sleep naked?" I had to pinch myself hard on the arm in order to not think about her slender body, bare and wrapped in silky sheets. That would be the complete undoing of me.

"I wasn't really planning on sleeping much tonight."

I stifled a groan. That was what I got for thinking about her naked. A firm slap in the face with a reminder she wasn't mine. "You want to borrow a shirt?"

"If you don't mind."

I reached across the bed and rifled through my bag, pulling out the old Wyoming Knights T-shirt that I slept in, and tossed it at her. She darted one hand out from behind the partially closed door and caught it, but not before I realized she was wrapped only in a thick white hotel towel. Her arms were bare and brown and still dotted with water droplets. The swell of her breasts dipped below the fabric, and her toned legs peeked out from below.

It was the sexiest I'd ever seen her, her hair wet, skin gleaming. I had to drag my gaze away by its ear and give it a stern talking to.

She wasn't with Austin anymore. That thought kept running through my head, and though it filled me with impatient excitement, I was smart enough to not let it give me hope. Tonight was not the night to make a move, and we were pretty firmly in the friend zone. I wasn't entirely sure we'd ever be able to make it out, even if she wanted to.

But I wanted to. Not tonight. Probably not even next week. But at some point soon, I was going to tell Summer Hunt exactly how I felt about her, and I was going to hope like hell that she felt the same way back.

"Thanks." She closed the door.

When she reappeared in my shirt, I knew it was time for me to go to bed before I made a fool of myself. The fabric skimmed the tops of her bare thighs, and there was no controlling my gaze as it rolled up her legs, settling on the hem. How easy it would be to lift it straight off her and see everything she had beneath.

Instead, I tossed her a blanket and a pillow and switched off the lights. It was still pretty early for a weekend, but I didn't miss the weary way she moved, and the yawn she'd stifled during dinner. Plus, I needed the darkness to cover the fact that Summer in close quarters, and wearing my clothes, was doing things to me. Things that were decidedly unfriend-like.

I slid beneath the blankets of the bed and undid my jeans, tugging them off, pulling them out, and throwing them to the floor.

Summer watched. "Didn't pick you for the modest type."

"I'm not, really. But I didn't think you'd particularly want to see me in my underwear either."

There was a momentary pause.

And hell if I didn't feel something change in the air between us. I couldn't take my eyes off her.

Her gaze burned through me like she was seeing me for the first time. "You might be surprised at what I want."

My breath stuttered in my chest, while my damn dick kicked to attention. "Summer..." Fuck, what was she saying? I was suddenly flashing back to the morning at the diner, and the brief moment of insanity when I'd taken the chance to shoot my shot.

She'd turned it down. And rightly so since she had a boyfriend.

She didn't have a boyfriend anymore.

Her eyes darkened in the already dimly lit room. "I hate him. I tried to wash the thought of him away, but the shower didn't work. You're here. I'm here. We're both adults." She shrugged.

Jesus Christ. I planted my fingers into the sheets, bunching them up until the veins in my forearms popped. I forced myself to remain still, but my heart thumped at the thought of what she was offering. Every part of my body wanted it. It would have been so easy to throw caution to the wind, to get caught up in the moment, and to do what came naturally. I squeezed my eyes tight, my dick throbbing behind my underwear. Then I drew up every ounce of willpower in my body and forced out the words I knew deep in my heart were right. "I think we should probably go to sleep."

I immediately wanted to punch myself in the balls. Going to sleep was the last thing I wanted when she was looking at me with eyes that begged me to fuck her. But dammit. She was angry, and she just wanted a revenge screw. I couldn't do that. Not with her.

I wanted more than that. So much more.

I respected her too much to take advantage of her tonight, no matter how much my body begged to cave in.

She nodded and sank down on the couch, the fire going out in her eyes. "You're right. I'm sorry."

"Don't be. It's not that I don't want to..."

Summer groaned and pulled the blanket over her head. "This is embarrassing. Please don't try to explain. Let's just pretend it never happened."

I frowned, but she wasn't coming out from underneath the blanket so there wasn't much else I could do but agree. "Goodnight, Summer."

"Night."

We lapsed into silence, but I couldn't sleep. I lay there, watching the dark lump on the couch twist and flail around.

The minutes became hours, and eventually Summer settled down.

Only then did I let myself relax.

I was verging on sleep when she let out a tiny sob. It was quickly followed by more, until they turned into heaving cries that racked her entire body, while she shoved the end of the blanket in her mouth, trying to muffle them.

I squeezed my eyes tight and hated Austin, with every inch of my body, for making her cry like that. Her tears were so filled with pain, each cry was a needle stabbing through my heart until I couldn't take for it a moment longer.

I pushed off the bed and stormed to the couch, crouching so I was eye height with her.

She didn't try to talk. The agony in her eyes was too overwhelming.

So I did the only thing I could think of.

I scooped her into my arms and held her to my chest.

Her head immediately fell to my shoulder, her good arm wrapping around me while she cried into my neck. All the anger from earlier had disappeared, leaving her a sad, broken shell of the woman I knew.

Before this, fragile was not a word I would have ever used to describe Summer. But in that moment, she was as breakable as glass.

But she'd let me in. She held me close as I took her to my bed, placing her gently down on the starched white sheets.

She stared up at me with big brown eyes, still filled with tears. "Did you change your mind?" she whispered desperately.

The question ripped through me. She wanted me to take the pain away, if only for a few minutes. But I couldn't. Not the way she wanted me to. It would end me. It would end us, before we'd even gotten a chance to start.

"No," I whispered. But I laid down and pulled her tight, wrapping my arms around her. "Sleep." I lowered my lips to press a gentle kiss on her forehead and breathed in her scent. I knew it would drive me insane all night. I already had my hips well away from her, because my damn dick couldn't be trusted. "Just sleep, Summer."

Her muscles relaxed one by one, until her erratic breathing slowed, becoming deep and even.

Safe in my arms, she fell asleep in minutes.

While I was just beginning the longest night of my life, in a hell of my own making. I had no idea how I was going to get through the next few hours without losing my mind completely.

Because my heart had already fled my body and was beating for her.

13

Dominic

In the middle of a new group of young cowboys, Summer was the shortest by more than a head. Those boys towered over her, but they may as well have been ant-sized, judging by the way they stared at her in a mixture of shock, awe, and more than a touch of fear.

She eyed each one of them, staring them straight in the eye as if she were taming a wild horse, letting each of them know exactly who was boss. "There are rules here," she yelled. "Me and the other trainers expect that you will follow them. Do not waste our time. If we say to be in the ring by 6 a.m., you're here at five to. Got it?"

Frost cleared his throat softly, and I glanced over at him. His eyebrows were drawn together, giving off a fierce vibe that was almost as scary as his daughter. If I'd been one of those brand-new cowboys, huddled in a group, I would be terrified of the two of them.

But I knew Frost better now. I'd been here almost a month, and I knew the face he wore in this moment had nothing to do with his new charges. And everything to do with his daughter.

Summer had been in a funk ever since we'd come back from the city. Her breakup with Austin had sent her spiraling, and as yet, none of us had dared approach her about it. It was the elephant in the room that we all tiptoed around.

"Right, so now that you know the rules, get your asses over to the seats, and listen, because I'm not going to say this twice."

Frost strode by me and muttered, "She's getting worse."

He didn't have to tell me. I could see it, too. She was sinking further and further into the anger that had bloomed around her that night in the city, and instead of it dissipating with time, as I'd assumed it would if we just left her alone, it only seemed to be getting worse.

My phone rang, and Summer shot me a dirty look for interrupting her class.

Thank God her facial expressions couldn't kill because if they could, my head would have been rolling on the ground, covered in dirt. "Lesson twelve," I joked to the group of cowboys, trying to lighten the situation a little. It was their first day, and I really felt sorry for how hard Summer was coming down on them. Half of them were ready to piss their pants. "Don't leave your phone on during class or Summer will have your head."

There was a titter of laughter.

Summer didn't even crack a smile.

"I'll go somewhere else to answer this then."

She glared. "You think?"

Yikes. The mood this morning was as bad as I'd seen her yet. I knew she wouldn't need me for a little bit, she still had some basics to run through with the group. I slunk away to the other side of the ring, so I could still watch and make sure she didn't try to dropkick a student, but I was far enough away that my conversation wouldn't upset her any further.

"Hello?"

"Hey, man, it's me."

Julian. I swallowed hard. "You got something for me? It's been weeks."

"Yeah, I know. Turns out it was a little harder than I expected, but I had a breakthrough last night. You sitting down?"

"No."

"Maybe you should."

"Just tell me."

"Fine. You do have a brother named Felix Kaur. He's older than you by—"

"Wait, what? He's older? I thought you said he was twelve?"

"I was getting to that. You have two younger siblings. Micah is eleven. I think he's the one I saw at your birth mom's house that morning. And you have a younger sister named Lila, too. She's nine. Their father is Maria Kaur's current live-in partner."

"So who the fuck is Felix?"

"It seems she had another son she gave up for adoption before you. He's about twelve months older."

"How does he know about me, though?"

"No idea, bro. All I could find was his name and date of birth."

I fell silent as Summer picked up a big inflatable exercise ball.

"Right, the first thing you ride is this." She pulled one of the guys out of the crowd and tossed it at him.

He caught it with both hands and put it down on the ground, then peered at her in confusion.

Her huff of irritation made it back to me across the other side of the ring.

Shit. This was getting out of hand. "Listen, man, I gotta go. Thanks for doing that for me. We'll catch up soon, okay?"

"You got it."

We hung up, and I broke into a jog, heading back to the group.

"Sit," Summer commanded. "Use your knees to grip the ball. Now get your feet off the ground and balance."

The guy did as he was told, managing to balance for a second or two before he put his feet back down.

He looked up at Summer.

"What, are you expecting a pat on the back? That wasn't even close to eight seconds! Awful!"

The guy's cheeks went red beneath his cowboy hat. A few others in the crowd laughed.

"What are you all laughing at?" Frost asked. "You think you can do any better?" He threw a few more exercise balls into the group. "Let's see it." But his concerned gaze immediately strayed back to his daughter.

Hallie watched quietly from where she was tying ropes at the top of the bucking chute, and when I glanced up at her, her teeth were sunk into her bottom lip, a worried frown creasing her forehead as she watched her best friend.

"Hey." I nudged Summer.

"You done with your phone call, Mr. Have A Chat?"

I ignored the jab. I knew it wasn't her, and there was so much more going on behind this bad mood. "Do you want to take the day off?" I asked carefully. "Your dad and I have this covered. You haven't had a break in weeks."

"I'm fine," she snapped.

One of the guys fell off his ball, landing on his back in the dirt.

"Fucking hell," she muttered none too softly. "What a waste of time this is."

"Okay, that's enough," Frost barked.

The guys all stopped and stared at him.

"Not you lot! Keep practicing! Staff meeting in the middle of the ring."

"Dad—"

"Now, Summer."

There was no arguing with Frost when he spoke like that. Summer and I ducked between fence railings, following Frost to the middle of the ring, and Hallie abandoned the bucking chute to join us. The four of us stood in a huddle.

I already had a good idea what Frost was going to say. Judging from the way Hallie stared at Summer, rather than her boss, I think she knew, too.

Summer glanced around at each of us, her frown deepening with each look. "What? Why are you all staring at me?"

"Because you're kinda being a bitch to the new guys," Hallie said. "Actually, not kinda. You are being a total cow. You're practically mooing."

"I'm not! I can't help it if they're terrible! What do you want me to do? Pat them on the head and tell them they're pretty?"

"Actually, yes," Frost spoke up. "You're supposed to be teaching them, Summer. Encouraging them. Not making them feel like shit because they don't know what they're doing."

She folded her arms across her chest. "Oh, that's rich,

coming from you. How many green riders have you yelled at over the years?"

"Not on their first day!"

Summer threw her hands up in frustration. "So what is this then? An intervention?" She glared at me. "Was this your idea?" She didn't even give me a chance to answer. "You know what? It doesn't matter. You all seem to think I'm doing such a bad job, then fine. You do it."

She stormed off toward the barn, while Frost, Hallie, and I watched her go.

Hallie's eyes shined with unshed tears. "I hate this. And I hate Austin for what he did to her."

Frost swallowed hard. "You and me both, kid. She hasn't been herself since." He sighed. "I'll go talk to her."

On autopilot, I grabbed his arm. "Let me."

To my surprise, he didn't fight me on it. Just studied me curiously, then nodded. "Go on, then."

Hallie smiled at me encouragingly, like I was going off to fight a lion.

Summer did look a little like a lioness by the time I found her in the barn. She ran her hand down her horse's neck, muttering something as she stroked him, her eyes wild with anger still.

"Patting an animal is supposed to help relieve stress, you know. Not make it worse. I think you're scaring him."

"Buck off, Dom. I'm not in the mood."

I folded my arms across my chest and leaned on the stall door beside her. "You know what? No. Not until you talk."

She only patted the horse harder and faster. His ears pricked up, and he tried to back away, but she held him by his halter. "What is there to talk about? I got dumped on my ass. It's just the way it is."

"Is that really what's bothering you most?"

She shrugged. "I don't know."

"Fine, don't think. Just answer. First thing that comes to your head. What's really got you in such a bad mood?"

"Austin."

"Why?"

"Because I can't yell at him."

"Why not?"

She raised sad eyes to mine. "He hasn't called me. Not once. He hasn't tried to come around. I'm pretty sure he went to the city and hasn't looked back."

I wanted to groan internally. "And that makes you sad?"

"No, it makes me fucking angry."

"That he left?"

"That I wasted years of my life with him. That I didn't stop all this before I became *that girl*." She said it like it tasted bad.

I pulled her hand away from the horse before she rubbed a bald spot on his neck. "You're not any 'girl,' unless you want to be."

"But I am! He made me into the stupid small-town hick I never wanted to be. I'm basically the plot of a Hallmark movie, Dom! How bucking embarrassing. Stupid naïve girl gets cheated on by her big city boyfriend. I'm a cliché."

I rubbed my thumb over the back of her hand, trying to soothe her. "Bullshit, Summer. You know who you are. And so do I. You're beautiful and smart and talented. You're Summer Hunt. The woman who can ride rings around the guys when she's on the back of a bull. The woman who can take a kid from the middle of nowhere and turn him into a champion." I couldn't help but grin. "Also, apparently, the woman who can make a group of new riders cry."

The corner of her mouth lifted a tiny bit. "Stop. I didn't make them cry."

"You sure about that? Pretty sure I saw moisture in a few of their eyes. You're a scary lady when you want to be, you know? I'd be scared. If I wasn't already an awesome bull rider and all."

We both knew I wasn't half as good as she was. She snorted on a laugh.

Her smile got me right in the feels. It lit me up from inside, just like it always had. I'd missed it, these last few weeks. I'd missed her. I'd been trying so hard to give her space, but now I saw that it had been the wrong thing to do. We'd let her retreat in on herself and wallow in her misery. No more.

"You know what also happens in those Hallmark movies?" I said quietly, looking down at her hand in mine.

"What?"

"The woman finds herself a kick-ass new life, and when the ex-boyfriend comes crawling back, she gets to tell him to go to hell."

Her smile widened. "You make a good point."

My gaze locked with hers, the laughter dying on my lips. I was dead serious when I said, "And in the process of building that new life, she meets a new guy. The right guy. The one who won't make her cry."

She froze. "Dom, I—"

I shook my head. "I'm done waiting, Summer. I'm pulling you out of your mood, whether you like it or not. Friday night, we're going out. Your new life awaits."

Before she could say no, I spun on my heel and went back outside to help Frost with the trainees. He glanced over at me questioningly, and I just shrugged in response. I really had no idea whether what I'd just said to Summer had helped or made things worse.

When she eventually came back and took her place

beside me, she stood a little closer than she ever had before. Our arms brushed, and sparks zipped along my skin.

She cleared her throat. “There’s a honky-tonk in Harlow County I’ve been thinking about trying.”

I glanced down at her, but she was steadfastly watching her father herd the group toward the bucking chutes.

I suddenly wanted to fist pump the air, but I kept myself in check and settled for grinning like a loon. “It’s a date.”

She didn’t argue.

14

I was so tired of being angry during the day and sad at night when I thought I could finally let my guard down. It wasn't even the fact Austin and I weren't together. I didn't even miss him. Not for a minute, which really showed me that this breakup was so very overdue.

But I'd been struggling with what to do next. In the space of twelve months, everything I'd planned for my future—bull riding, Austin—it was all gone. That had taken me more than a hot minute to get over. I ran the full gauntlet of emotions on a daily basis, until all I had left was exhaustion, a short fuse, and a bad temper I took out on our students.

I'd been spiraling and I knew it. I'd needed Dom to kick me in the ass and tell me to pull my head out. I didn't want my family and friends and the young men we taught to have to walk on eggshells with me, or whisper behind my back about what a cold, hard bitch I was.

I wanted to get back to me.

The me I was without Austin.

It was about fucking time.

Going out with Dom tonight was the first step. Nerves churned through my stomach, turning it over and sending jitters into my extremities.

Hallie flopped on my bed behind me, watching me put makeup on. "You look so amazing, hottest woman at the bar for sure."

My fingers trembled as I put on my eyeliner. "You're a great liar, but thank you."

"Have you not seen how Dom stares at you? He'd think you were hot in a paper sack. Actually, if that's all you were wearing, he'd probably like it more." She wriggled her eyebrows suggestively.

I tossed a tube of mascara at her. "Stop. It's not like that." But it sounded like a weak protest, even to me. And I couldn't help the little smile that pulled at my face.

She let out a holler. "Totally is like that and you know it. You like him!"

"Of course I do. He's my friend."

She waggled a finger. "Nuh-uh. Cut it out with that bullshit. It was understandable that you had to keep him in that box while you were dating Austin. But Austin is nothing but a stinking memory now, one I hope we all get amnesia and forget completely. But Dom is different. You gotta get that man out of the friend zone and into the boyfriend zone."

I wrinkled my nose. "I just came out of a very long relationship."

"Into the friends with benefits zone then?"

I shrugged. "I honestly don't know if that's what he wants. I already sort of tried that—"

"You what?"

"That night in the city, after Austin broke up with me. He turned me down." I still cringed at the thought of that night. "Totally rejected me."

Hallie sat up on my bed and glared at me in the mirror. "Oh my God, you've been with that douchebag Austin for so long you've forgotten what it looks like when a guy treats you with respect. That wasn't a rejection. I'll bet you anything he was dying to do anything you asked him to do that night. But he didn't because the man cares about you, and that would have been taking advantage. Imagine how much worse you'd feel right now if you had slept with someone the night you broke up with Austin."

She had a point. "He's been avoiding me, though."

"He's been giving you space to work through your shit. Just like I have. Just like your parents and sisters have. We thought that was what you wanted."

"It was."

A knock came from downstairs, and Hallie bounced a little on the bed in her excitement. "Go! Have an amazing time. Have some hot sex in the back of his truck!"

I spun around, eyes wide. "What? I'm not having sex with him in the back of his truck. Oh my God, is that what he thinks is going to happen?" I'd literally slept with one guy in my entire life. I had no idea what to do with someone who wasn't that guy, and the thought of it was suddenly terrifying. It was a completely different prospect to hitting him up for sex when I'd been so lost to my own misery.

Hallie rolled her eyes. "Stop psyching yourself out. He doesn't expect anything. I bet he won't even try to kiss you. It'll probably be you who has to make that move."

I widened my eyes. "Are you serious?" I wasn't sure if that was better or worse.

She shoved me toward the door. "Just go. Turn your brain off for one night, okay? You're overthinking."

She towed me down the stairs, and it was a good thing she did because I was suddenly contemplating running out the back door. This all seemed like a lot. I hadn't even considered that we might have sex tonight. Buck!

A warmth rolled through me at the thought of Dominic and I getting naked together. That heat only intensified when I got downstairs and found Dominic standing in my living room, talking to my mom.

I swallowed thickly.

"Girl, you got your work cut out for you tonight if you're really going to try to stay in that friend zone. Damn," Hallie mumbled.

He'd gone casual. Boots, jeans, and a V-neck black T-shirt. It wasn't tight, but it did cling a little tighter around his biceps. Lucky T-shirt.

He peered out at me from beneath a black cowboy hat, his gaze sweeping my body slowly, before returning to my face. There was a distinctly unfriend-like glimmer there, and I was glad I'd gone for a dress instead of my usual jeans and top combo.

The heat in his brown eyes warmed my blood, and suddenly, I was very aware of what had been under my nose for such a long time. Hallie was right. The man was gorgeous.

"You ready to go?" he asked.

"Yep." I couldn't take my eyes off him. His dark hair poked out from beneath his hat, his tattoos curling up the side of his neck and into his hairline.

"Wait!" Hallie cried. "Photo or it didn't happen." She grabbed Dom's phone from his hand.

He raised an eyebrow.

She shrugged. "What? Mine is upstairs, and Summer's is probably buried at the bottom of her purse. You can send it to us. Ooh, no passcode? Trusting sorta guy, huh?" She gave me a look that somehow made me feel like I should be writing it down on some sort of 'Dom's best characteristics' list.

"Stand together," she instructed.

Dom moved in but kept a tiny gap between us. I appreciated that he wasn't trying to get all up in my space. Austin had been the complete opposite the first time we'd taken a photo together. It had been after prom. I'd gone with Tyler, but he had been a complete dud, and I'd found myself talking to his friend instead. When someone had called for a photo, Austin had immediately put his arm around me, his hand dipping low and squeezing my ass. It had happened so quick and I'd already been a little bit drunk, so I'd laughed it off, flattered by his attention.

Now, older and wiser, I appreciated that Dom was more of a gentleman. I wasn't the same stupid kid I'd once been, who'd been a little in awe of Austin and willing to be steamrolled because he had a pretty face.

Dom was no slouch in the attractiveness department either, but it was going to take more than that to win me over now. I was old and jaded in comparison to the girl I'd been on prom night. But the fact Dom had manners, and he wasn't Austin, was two big checkmarks in his favor.

"You two are going to make gorgeous babies one day," Hallie declared, turning the phone back over to Dom.

"Hallie!" I hissed. "Stop."

When I glanced up at Dom, the apples of his cheeks had tinted pink. I couldn't help but grin and tease him. "That embarrass you?"

His gaze met mine, and his voice lowered so only I'd hear it. "Only in that I like the sound of it."

My gaze widened, and I choked on a cough.

He grinned, obviously enjoying that he'd caught me off-kilter. He stared down at the photo then held it out to me.

Hallie was right. We did look good together.

"Can I post this on Instagram?" he asked politely.

I nodded. "And send it to me so I can post it on mine."

His smile widened. "Austin will probably see it if you do that."

"I know. I don't care if you don't."

He chuckled. "Post away."

We both fiddled with our phones on the way to the truck he was using. I immediately went for the driver's side door and only stopped when he jingled the keys. "You want to drive?"

"Sorry, work truck. Force of habit."

He cocked his head to one side. "I don't mind."

Austin had always preferred to drive me around. We always took his car, because he didn't like my truck, and though he'd never come right out and said it, he'd have never let me drive his ride.

I mulled on that as Dom threw me the keys. I stared at them for a second and then got in behind the steering wheel.

I started the engine and let the noise thrum through me. It was comforting and familiar. As was Dom himself. A constant figure throughout my entire life that I'd never associated with anything but friendship.

Until now.

We got on the road, driving in the sort of comfortable silence you only had with people who'd known you a long time.

Eventually, my thoughts spilled over into words. "I never noticed all the ways Austin was bad for me, you know? They didn't happen all at once."

Dom glanced over at me. "Some guys are good at that.

Making little moves, inch by inch, so small you don't notice until they all rain down on your head."

"He never said sorry. Not just that night I walked in on him. But over all the years we were together, he never said it. Even if he didn't spin it so it was my fault, he'd just change the subject and talk about other things until I gave up being angry. I never noticed it at the time, but now..."

"Hindsight is twenty-twenty."

"I guess so." I sighed. "This is a shit way to begin an evening, isn't it? Let's not ruin this night before it's even begun by talking about Austin."

"You can talk to me about whatever you need to talk about, Sum. I'm not threatened by Austin."

Something inside me clenched. Why was that so hot? Austin was the complete opposite. He hated it whenever I'd even mentioned another guy's name, and Dom had been a source of conflict every time he'd been around. Dom's confidence was a breath of fresh air. "Good. But still, I'd rather talk about slugs than my ex."

"Slugs are nice. Good for your garden."

I stifled a laugh. "Okay, maybe something slightly more interesting than slugs. Have you called your brother yet?"

"From one frying pan straight into another, huh? If I didn't know better, I'd think you were deflecting."

"I've no idea what you're talking about," I said in an overly innocent tone. "But seriously, did you?"

"Not yet."

"Yet? Meaning you still plan to?"

"Yeah, I think so."

I grinned at him. "That's awesome."

"What's awesome is seeing you smiling again."

I realized he was right. I was sick of moping, and I was sick of being angry. Smiling felt good. "I needed this. I hope you're ready for bad karaoke and my awful dance moves."

"Have you seen me dance?"

I thought about it for a second. "Actually, no."

He cringed. "Well, get prepared to turn that smile into a laugh, because it ain't pretty."

The inside of the bar was dimly lit by small spotlights in the ceiling and wall sconces in the shape of bull horns. It was wood as far as the eye could see, wood floors, chairs, bar top, wall paneling. The place was jumping by the time we got there, and for half a second, we just stood in the doorway, taking the whole thing in.

Dom glanced over at me. "Drink or dance?"

"Definitely drink." But I eyed the dance floor and the couples spinning around it. The thought of getting close to Dom and having his arms around me was also a compelling idea. "Then dance. I want to see your two left feet." Because I had a feeling he was just being modest. I'd seen him on the back of a bull. He wasn't lacking for coordination.

"Lucky for you, my dancing gets better the drunker I am. After you." He motioned toward the bar and walked close behind me, his hand at the small of my back. His fingertips brushed my skin through a cutout in my dress, and it sent an unexpected tremble through my body.

"You cold?" he asked, leaning in closer.

I caught a whiff of his aftershave and hauled the delicious scent of clean man deep into my lungs.

I didn't want to be blatantly obvious about how his touch affected me. "Uh, yeah, just a little. But I'll warm up once we get drinks."

I found a tiny table to the far side of the bar, and Dom ordered us a couple of beers, putting one down in front of me. I picked it up and took a long swallow, grateful for the cold liquid sliding down my throat. I was such a liar. I was the complete opposite of cold. If anything, being in Dom's presence, just the two of us, alone like this, was heating me up.

Dom moved his chair so he was sitting beside me, rather than across from me, and sank into it. "Cheers."

We clinked our bottles together, smiling at each other as we took another drink.

"So, why this bar?" Dom asked. "Not exactly the local. I mean, do you even know anyone in this room?"

I gazed around before I landed back on him. I lifted a shoulder. "Not a soul. And that's exactly why I chose it." It had taken us over an hour to drive here, but it had been worth it to get outside our gossipy town. "I just hate how everyone is all up in my business at home. Do you know how many little old ladies have stopped me in the streets to tell me how sorry they are that Austin dumped me? I have no proof, but I'd bet anything he's spreading rumors to anyone who'll listen." Irritation rolled through me at the memory. There'd been three just yesterday, and all of them had patted me on the arm, and told me what a shame it was, and how he was such a nice boy. "I would have loved to have told them all what really happened."

Dom sat back, eyeing me. "Not you, though, is it?"

I huffed. "No. Why can't I be a petty bitch just for once, though? Why do I always have to be the bigger person? Ugh, how did we start talking about him again?"

"Okay, so let's talk about the reason I wanted to come here then. I Googled it after you mentioned it."

"Great, excellent. Shoot. Why?"

"That." He pointed to the corner of the room.

It took me a moment to look through all the bodies and see the mechanical bull on the other side. "You don't get enough bull riding at work? Or are you just showing off for the ladies?"

He finished his beer and held a hand out for me. "Only one lady I'm interested in impressing tonight."

I grinned and put my hand in his, letting him pull me up. I spotted an older woman, with a silver perm fluffed up around her face and enough makeup to give Dolly Parton a run for her money. "It's that one over there, isn't it?" I asked quietly. "I think you're in luck, she's definitely checking you out."

He sniggered and tugged me toward the fenced-off area. They had the whole thing decked out like a real bull riding ring, though the floor was covered in padded mats. Dom's fingers threaded through mine as we found the entry gate. His hand was rough and warm, calloused from a life of physical work.

Sexy.

Shit. I needed to get my mind out of the gutter. It had obviously been too long since I'd had sex. Or maybe that one beer had gone to my head? I leaned on the fence. "Go on then, cowboy. Go show the room what you got."

But a band had started up across the other side of the room, and nobody seemed particularly interested in watching Dom ride a mechanical bull.

Nobody but me, anyway. I was very interested.

Dom took a few coins from his pocket and crossed the mats, his weight forcing his boots to sink down into the foam.

"Dominic West with his first ride of the night," I called in my best announcer's voice, trying not to giggle. "He's had some pretty piss-poor form over the last few weeks of competition, but let's see what he's got in the bag tonight."

He shot me a dirty look.

I dissolved into laughter. "What? You have!"

"I've been teaching more than riding, get outta here." He grinned at me.

"Come on then, hot shot. Let's see what you got."

He swung a leg over the back of the fake bull and got himself settled, twisting his right hand around the rope and frowning at it like it wasn't quite up to his standards. "Rope is loose," he complained.

I snorted. "This isn't the WBRA, Dom. Stick your money in the slot and get on with it."

The band started a cover of Brantley Gilbert's "Bottoms Up" and I couldn't help but sway my hips a little. I loved this song.

Dom put his money in the slot, and the bull jerked to life, starting a slow spin and rock that even a three-year-old could have ridden. Dom raised an eyebrow. "How's my form?"

I snickered. But I wasn't going to pass up the opportunity to check him out either. His form was pretty damn fine, with his T-shirt clinging to his biceps and jeans tight against his muscled thighs. "Don't know if you're going to make it to the WBRA with that sort of posture. Sit up straighter."

The bull did a few more slow rounds of spins and jerks, all of which Dom handled without a problem. But then it sped up, each round getting faster and faster, the machine doing its best to actually knock him off. To my surprise, he went sailing over the top of the bull's head, landing harmlessly on the mats.

I burst into laughter. "Nice ride."

"At least I made the eight seconds?"

"Wasn't pretty, though. I give you a sixty-two at best."

His mouth dropped open in mock outrage. "A sixty-two! I demand a recount. The judge is biased."

"I'm your friend. The judge is biased in your favor. Anyone else would have given you a fifty."

He pressed some coins into my palm. "Your turn then. Let's see you beat me." He was joking and laughing, but I didn't miss the tiny flicker of worry that shone through.

I shook my head, smile falling off my face. "No."

But he wrapped his hand around mine, closing the money in my palm. "Come on, Summer. I know you've been cleared by your doctor. Just get on and have a go. It's a bit of fun."

I swallowed hard. "Everyone is watching."

Dom cast an eye around. "Everyone is watching the band or dancing. We're barely drawing a glance. But who cares anyway? Nobody knows who you are here. You're just some wasted girl, having a good time on a Saturday night."

"I've got a dress on!"

"All the more reason not to fall off, huh?"

There was a challenge in his eye that made him devilishly cute. He was right about no one watching. The main attraction really was the band, who were amazing, the lead singer belting out popular country songs in a gravelly voice that probably had every woman's toes curling.

Meanwhile, mine were curling in fear. But I also didn't want to back down from a challenge. It was a mechanical bull in a bar. I was a better rider than Dom. I had this. We were here for fun, and that was all this had to be. It wasn't an audition for the WBRA.

My boots had a heel, so I toed them off and padded across the mats, ignoring the slightly sticky feel of them beneath my bare feet. I hoisted one leg over the back of the bull, hoping it was dark enough that I wasn't flashing the entire bar in the process. I wriggled, trying to get comfortable. It wasn't warm beneath me, like when you rode a real bull. And there was no jostling of the restless animal in the chute, ready to burst out and do his job. It was completely still, giving me all the time in the world to get myself into position.

So I took it. Dom didn't rush me. He just watched on silently from the sidelines.

"You're right, the rope is loose."

"Not the WBRA, Summer," he mimicked.

Fine, I deserved that.

I sucked in a deep breath and dug my knees in. I still remembered what had happened the last time I'd ridden. How I couldn't do it, no matter how hard I tried.

I raised my bad arm experimentally and felt that same familiar flash of blinding fear mixed with a shot of pain.

I shook my head frantically. "I can't. I can't get my arm up. This is a bad idea." I scrambled to get off.

Dom jumped the hip-height fence and in two strides was swinging his leg over the back of the bull and sliding in behind me. He wrapped his right arm around me, reaching low to grab the rope with me. His chest molded to my back, strong and warm.

"What are you doing?" I asked.

He plucked the coins from my hand and slammed them into the slot. The bull immediately lurched to life, and years of training and muscle memory kicked in. We both went with it, Dom's body pressed hard against mine. "Getting you back on the horse. Or the bull, as the case may be."

"I can't. I can't get my hand up."

He grabbed my free hand as the bull rolled into a deep low, both of us easily countering by leaning back. He crossed my bad arm over my body, holding me tight. "You don't need this hand. You're good, Summer. Amazing. You're one of the best natural talents I've ever seen and I know you want this. I know you want to ride. It's only your head stopping you."

Deep in my heart, I knew he was right. "I don't want to fall."

"You will fall. You know that. But you'll get up."

"What if I don't?"

That was at the heart of my problem. I was scared of being hurt again, just as much as I was scared of never making the pros. One I wanted so bad, but the ache in my shoulder, and the movement I knew I'd never regain were constant reminders I wasn't the same girl.

I'd lost my confidence so thoroughly I barely recognized myself.

"Close your eyes. Shut off your brain. Your body knows what to do, Summer. I know it does. You just have to give it a chance." His voice was a low, deep murmur in my ear.

I wanted it. So bad I was willing to close my eyes, in the middle of a honky-tonk bar, and try to ride this fake bull in a way I never had before.

I shut out the world.

All my other sense heightened, and I breathed in Dom's scent, and the feel of him at my back, steady and reassuring. For a few seconds, my left arm fought to go up in the air, a force of habit that helped keep my balance, even if it did cause me pain.

But Dom only held me tighter, refusing to let my arm move, and forcing me to rely on the rest of my body.

The strength in my good arm, stronger now after a year of physical therapy and weight training than it ever had been.

My core muscles contracting, compensating to keep me balanced, my thighs holding tight.

Every time my brain tried to yell a reason why I couldn't do this without my arm, I focused on the man at my back. On the roll of his hips and the strength of his embrace. The way he made me feel like I could do anything, even ride again, because that's how strong his belief in me was.

I wanted that belief in myself. I'd had it once, and I'd lost it. But here was Dom, trying to give it back to me.

The bull came to a stop, and I opened my eyes. "What happened?"

Dom got off, a huge beaming smile across his face. "What happened? You, Summer. You happened. You just beat the bull. Without using your arm for balance."

I blinked. It was as if I was waking up from some sort of fog, or an out-of-body experience. I smiled, and when he grabbed me by the hips and lifted me, I threw my arms around him, squeezing him tight. "I beat the bull," I said, still kind of in awe.

His stubble brushed my chin, and he leaned back, grinning at me. "I give you a perfect score. That was a hell of a ride."

I shoved at his chest. "Nobody has ever ridden a perfect score."

He only pulled me closer, his gaze dipping to my lips. "I'm the judge. And I say you're perfect."

I swallowed hard. "Are we still talking about how I ride?"

His head bobbed lower. "No."

I sucked in a breath. "Dom...we're friends."

"We're more than that and you know it."

The breath rushed out of me in a whoosh.

Dom's eyes lit up, determined and honest, a fire burning behind them that roared of mind-numbing kisses and long nights between the sheets. "I want to kiss you, Summer. I'm just waiting for you to say I can."

My knees wobbled. "I—"

"Excuse me? Sorry to interrupt, but are you Dominic West?"

Dom and I jumped apart like we'd been electrocuted. Both of us spun to find a guy about the same age as us, staring at us curiously.

Dom's fingers found mine and entangled around them. He muffled a groan of frustration. "Yeah, that's me."

The other man broke out into a wide grin and put his hand out. "I'm Felix Kaur. I'm your brother."

15

Dominic

I stared at the man through the smoke haze, taking in each of his features. I stared so long the smile fell from his face, and his outstretched hand fell back to his side. "Shit. I'm sorry. This was a really bad idea, but when I saw your Instagram and it said you were coming here..."

"You follow my Instagram?"

The guy shoved his hands in his pockets and studied his feet awkwardly. "Sounds kinda stalkerish now that you say it like that."

Yeah, it did. But that didn't stop me from taking in the man's dark eyes, and his olive skin, and our near identical builds.

He screwed up his face. "I've really sprung this on you, haven't I? Can I buy you both a drink? Maybe my behavior will be more easily understood if we're all a little buzzed."

He chuckled awkwardly, but I had to be in some sort of shock because I couldn't move.

It took Summer squeezing my hand for me to jerk to

attention. I looked down at her, her fingers entwined between mine, and she nodded at me encouragingly.

"This is my friend, Summer," I said to Felix.

He held his hand out to her with an easygoing smile. "Good to meet you."

She shook his hand. "You, too. I think Dom could really use that drink."

She was right. My mouth felt like it was stuffed full of cotton balls. I nodded, and Felix grinned, heading for the bar.

"Beer?" he called back over his shoulder.

I let Summer answer for us. Then she guided us back to the table we'd been sitting at earlier and eyed me cautiously. "You okay?"

"No." I suddenly realized this was exactly what I'd done to my birth mother. I'd jumped out of the damn woodwork and accosted her completely out of the blue.

It wasn't a good feeling.

I groaned, keeping one eye on Felix at the bar. "Is he for real?"

She shrugged. "He seems pretty real to me. And I don't know if you want to hear this, but you two look alike. At least a bit."

I took my hat off and ran my hand through my hair before putting it back on. Felix came back with beers for all of us, and I took a long swallow of mine.

He didn't say anything. Just watched for a moment, giving me time.

"I'm sorry," I said eventually, after I'd downed half my drink. "It's just, this was the last thing I'd expected to be doing tonight."

"I tried to call you, a while back. I wasn't sure if you got my message."

"I got it. I just wasn't sure what to do with it."

Felix grimaced. "Ouch."

"He was going to call," Summer jumped in. "He just got burned by your mother so..."

Felix tapped his beer on the table, rolling the bottom of it from side to side. "Yeah, our dear old mother."

I swallowed hard. "You know her? Did you live with her?"

His eyes widened. "Maria? God, no. My grandmother is the only parent I know. You're what, twenty-four?"

I nodded.

"I'm a year older. Maria got knocked up with me when she was too young to look after herself, let alone a baby. My grandmother, her mom, took me in and raised me."

"But they gave me up for adoption." I swallowed hard. The words shouldn't have gotten stuck in my throat. I had an amazing family. But this was still a hard pill to swallow. I'd not only been rejected by my birth mother, but by my extended family as well.

Felix nodded. "I've always known about you. Not that I could remember when you were born or nothing. But Grandma tried to keep you, or so she says. But it was too much, two young babies. Maria just dumped us both and then went right back to her deadbeat boyfriend. Grandma was already in her fifties when I was born, and her husband had left years before."

"That's understandable," Summer said, squeezing my hand. "That would be a lot for anyone to take on."

I gripped her fingers tighter and tried to get myself under control. "So how is it that you're here right now?" I asked Felix.

He relaxed back in his chair. "I work on a ranch in Masonville."

"No shit?"

He chuckled. "My grandmother—our grandmother? Shit, sorry, man. I don't know how to phrase it. She grew up out here. I was a bit of an unruly teenager, so she sent me out here to work on her brother's property after I dropped out of school. Was supposed to just be a few months of hard work to set me on the straight and narrow."

"Did it work?"

Felix put his beer bottle down on the table. "Maybe a little too well. I never went back. Liked it so much out here they offered me a full-time job and I took it. Nothing fancy. I just do whatever needs doing around the place. But I like it."

I could relate to that. Country living and working on the land every day had a way of getting inside you. Something settled at the thought that Felix had found a love of the land, just like I had. I'd thought maybe it wasn't in my blood, but if he loved it, too, then maybe it was?

"Maria called me after you went to see her. Gave me the details on your card. She won't tell her kids about you. They don't even know about me, I don't think. She's estranged from her mother. She keeps her new life completely separate. Can't blame her really. She royally fucked up. Still breaks my grandmother's heart, though. But at least she thought I might want to know you. I called the ranch you were working at, but they said you'd moved out here." He grinned and held his hands up. "I swear, I only got social media stalkerish after I realized how close you were."

I blew out a long breath. There was so much rejection in everything he was saying, and yet, Felix was right here in front of me, actively seeking me out, calling me, checking my social media, then driving all the way here from Masonville so he could meet me.

I didn't think anyone had ever gone so out of their way

for me. With his friendly smile it was impossible not to like the guy.

I was leaving him hanging. I could see the worry in his eyes, that I was going to tell him to leave. I could see him waiting for it, another rejection in a long line of them.

I wouldn't do it to him. "Another beer?"

He looked at me, the fear leaving his eyes. "Hell yes. I got all night."

I glanced over at Summer, questions and an apology in my gaze, but she shooed me toward the bar. "Go! Get more drinks while I grill your brother."

There was nothing but pure excitement in her eyes. On impulse, I leaned in, took her chin between my fingers, and brushed my lips over hers.

It was barely more than a peck, not even long enough for either of us to close our eyes. Summer's went wide.

I just grinned and went to get a drink, knowing I'd caught her off guard, and feeling her gaze on me as I walked away. It had been a thank-you kiss. A thank-you for her understanding. For her excitement. For caring enough about me to happily turn our date into a family reunion.

But the next kiss I gave her would not be in front of my long-lost brother.

It wouldn't just be a peck on the mouth.

The next time I kissed Summer Hunt, I was going to do it properly. And it was going to blow her mind.

16

Felix was amazing. Genuinely one of the nicest guys I'd ever met. He kept me and Dom entertained all evening, telling us stories about the ranch he worked on, and growing up with his grandmother, and the trouble he'd gotten into when he was younger. Once Dom loosened up, the two of them talked like they'd known each other all their lives.

The three of us laughed until two in the morning, when the bar closed, and they kicked us out.

But even as we said goodbye to Felix in the deserted parking lot, Dom's kiss was still playing over and over in my head.

My mouth still tingled from that tiny brush from his. My lips were still seared with his touch and aching for more of it. Heat still pulsated up my arm, from where our fingers were joined.

He barely let go of my hand all night. Every time he'd gotten up to go to the bar, or the bathroom, as soon as he'd returned, he'd picked my hand right back up and stroked his fingers through mine.

It was the most innocent of touches, but between that, and the brief preview of what kissing him might feel like, and beating the bull, tonight had been the best date of my life.

We waved as Felix drove away, and then Dom turned to me.

I grinned at him. "Well, that was a bit amazing."

I'd never seen Dom smile so big. He threw his arms around me, picking me up and twirling me around, both of us laughing.

"He's great, right? You liked him?"

I nodded. "Definitely. I'm so happy for you."

His gaze darted all over my face, his excitement palpable. But then it dimmed a little. "Shit, though, Summer. I completely ruined our date."

"Not a chance. I had an amazing time."

A little of his smile came back. "I did, too. But there was one thing I wanted to do tonight, that I didn't get to."

"Eat the nachos?" I joked. "Really, they were way better than what you ordered."

He shook his head, that tiny smile playing around his lips again. "No, not that. I didn't get to dance with you."

"It's okay. Next time." I blushed at how presumptuous I was being. But I also really wanted there to be a next time. I wanted him to know that.

"I don't want to wait until next time. I don't want to go to bed tonight, kicking myself for missing my chance." He tugged me toward the truck and leaned through the open window, hitting a button on the dashboard. It lit up, and a fast-paced, boot-scooting song blared through the speakers.

I did a little jig, trying to keep up with the incredibly fast notes.

Dom sniggered and took his phone from his pocket,

switching the stereo to Bluetooth. In the next moment, the song changed abruptly, and "Slow Dance in a Parking Lot" by Jordan Davis started playing.

I raised an eyebrow. "You trying to tell me something with this song choice, cowboy?"

He grinned and stepped in close, pulling me into his arms. "Yes. I'm trying to tell you that I want to dance with you. Right here. Right now. At 2 a.m. In a parking lot. How about it?"

I grinned up at him, my heart thumping. "The bouncer is probably watching."

"I don't care who's watching, Summer. I just want to dance with you."

My knees went weak. "I'd like that."

The lyrics washed over us as he spun me around beneath a sky full of stars, with the warm, summer night air misting over our skin. I leaned into his body, resting my head against his chest, and he slowed it right down to a sway. His fingers brushed the bare skin at my lower back, sending delicious trembles through my entire body.

"I need to ask you something," he murmured into my hair.

I leaned back an inch and stared up at him. "What?"

"Is this thing with you and me a rebound? If I kiss you right now, will this be a one-time thing that is all mixed up with your feelings for Austin? Because I don't want to be that guy for you. If you need a rebound, I get it. But it can't be me." He stopped dancing and tilted my chin up, his eyes burning into mine. "I'm not a one-night stand. Not for you. I'm the guy you fall in love with, Summer. That's all there is to it."

Shock punched through my gut, stealing my breath. I clutched him tighter while my head spun with the enormity of what he'd said. I opened my mouth to answer, and his gaze dropped to my lips. A growl of need reverberated from his chest, and his hand snaked into my hair, tugging it back so my face was fully lifted to his.

I closed my eyes, a throbbing starting up in my core.

"I want you, Summer," he murmured. "Don't say no."

I pulled his head down to meet mine, but his lips hovered just an inch away, our breaths mingling.

"Say it. Say yes," he whispered.

I couldn't give him promises. Not the sort he wanted. This wasn't one night for me, but I'd been burned so bad. I couldn't promise him a forever. I couldn't promise him I could fall in love with him when I had no idea if that part of me had been obliterated by someone else.

So I gave him what I could.

I gave him the truth. "I need you," I whispered.

Then I waited to see if that was enough.

His lips slammed down on mine, and his fingers dug into my hips, picking me up and pressing me back on the truck.

His kiss stole the breath from my lungs, leaving me hungry and desperate for more, and when his tongue ran the seam of my mouth, I opened for him, letting him in, letting him feel how bad I wanted him. I clutched at him, kissing him desperately, wanting his body against mine, his dick hard behind his jeans, teasing the softness at my core. Our mouths moved in effortless synchronization, while my head fought to lose it completely and entirely, over a man who'd been my friend for the longest time.

In that moment, I realized I'd never been kissed before. Not like this. Not where kissing became a whole-body experience that blocked out everything around us. The parking lot disappeared in Dom's kiss, the bouncer, the music playing on the truck speakers. All of it paled in comparison to the way Dom held me, and the way his body felt, moving with mine.

He was right. He wasn't a one-night-stand sort of guy.

He was the sort of guy who had the power to make you fall in love right there and then, with a solitary kiss.

He was the sort of guy whose kiss made you realize there would be no other kisses like it, no matter how long you lived.

He was the sort of guy who kissed you, then broke your heart, if he ever decided that what he wanted wasn't you.

And I was the sort of girl who didn't care. Because in that moment, he was everything. And I was the girl who was willing to open up her heart again, willing to fall, no matter how much it might hurt if the day ever came when he changed his mind.

17

Dominic

In an effort to not appear completely desperate, I promised myself I wasn't going to call or try to see Summer until Monday. I'd really put myself on the line before our kiss the other night, and though I'd meant every word, I'd seriously gone from zero to one hundred in the space of an evening. Now I was kind of worried I might have scared her off.

I managed to keep myself away from the main house on Saturday, and instead laid low, with a stupid grin on my face every time I thought about Summer. I called my parents and talked to them for a while, watched some Netflix, texted Felix, and had beers with Preston and a couple of the other guys who were living on the property.

But by Sunday morning, I knew I wasn't going to make it through the day without seeing her. If I looked like a desperate fool, then I'd wear it with pride.

I wanted to see her. I wanted to pick right up where we'd left off, kissing beneath the stars. That wasn't going to happen if I hid out in my cabin all weekend. I picked up my phone and shot her a text.

I can't stop thinking about you.

My thumb hovered over the 'send message.' "Going a hundred miles an hour again," I muttered. But fuck, I'd been patient so long. Years I'd waited for her, barely dating because nobody ever interested me the way she did.

Then I remembered the way she'd felt in my arms and I took a chance. I hit 'send.'

Then I stared at my damn phone, desperately waiting for those little dots to appear that signaled she was typing back.

Nothing came.

I groaned and got my ass out of bed, dragging it into my shower. I turned it all the way to cold, but even the barely room temperature water cascading over my head did nothing to get me thinking any more clearly. My mind just started drifting to what I could be doing if Summer were here with me right now, instead of just a few hundred meters away, in her bedroom.

I wanted to know if she was thinking about me. If she was reliving that kiss in the parking lot and wishing we'd taken it further. We had time. There was no need to rush, but fuck. It was so hard to keep myself in line.

The moment I got out of the shower, I wrapped a fluffy white towel around my torso and padded barefoot back into my bedroom to check my phone.

Still no message.

I got dressed and wandered over to the training rings, pleased when Frost was sitting high on the bleachers, watching a couple of guys practice. I climbed the stairs to sit beside him, neither of us uttering a greeting. We both watched in silence for a while, Frost jotting down a few things on a notepad.

"Heard you took Summer out."

"Yes, sir." We'd ditched the formalities at work a long time ago, but I was well aware he wasn't speaking to me as a boss, but as a father. That commanded a different sort of respect.

"Good. She needs a friend right now."

Warmth crept up the back of my neck. I wasn't a good liar, but it also wasn't my place to tell Summer's dad about us. Summer and I hadn't even discussed it, so there was no way I was going to do that with Kai.

My phone buzzed in my pocket, and I pulled it out, a grin spreading across my face when I realized it was Summer. I angled my phone away from Frost before I opened her message.

I spent the night at Hallie's place. Girl talk was needed. But I can't stop thinking about you either.

I leapt to my feet and punched the air. "Yes!"

The guys down in the ring looked up at me in confusion.

Kai frowned. "What the fuck are you doing? That ride was awful."

"The ride? Oh, right. Yeah. Terrible." I hadn't seen a second of it.

"So what are you cheering about?"

It was all I could do not to blurt it out. "Nothing. Uh. My favorite football team back home just won a game. I gotta go." I wasn't scheduled to work today, there was no need for me to be here. I was just going to put my foot in it with Summer's old man if I kept trying to lie. Now that I knew she wasn't here anyway, it was better if I avoided Frost for the rest of the day.

I jogged down the stairs again before he could stop me. I had one to go when he called out.

"Dinner at our place tonight, Dom."

I swiveled on my heel. "Huh?"

Frost was gazing at me intently from beneath his hat. "Sunday night family dinner. You haven't been to one since you got here. Seven. Be there."

"Yes, sir."

He gave a 'you're dismissed' flick of his head, and I went back to my cabin. Despite the fact I'd been invited to Sunday night dinners from the day I'd arrived, I'd felt like I was intruding. But now it was the perfect opportunity to see Summer. Because there was no way I could wait until Monday morning.

18

Hallie peered over my shoulder as I sent the text message to Dom off into cyber space. Then she rolled her eyes. "You two are so wholesomely cute, with your 'can't stop thinking about yous.'"

I flopped back on her super-soft couch and tucked my feet up beneath me. "I know."

"I still can't believe all you did with him the other night was kiss, after he danced with you in the moonlight. If Nate had done that, I would have done him on the back seat."

We both laughed, but then I sighed remembering the world's most amazing kiss, and the way it had made me feel. I'd gone to bed the last two nights desperately happy. And desperately horny. I'd definitely been thinking about doing Dom on the back seat. In a bed. In the barn. Pretty much everywhere. My body still remembered the feel of Dom's erection pressing against me in the parking lot. And my body had reminded me ever since that it had been ages since I'd had sex, and even longer since I'd had *good* sex. The kind of sex that Dom's kiss had promised. "Trust me, Hallie. I've got a severe case of blue balls. I'm so horny, I might even look at you twice right now." I winked at her.

She tossed a pretzel at me. But then she put the bowl of snacks down and held out a hand to me. "Come on, let's get you laid."

I squinted at her hand, not daring to touch it. "I was joking. I love you, but not like that."

She rolled her eyes. "Stop. We're going shopping."

I got off the couch and followed her, picking up my purse as my phone buzzed again.

I want to kiss you again. If you were here right now, I would.

Heat bloomed in my cheeks, and I got into the passenger seat of Hallie's green Volkswagen Beetle. Hallie raised an eyebrow, and I flashed the screen at her.

She grinned. "Write something back already!"

"What, though?"

She snatched my phone from my hands and typed something in, while I grappled to get my phone back.

"There! Sent!" She tossed it back at me with a huge grin and started the car.

I frantically read the message.

What else would you do if I were there?

My eyes widened. "Hallie! Jesus, now he's going to think I want to sext him!"

She laughed her head off. "I know! Because you do! You just told me how horny you are, when you should be telling him!"

Heat burned in my cheeks, but there were those three little dots on the screen, and I couldn't deny that a huge part of me desperately wanted to know what he was going to say.

When the phone buzzed again, I made sure it was well free of Hallie's grabby hands before I opened it.

I'd brush your hair off your neck, gathering it up so I could tilt your head to one side. I'd come in close behind you, and kiss that spot right below your ear. Then I'd move lower.

I blew out a slow breath, almost able to feel exactly how that would feel even without him there.

Hallie glanced over at me. "Good response?"

I grinned. "Very good."

Her smile turned smug. "Dirty text messaging is the best foreplay. Write something back."

You were hard when you kissed me the other night.

The miles flashed by outside, and Hallie sang along with the radio until we made it into town. She parked the car and took my hand.

"Where are we going?" Nerves still fluttered through me at what I was doing with Dom. He still hadn't written back.

"You'll see. We're just about there." She dragged me a long for few more steps before dragging me into a women's clothing store and leading me all the way to the back where they stocked underwear.

Hallie immediately started pulling sets of bras and panties out and tossing them in my direction. "What do you think he likes? Black? Red? Virginal white? See-through?"

I watched the pile in my hands grow. "I've no idea. But I am not wearing those." I passed her back a set that was nothing more than a scrap of lace and considered a pair that were much more sensible-looking. Much more me.

Hallie steered me right back to the sexy stuff. "How about these?" She took out a low-cut black lace bra with a matching thong.

I eyed the set. "There's no ass in it."

"Because your ass is smoking all by itself. Flaunt it."

My phone buzzed again, and I glanced down at it.

I'm hard every time I think about you.

Heat flushed through me. I snatched the underwear

from her hand and tossed it at the cashier. "I'll take those please."

Hallie grinned. "You're so getting laid tonight."

I bit my lip, trying to hide my smile. I could only hope she was right.

19

Dominic

I was already standing in Summer's parents' living room when she made it home from Hallie's place. She slammed through the front door with an armful of shopping bags slung over one arm and a takeaway coffee in her free hand. "Sorry I'm late, I went shopping with Hal—"

She stopped dead when she saw me.

"Hi!" she squeaked, her cheeks going pink.

"Hi."

The phone in my pocket still burned with the messages we'd been sending each other all afternoon. They'd gotten progressively dirtier as the afternoon had worn on.

"What are you doing here?"

Frost looked up from the drinks he was pouring and eyed her shopping bags. "He's here for dinner. You want a hand with those bags?"

She clutched them tighter to her side. "No! It's fine. I'm just going to get changed. I'll be right back."

Her gaze lingered on me for a moment, her mouth turning up at the corner before she ran upstairs.

It took everything in me not to run after her.

Mrs. Hunt took a drink from her husband and then passed one to me. I took a hefty swallow.

"I spoke to your mother last night." Addie patted my arm. "I think she might be missing you a bit."

That old familiar guilt rolled through me. "I know. I spoke to her yesterday, and she kept telling me all the things I was missing out on at home. I think she's hoping if I miss it enough, I might go back."

Addie shot a look toward the stairs her daughter had just disappeared up. "Will you?"

I shook my head. "I've no plans to leave anytime soon. I'm happy here. There's a lot to like about living on your property." I didn't mention that my biological brother being only a few hours away was one. And that their eldest daughter was very much the other.

I eyed the stairs again, impatient to see her walk down them.

A timer went off in the kitchen, and Addie excused herself to go check on the oven. Frost had flicked on the TV to a baseball game, so I sat on the other couch and got out my phone.

With a smirk, I sent Summer another text. *Get down here before I come up there after you.*

Immediately the little text bubbles appeared, and a second later, her message. *I bought you something while I was out.*

Yeah? What?

I'm putting it on. But you can't see it until later.

Holy shit.

Did that mean what I think it did? My head snapped up as she walked down the stairs in a blue cotton summer dress, our gazes clashing. It was pretty and free flowing with tiny little flowers, but I could see that...her message had said I couldn't see it until later. So she must have been talking about what was under it. I took a long swallow of my drink and a few deep breaths in order to keep my dick under control.

The doorbell rang, and Frost looked toward it with a puzzled expression. "Who the hell uses the bell around here?"

Summer shrugged and took a step toward the entranceway, but Lennon and Callie came thundering down the stairs, pushing and shoving each other out of the way, both of them scrambling to get it. Summer had to take a giant step back and plastered herself against the wall so she wasn't mowed down by her sisters.

Callie got to the door first and yanked it open. "Hey! You made it."

She stood back, and Preston walked in, taking off his baseball cap and smoothing his hair out. "Yeah, thanks for the invite."

Summer raised an eyebrow in my direction, and I just shrugged. I'd had no idea Preston was coming either. Or what was going on with him and Callie. Or Lennon? I had no idea.

"Food's ready!" Addie called from the kitchen.

Preston was the first to head in that direction, traipsing out of the living room with Callie and Lennon following him. Frost shot Summer a confused look, but she just shrugged at him. He sighed and trailed after, seemingly resigned to the fact that his younger daughters might be harboring a crush on one of his cowboys.

Summer and I took up the rear, moving slowly to give us a few seconds alone.

"What did you buy?" I whispered.

She bit her lip. "I told you, I'll show you later."

Damn if that didn't make me want to pull her straight out of this house and back to my cabin. I groaned beneath my breath and linked my pinky finger through hers. I just wanted to touch her. Even if only for a second.

She glanced down at our joined fingers with a soft smile, but then it fell an inch. "I don't want to make this a big deal in front of everyone just yet. I'm so sick of being the center of attention. And you know the town will explode once news of this gets out."

"This?" I questioned with a grin.

She swatted my arm. "Yeah, this. Whatever this is. You and me. We're a this, aren't we?"

"Dominic! Summer! Hurry up, we want to eat!"

I dropped her fingers and entered the kitchen a step or two ahead, without answering her. The Hunts' dining room was around a corner from their kitchen. The big, solid wooden table was the centerpiece of the room, the top covered by a sunny yellow cloth, only the thick wooden legs poking out from beneath the hem. Food filled multiple platters, roast meats and vegetables emitting a taste bud tantalizing smell that had me drooling.

My stomach rumbled. I was suddenly starving for more than just Summer.

Frost sat at the head of the table, already helping himself to a platter of roast beef, while Addie sat at the other end, sipping her glass of wine. She smiled as Summer and I took the only two remaining seats, sitting side by side. The twins had situated themselves next to Preston, squishing together a little because the table really wasn't made for seven. Callie dominated the conversation, asking Preston all about his training, while the rest of us got started on the food.

I was more than happy about the seating arrangement.

Summer moved her chair an inch closer, her bare leg brushing mine beneath the table. I glanced at her, but she was steadfastly concentrating on putting mashed potato on her plate.

"Dominic, Kai said the two of you have been hatching plans to move into getting our bulls on the rodeo circuit?" Addie passed me a bowl of green beans, distracting me from the warmth of Summer's leg.

"Yes, ma'am. Grave Digger made a bit of a name for himself last month. Got people buzzing about y'all."

She beamed at that. "Fantastic news."

Kai cleared his throat. "I actually had a call this afternoon. A stud service offered to buy him."

Summer paused. "How much?"

"A lot more than I would have thought he was worth."

I shook my head. "He's good. He's got raw potential. Don't sell. You could make more money from his offspring. Get him with a cow whose sire was a good kicker and you could have yourself a nice little money-making pot."

Callie spoke up, steering the conversation to one of the times she'd seen Preston ride Grave Digger, and Kai and Addie both turned their attention back to their younger daughters.

Summer's leg brushed against mine again, and the tiny grin on her face told me she was doing it deliberately to tease me.

Two could play at that game.

Switching my fork to my right hand, I stabbed at a bean innocently, while my other hand drifted beneath the table and clamped over Summer's knee.

She froze beside me, her breath hitching.

Good. I pulled her knee toward me ever so slightly, while still eating my dinner. But she'd faltered in her chewing. I kept moving her leg closer and closer to me until I knew that they were spread wide beneath the table. If anyone had stuck their head beneath the tablecloth right now, they'd have been flashed with Summer's panties and my hand on her thigh.

I relaxed my hold for a moment, giving her the chance to move away. But I roared inside when she didn't. Preston droned on and on about his last competition, and I trailed my fingers over the silky softness of Summer's thigh, slowly inching higher and higher, pushing the hem of her dress up.

Her skin was so smooth. And warm. Her uneven breathing beside me only increased while I walked my fingers farther up her leg, until they brushed over the fabric of her panties.

Summer shot to her feet. "Wine. We need more of it."

I stifled a grin, watching her run out of the dining room and disappear around the corner.

There was an almost full bottle of wine on the table.

Nobody else seemed to notice. Preston was too busy entertaining them with the story about how a bull had ripped the back of his jeans and left his ass on display for an entire rodeo audience. He was a good storyteller, and his personality was larger than life, commanding attention.

Nobody even looked my way as I stood and mumbled something about helping Summer in the kitchen.

She was fumbling with the cork on a wine bottle when I walked in. Her head snapped up, and our gazes clashed.

Fuck, she was beautiful. A fire burned behind her eyes, and with her breaths still slightly erratic, her chest heaving, I'd never wanted her more.

"Dom," she warned feebly.

I wasn't listening. I closed the gap between us, put my hand to the back of her neck, and hauled her in, devouring her mouth with my own. She melted into me, a tiny whimpering noise of need escaping her chest, our tongues moving in unison.

She wanted more. I could tell by the way she pressed herself to me, desperate and needy, and I dipped to grab her thigh again, slipping my hand beneath her dress. But this time, there was no slow wandering of fingers. I dragged my hand up her leg and cupped her mound.

She moved away an inch, tearing her lips away from mine. She darted wild, unfocussed eyes toward the dining room. "Not here."

I backed off straightaway, more than willing to save it for when we were alone, but then she bit her lip and let out a groan of frustration. "Fuck. Okay, yes. Just a little bit here."

A grin spread across my face. I backed her up against the kitchen cupboard and snuck a look at the doorway. But the sounds of laughter still rang out from dining room. And there was no way I was turning her down now.

I kissed her hard, her head hitting the cupboard behind her, and slid my hand up her dress once more, but this time I went beneath her panties to cup her pussy. Her fingers clenched into my biceps, and I stifled her moan, finding her clit with one finger.

"Hurry," she murmured over my lips.

I dipped my finger lower and let it slide through her folds.

There was no managing my erection. She was so soaking wet, all I wanted to do was rip her panties off and slide my dick right inside the pool of arousal between her thighs. "You're so wet," I whispered in her ear. I pushed one finger up inside her tight slit and was rewarded with the rocking of her hips and her teeth biting down on my shoulder.

God, I would do her right here, right now, if I thought that was what she wanted.

But I knew it wasn't. The first time I slept with her wasn't going to be a three-pump quickie in the middle of her kitchen.

No, I was going to take my time with her. I'd waited all these years. I could wait a little longer.

I pulled my finger from inside her and stepped back. Her gaze lifted to mine, her breath coming in pants.

I put my finger to my mouth and licked her off it.

"Fuck, that's hot," she whispered.

I leaned in, moving her hair aside, so I could whisper in her ear. "Go finish dinner. Do whatever you need to do. Then meet me at my place."

She brushed her lips over mine. "I think I like it when you're bossy."

I swatted her on the ass. "Get out of here."

"Aren't you coming? Your dinner will be getting cold."

I shook my head and looked down at the erection straining behind my fly. "I can't come out until you leave and that goes away."

She sniggered. "What am I going to tell my family?"

"That I need a cold shower because all I can think about is bending you over this countertop?"

We both eyed it, like I might actually do it.

I groaned. "Seriously, Summer. Go."

With a final, longing glance at me, she left the room. I slumped back on the cupboards and took a deep breath.

My cabin had a countertop, too. I could wait.

20

Dom excused himself not long after the meal came to an end, and with a final secret glance in my direction, disappeared into the night. I clenched my legs together and tried to patiently wait an appropriate amount of time to go after him.

On the couch, Callie and Preston chatted animatedly, both their outgoing personalities competing for the limelight, while Lennon sat quietly, watching them.

When she got up and left the room without a sound, my big sister senses went off, and I followed after her. I knocked on her door, but when she didn't answer, I let myself in.

She glanced up from where she was flopped across her bed, but she didn't say anything.

"You like Preston?" I asked.

She shrugged. "It's not that, exactly. I just wish I were more like Callie."

I tilted my head. "Why, though? You're pretty great as you are. If Preston doesn't see that, it's his loss."

She sighed. "You're my sister. You have to say things like that."

"Not true. I could have just ignored the fact you slunk away up here."

She eyed me. "Why aren't you off with Dom?"

I tried to shrug casually. "Why would I be?"

Lennon rolled her eyes. "Because you want to get all up on him, as much as Callie wants to get all up on Preston."

I cringed. "That obvious?"

"To me it is. But I pay more attention than most people."

She did. She was the most introverted of the three of us. Callie was the complete opposite and forever the life of the party.

"You think Mom and Dad noticed?"

She shook her head. "Nah. They've got their own things going on. They're just happy you're not moving to the city anymore." She smiled softly. "So am I."

That actually took me by surprise. "But you liked Austin."

"I like Dom more. And I like having you here."

A warmth radiated through me. The twins had always been close, and they had a bond I'd always felt like I couldn't worm my way into, no matter how hard I tried. For the most part, it hadn't seemed to matter. I had a bond with my dad that neither of them had. Things all seemed to work themselves out in the wash. But it was nice to hear she was glad I was staying.

"Just one thing, though. If you're going to have sex with Dom in the kitchen, sanitize afterward, okay?"

My eyes went wide. "I didn't have sex with him!"

She shrugged. "What the hell were you doing in there then? Wasted opportunity if you ask me."

I was suddenly not sure I knew my quiet youngest sister at all.

Claiming the need to walk off a food coma, I left my parents, Callie, and Preston playing a game of charades. The night air was muggy, but it was soft after the noise of the house. Each step I took toward Dom's cabin had me moving a little bit faster, a little more eager to see him with every passing minute.

My core still throbbed with the beginnings of an orgasm that had never been achieved. My panties didn't help, slick and rubbing over my mound with every step, a constant reminder of how damn horny I was.

I'd completely lost my head back there in the kitchen. Dom had his fingers inside me, working me toward a climax with a roomful of people just feet away. Thank God he'd stopped because I didn't think I would have. I would have just let him keep doing what he was doing, his fingers deep inside me, hitting the spot that sent trembles through my entire body.

I'd wanted him to fuck me. I'd wanted him to push me up against the cupboard and take me right then and there.

Something deep inside me clenched, and by the time I got to his cabin door, I was breathless, but it wasn't because I'd broken into a run.

It was purely because I needed him so badly.

The door opened as my foot hit the top step, and then he was there, door open before I could even knock, like he'd been waiting for me. Dark eyes shining in the moonlight, drinking me in, turning me to liquid with the fire in his gaze.

I stopped dead, suddenly unsure of what to do. Did we just go straight back to where we'd been in the kitchen? Or did we need to sit and talk first?

Dom didn't have any of the same hesitations as I did.

"What took you so long?" he growled, striding out into the night and hauling me to his chest.

His lips came down on mine, hungry and demanding, and everything that had been tense and hesitant unfurled for him. "I don't know," I mumbled between fast, hard kisses. "I'm an idiot."

His fingers gripped my hips, and he picked me straight up off the ground, sitting me on the porch railing. My knees opened on instinct, welcoming him between my legs like he'd always belonged there.

"Not an idiot," he murmured, lips trailing off my mouth and across my jaw to my neck. "But that was the longest thirty minutes of my life."

I dropped my head back on my shoulders, giving him better access to bite and suck and lick my neck. I clutched him tighter, digging my fingers into his shoulders, while wrapping my legs around his waist.

His erection pressed against my panties. "You're hard again."

"Been hard the whole time, just remembering what you taste like."

Heat flooded my cheeks. His fingers slipped beneath the hem of my dress again, this time running up the outer sides of my thighs, until he got to two ribbon ties at my hips.

His head jerked back in surprise. "What the hell kind of panties are these?" he groaned. "If I pull these ribbons..."

I grinned at him in the darkness and leaned closer. "You should probably pull them once we're inside..."

He glanced around, but the night was thick, and there were no lights on in the nearby cabins. I knew the guys were probably all at the Black Bull Bar, like half the town was on weekends. Slowly, defiantly, Dom pulled the ribbons, and the fabric fell away.

I raised an eyebrow, my system flooding with adrenaline at the idea of getting caught out here. "Dom..."

My dress still covered me, offering some sense of security. Dom's fingers found my clit, and I gasped at the contact. He rubbed it, slowly working the tiny ball of pleasure and spreading a tingling warmth through my entire body.

He kissed me again, his tongue plunging inside my mouth, taking control, and showing me that while I might be the boss at work, I wasn't here.

I kept my eyes open, glancing around for movement, but my body grew more and more relaxed the more Dom touched me, and by the time he plunged two fingers up inside me, I'd all but forgotten my name. I was so wet, so ready, and the orgasm that threatened had been building inside me for hours.

In a sudden jerk of movement, Dom swept me from the railing and carried me through the open door. I wrapped my arms around his neck, yanking him in for another kiss as he kicked the door shut behind us.

"I wanna make you scream, Summer. I can't have you screaming out in public where people might come running." He tossed me onto his bed, the mattress dipping beneath my weight, then followed me with his big body looming over me.

I had no idea where my panties had gone. They' fallen off somewhere between the porch and the bed, and I didn't even care. I just wanted him to go back to what he was doing.

He didn't disappoint. He kissed me long and hard while he hauled the skirt of my dress up, putting me on display for him.

His cabin was lit only by the dim light of a lamp, but it was enough for him to rear back and feast on me with his gaze, his eyes traveling all over my body and lingering on the glistening junction of my legs.

He slicked one finger between my folds, watching me intently, and gripping my thighs when I bucked my hips off the bed at his touch.

"Part those pretty thighs for me, Summer."

My core throbbed at his dirty words, but fuck, I liked it. He drew my legs up, so my heels were on the bed, then he knelt on the floor and put his mouth to use. His tongue speared straight to the center of me, sliding over my clit and lower to my entrance.

I closed my eyes, my hands grabbing his head as if they had a mind of their own, holding him to my pussy like I was scared he might leave.

He wasn't going anywhere.

He moved me closer, putting one leg over his shoulder and tongue-dived inside me. I moaned loudly, but he didn't need my encouragement. The man knew exactly what he was doing. He slid two fingers inside once more, building me higher and higher, massaging my clit with tiny licks.

I wanted to come but didn't want it to end all at the same time. I writhed against his mouth, gyrating my hips on his fingers, taking more and more of him with every stroke.

There was no stopping the orgasm that shattered through me. I screamed out his name as it crashed down hard, my internal walls clamping down on his fingers. Blinding flashes of color lit up behind my eyes, and sparks of electricity pulsated through my body, taking pleasure I'd never known before with it.

He didn't stop. His fingers and mouth moved in unison, working me through the orgasm until I couldn't take another second. I pulled his head up to mine, and leaned into the kiss, tasting myself on his lips and not caring.

"I can't believe you made me wait this long," he murmured between kisses. "I've waited years to do that."

I looked him in the eye. "Years?"

He nodded. "Ever since I saw you in your prom dress. We'd only just arrived for a visit, and you were just leaving. Your friends were already arriving in a limo, and you had some deadbeat date, but that night, all I saw was you."

I swallowed hard. "You never said anything. That was the night I met Austin."

He nodded. "I know. By the time you came home the next day, you and he were together. I never got a chance."

Gone was the dominating man who'd just rocked my world and filled my ear with dirty talk. In his place was this kind, sweet man, open and vulnerable.

That was all it took for me to fall the tiniest bit in love with him.

But that tiny flicker of a feeling couldn't be relied on. Not when this thing between us was nothing more than days old.

But it was years old to Dom. Years he'd waited for me. My heart flickered again.

I tugged him down on me and kissed him once more. This time our kiss was softer, sweeter. I rolled us so his back was to the mattress, and he let me have the upper position, taking control.

"Am I why you haven't dated much?" I asked, kissing my way down his neck, tugging at his shirt.

I lifted it higher, running my hands up his abs, the same way he'd run his hands up my thighs. I followed with open-mouthed kisses, tonguing the ridges of his abdominal muscles and nipping at his skin.

"You're why I haven't dated seriously," he corrected.

Then he grinned. "I've dated enough to know how to make you scream. As you just found out."

I ran my tongue around his nipple and enjoyed the way his head flopped back against the mattress. "Cocky."

"Confident."

He was right. There was a difference. But I still wanted to wipe the smug grin off his face.

I popped the button on his fly.

"Summer," he husked out.

I undid the zipper. "Lift up."

He did as instructed, chuckling. "Apparently I'm not the only bossy one."

I dragged his jeans off his legs and took half a second to admire the bulge behind his boxer briefs before hooking my fingers in the elastic and taking them off, too.

His cock was as big as the rest of him. Hard and thick, precum glistening at the tip, just begging for me to taste. I wanted to make him feel as good as I had. But I was in a tangle of my dress, and it needed to go.

I stood to pull it off, reaching for the zipper at the back, but Dom stood and covered my hand with his own.

"Let me," he whispered softly, breath misting over my skin.

I dropped my hand to my side and pressed my lips to his bare chest instead.

He reached around me and drew the zipper down, his hand slipping beneath the fabric to mold against my lower back. He smoothed his palm in a warm trail up my spine, until he reached the straps of my dress, slid his fingers beneath them, and drew them down my arms. The dress puddled on the floor.

"Was this my surprise?" His fingers trailing across my collarbone and over the swell of my breasts. The new bra

Hallie had encouraged me to buy dipped low in the front, giving me killer cleavage, with a sweet satin bow in between that matched my long-gone panties.

The material was just sheer enough to see my nipples through. "Do you like it?"

He didn't answer. Just dipped his head to suck my nipple through the fabric.

"Oh God," I moaned, my head tipping back.

My core still throbbed pleasantly from my orgasm, and his tongue rasping over my nipple, with the thin fabric in between, only made a second rush of arousal roll through my body. He unclipped my bra and slid it off, so we were both completely naked.

It should have been strange. We'd been friends for so long, and we'd stepped so far over that line tonight that I would have expected at least a little hesitation from one, if not both of us. But if there was anything on his side, he didn't show it.

And there was nothing on mine. Nothing except a pure need to touch him. Taste him. Own his orgasm the way he'd just owned mine.

I dropped to my knees before he could distract me again.

The wooden floorboards were hard, but I barely felt them as I wrapped my lips around his cock. God, he was big. At first, I just took in the head of him, thick and blunt, and ran my tongue over the ridged underside, working my hand up his length to compensate.

He groaned and speared his fingers into my hair, but instead of thrusting his dick deeper into my mouth, or trying to control my head, he kept it light, massaging my scalp until my eyes were rolling back with how good it felt.

"You like that?" he asked me.

I pulled away. "Sucking your dick?"

He chuckled. "I meant when I play with your hair like this."

"Oh." I laughed. "Yeah, I do. You might have missed your calling as a hairdresser."

He grinned and gathered my hair up in one hand, wrapping the long lengths around his fist. "Nah, I don't think hairdressers get to do this."

He gripped my hair harder, tugging it back so I had to look up at him. Sparks of pleasure shot through my scalp and straight to my core.

Holy shit. That felt entirely too good.

He knew it. But he dropped down to his knees beside me and followed it with a long, searing kiss, his touch at my head going back to soft.

The man knew what he was doing. There was no doubt about that.

But I'd barely started. He kept trying to distract me from what I'd set out to do.

I pushed him back on the floor and then settled between his widespread legs, gripping his cock once more and running my fingers over it. He put his hand behind his head, propping it up a little so he could watch me.

Our gazes clashed, his turning fiery as I held it, my head bobbing over him. I sucked him as far I could into my mouth, his erection pressing to the back of my throat.

My core ached, just begging me to straddle him and sink deep onto him.

"Come here," he groaned out. "I want to taste you while I come."

I crawled up his body, but when I got to his lips, he grinned. "I didn't mean your mouth, Summer."

Heat flushed through my body, realizing exactly what he

meant. Oh my fucking God. Who knew what Dom was hiding behind his nice guy persona?

"Turn around."

A tiny sliver of self-consciousness rolled down my spine. I'd be *so* on display for him if I did that. But my core was so slick with arousal again and throbbing for more. The heat in his eyes was impossible to deny. I spun around, and he grabbed my thighs, making me squeal as he pulled them over his face.

"You act like you've never done this before," he laughed, before running his tongue through my folds.

"I haven't," I moaned.

He paused, and I looked backward at him, along the ridged planes of his belly to his face between my legs.

"Are you serious?" he asked.

"Yep."

"Jesus Christ, he's an idiot." He licked me again, rolling his tongue between my thighs, tasting my arousal. "Suck my dick, Summer. Just concentrate on that for as long as you can."

I took his dick in my mouth again. Each time I took him in, I took a little more, working more and more of him into the back of my throat.

But fuck, he made it hard to keep a rhythm. He dragged me down over his face and licked me mercilessly, until my hips were gyrating with a need of their own and a second orgasm built from the base of spine.

"Summer," he warned, his voice muffled between my thighs.

I barely heard him. I was so on the edge, it was hard to think of anything except the rhythm I was trying to keep on his dick, and the matching pace I was working over his face.

I cupped his heavy balls, squeezing them gently.

He speared two fingers up into my pussy, hitting that spot inside me.

Both of us fell over the edge at the exact same moment.

Pleasure speared through my core, and my legs wobbled in a full-body tremble that couldn't be controlled. I cried out around his dick, his hot ejaculation hitting my throat and sliding down while I worked myself mercilessly on his fingers and his mouth. The second orgasm was more powerful than the first, everything still tender and throbbing from the first round. I never wanted it to end.

It wiped out every thought, every worry, until all that there was, was me and Dom, and pleasure, and a connection I'd never known was there between us.

I flopped off him, lying on my side on the floor, while both of us tried to catch our breath. His fingers trailed idly over my hip as we both lay spent. Eventually, I flopped onto my back and stared at the cabin ceiling. "Well, aren't you full of surprises."

"Because I like going down on you?" He lifted his head to see me blush. "That blush tells me I need to do it more. What the fuck has he been doing with you for the past five years?"

He actually seemed kind of angry to learn that Austin and I had never had particularly good sex. Definitely not the sort where I came in the space of minutes, without his dick even getting near me. I'd never come so hard, or fast, or twice, ever.

Dom slid down my body with a promising grin.

I laughed, and then I let him start all over again. Because I wanted it. And he wanted me. Because Dom was nothing like Austin.

I'd never been so glad of something in my life.

21

Dominic

I made Summer come several more times during the night. Tucked into my bed, wrapped in my sheets, I couldn't get enough of her. If I could have taken up a full-time job just going down on her, I would have given up ranch work in a heartbeat.

Her taste was addictive, but the real thing I couldn't get enough of was the way she screamed my name every time she came. The sound worshipped my ears and branded itself across my heart. Her body was so responsive, like she'd never really been touched, and was suddenly coming alive with a partner who knew what the fuck he was doing.

Fuck Austin. He'd never deserved her. I was going to show her each and every day, for as long as she'd let me. I was going to make up for every time he'd come before her. I was going to prove to her that it would never be that way with me. I knew how to treat her right, and getting her off would always be my number one mission when we were alone in my bedroom.

So when my alarm went off and Summer was still very naked in bed beside me, I made her come hard once more, just so she'd have something to think about during the workday.

Her eyes were unfocussed when I was done, and we were already five minutes late.

For the first time in my life, I was okay with that. We struggled into the shower, and it was only a stern look from her that had me keeping my hands to myself.

"Seriously, Dom! I need to be able to ride today. I can't be so sensitive that the damn saddle makes me come again!"

I chuckled and kissed her mouth instead. "I'd kind of like to watch that."

She swatted me away and stepped out of the shower, water still rolling down her back and over the lush curve of her ass before she grabbed a towel.

She was gone by the time I got back into the cabin, and I knew she'd left to get clothes. Her dad would already be at the training rings, but hopefully it would still be early enough that her mom and sisters might not notice her walk of shame.

I hurried to get dressed and over to the training rings, not so much because I was late, but because despite being with her all night, I just wanted to see her again.

Smitten didn't even begin to describe how I felt about her. I just wanted to fast forward through the working day so I could get her back to my cabin for round two. Maybe we'd even get around to sex this time. But maybe not. I'd be more than happy to just live between her thighs for the rest of all eternity.

The training yards were quiet when I got there. So incredibly quiet that I stopped and looked around, wondering if I'd got my days wrong and it was actually Sunday. But no, we'd had Sunday dinner last night, so I was definitely scheduled to be at work thirty minutes ago. I strode across the yard to the office and let myself in, but it was as empty as the ring had been. There was a sheet of paper on the desk, though, and I picked it up, my gaze rolling over Frost's scrawly handwriting.

Taken the group down to the back pasture. Took Hallie with me, since the two of you couldn't be bothered getting out of bed. Lucky it's your birthday, Dom, or I would have fired you.

Oh yeah. Birthday.

Summer strode in, the dress she'd worn last night replaced with much more sensible jeans and a tank top that showed off her brown arms. The muscle tone and definition from a life of working on the land distracted me long enough that she grabbed the piece of paper from my hand and skimmed it while I was still checking her out.

"We're in trouble," I summarized the note, a smidgen of worry creeping in. I'd been on such a high after finally getting to see Summer naked that I'd shirked my responsibilities. That wasn't like me.

She blew it off. "Never mind that. It's your birthday?"

I shrugged. "Yeah, I guess so. I'd kind of forgotten to be honest." The days since I'd come here had been so heavily focused on work and Summer, I'd completely lost track of the date. Though I knew for sure that my parents and brothers would all be calling before the day was out, I wasn't particularly big on birthdays. But my dad loved to make a fuss over things. Christmas was his big hurrah, but birthdays were up there, too. He always made some sort of extravagant gesture, and each year he'd count down the days until our birthdays, so I'd never had the chance to forget about it before.

She clapped her hands together. "So, party then, right?"

I stepped in closer and wrapped my arms around her. "Only if it's a party for two."

She grinned and wrapped her arms around my neck. "We partied for two all night long."

I chuckled. "Better than a rave, don't you think?"

Her lips skimmed over mine. "Much." Then she pulled back. "Doesn't mean we aren't celebrating outside your cabin, though. Party for everyone, then a party after, just you and me. Deal?"

I screwed up my nose. "We only just had a party in my honor less than two months ago. We can't have another one. I'd feel like such an attention whore."

"What about a cookout then? Something low-key, casual. Just Hallie and Nate and a few of the guys." She raised an eyebrow. "And Felix?"

That actually wasn't a bad idea. I definitely wanted a reason to see my brother again.

Huh. So weird to think of him like that. But I liked it, too.

Thinking of Felix made me think of that night in the bar, where Summer had smashed a ride on the mechanical bull with only one hand. I needed to get her on the back of a real bull now and see what she had.

"You really want to have this cookout?"

She nodded. "Yep. I really do."

"You get up and ride again, and I'll agree."

She raised an eyebrow. "Blackmail, huh? And here's me, thinking so highly of your moral character."

I sniggered. "Did I not ruin my good guy persona when I had my mouth on your p—"

"Okay!" She laughed. "I'll ride."

I folded my arms across my chest. "You agreed to that way too easily."

She pressed up on her toes and kissed me again. "Probably because I'd already decided I was riding again today."

I swept her off the floor and kissed her hard in victorious excitement. "Let's do it."

"We're supposed to be working!" But she wanted to. And I knew how bad Frost wanted this for her. I was pretty confident he'd agree that getting Summer on the back of a real live bull again was more important than mucking out stalls or trying to fix the engine on the tractor.

"Just a couple of rides. Then we'll get back to work, deal?"

She bit her lip, but I could already tell she was going to say yes. I fist pumped the air, and we both ran to get a bull from one of the pens.

"Get Axel," Summer called, climbing to the top of the chutes to get her ropes organized. "Grave Digger is too much right now. But Axel is a good ride."

I almost argued with her, because I had every confidence in her ability to ride Grave Digger. But I respected her decisions, and if she said she wasn't ready for Grave Digger yet, then I wasn't going to fight her on it. At this point in her comeback, because that's what this would be, I would be happy if she rode a freaking dairy cow. I just wanted her to get back on the horse. Or the bull, as the case was here.

I shooed Axel's big tan ass up into the chute and then climbed it myself to help. We worked as an effortless team, not needing to talk in order to get the ropes on and get Summer on the bull's back.

Like a good boy, he just stood still and let us get on with it. Summer took the rope from my hand, running hers over the resin that helped her glove stick.

But then she started fidgeting. Moving around, adjusting herself then shifting back to where she'd begun. She was overthinking it. Overcomplicating things instead of just letting muscle memory kick in and take control. I could see her brain whirring a mile a minute, and pretty soon, she'd psych herself out. She just needed to rip off the Band-Aid.

The bull lurched, and when Summer lifted her head to counteract his movements, her eyes were full of fear.

She needed to get out of her head. A distraction. Something that pulled her out of wherever she'd just gone.

"Right, so no going down on you all night when you have to ride the next day?"

Her head snapped up. "Huh?"

"You're moving around on that bull like someone's tongue was on your clit all night. Seriously, Summer, quit being so obvious. If we were at a rodeo, you'd have totally given us away."

She glared at me, but the corner of her mouth curved up, and she jerked her head toward the dirt. "Go open the damn gate, then!"

She didn't have to tell me twice. I jumped the fence, grabbed the gate rope, and double-checked she was ready. She crossed her bad arm over her chest, her fingers as tight around the strap of her tank top as her other hand was on the rope.

She nodded.

Of course she fucking did. Because she was a badass like that. She was scared, but she wasn't letting it own her. Not anymore.

I yanked open the gate, and Axel burst into the ring with a strong kick of his back legs.

Summer shifted her weight, leaning the opposite direction to keep herself balanced. He spun into an easy right-hand turn, jerking his head, his tail swishing like a whip through the air.

"Come on!" I yelled.

She so had this.

The timer, automatically set off by the opening of the gate, counted up to the five-second mark.

But then Axel abruptly changed directions, catching Summer of guard. She slumped forward and then somersaulted over the bull's shoulder, landing on the ground.

Disappointment flooded me, but I couldn't let that distract me. My job wasn't done. I ran out, running a circle around Axel, drawing his attention away from Summer and onto me.

To my relief, she popped straight up from the ground and easily made her way to the other side of the ring, well away from where Axel trotted back to his pen.

As soon as he was safely out, I ran straight back to Summer's side. "Hey. You okay?"

I expected defeat. I expected the fear to be back, only tenfold.

But Summer's eyes glinted with determination. "Get me another bull."

I stared at her, my complete and utter admiration for her growing in every second. "Yeah?"

"Fuck yeah. That was amazing. I need to do more core work. It's harder without my arm for balance. And my legs aren't as strong as they were."

"But they will be," I said fiercely.

She turned wild, excited eyes on me, and her smile grew until it took over her entire expression. "I know hard work."

"I know you do."

"I'm not scared of it."

"Fuck no."

Her expression was fierce. "We're going to have to get approval for me to ride."

"Brad Pruitt ain't going to say no to this, Summer. He'll

milk your story to every news outlet there is, because your comeback is going to be huge."

Her eyes lit up with the thought. "You really think I can ride like this?"

I cupped her face with both hands and tilted her chin up to face me. "I think the boys on tour better watch their starting spots. Because Summer Hunt is back and coming for them."

She threw her good arm around me, and I swept her tiny frame off the ground and into a bear hug.

She was going to take the bull riding world by storm once more. And I was going to be the guy who stood at her back and cheered her every damn step of the way.

I was the guy who should have been there all along. I was just taking my rightful spot. And I wasn't going to give it up to anyone.

22

Dominic

"Happy birthday! Again." Hallie drew me in for a hug, kissed my cheek, and handed me a gift-wrapped package that was suspiciously shaped like a bottle of bourbon.

"Thanks." I hugged her back. She'd already wished me a happy birthday on Monday, when she'd come back from riding with Frost and the trainees. But Summer had decided it would be better to have a weekend cookout, rather than try to fit it into a weeknight, so it had actually been several days since my birthday.

I shook hands with Nate who came out to the back of Frost and Addie's house, a case of beer tucked under his free arm. "Ice in buckets over there," I directed. "Summer already has the grill going, so won't be long until food is up."

The two of them wandered off, threading their way around a group of the trainees who were talking and drinking in a huddle, in between shooting secretive little looks at Callie and Lennon. Neither seemed to notice. Callie was deep in conversation with Preston again, while Lennon pretended she didn't see. I shrugged. Whatever was going on with the three of them was too complicated for me.

I beelined for Summer and stood next to her, watching her cook hamburgers. When I thought no one was paying attention, I nudged her, letting my arm linger against hers a moment longer than necessary. “Looks good.”

She darted a glance around us, making sure no one was in earshot before answering. “So do you.”

It was a casual get-together, despite the gaudy decorations and fairy lights Summer had strung across the backyard. But I’d still wanted to make an effort for her, so I’d showered and trimmed the stubble beard I’d been rocking ever since I got here. Splashed on a bit of cologne and done my hair for once, instead of putting on a hat. I liked that she’d noticed.

But I didn’t look half as good as she did. A tiny pair of cutoff jeans hugged her ass and revealed long brown legs. Her tank top was just the tiniest bit too short and showed a sliver of toned belly whenever she reached to flip the burgers at the back of the grill.

I leaned in closer and whispered, “How much longer are we doing the secret sneaking around thing? Because I really want to kiss you right now.”

She grinned up at me, and damn if her smile wasn’t perfect. It had my heart thumping triple time, and I really wanted nothing more than to lay my lips down on hers, in front of all our friends and her family. I wanted them to know we were together. But I got why we were on the down-low. Just yesterday, I’d gotten stuck in the feed store while Mr. Morrison grilled me about Summer and Austin’s breakup. Around here, the men were as big of gossips as anyone. In a way, I couldn’t blame them. There wasn’t a lot else to do, and the breakup of a long-term relationship, especially from a family as high-profile as the Hunts, was big news.

"Yeah?" she whispered. "What else do you want to do?"

What didn't I want to do with her? I'd spent all week learning how best to get her off with just my mouth and my fingers, but I'd held off on actually sleeping with her. I didn't want to rush her, but damnit, when she gazed at me the way she was right now, all I wanted to do was throw her over my shoulder, storm back to my cabin, and spend the night deep inside her. I clenched my fingers around my beer bottle a little harder to keep from actually doing it. "Playing with fire, Sum."

She motioned to the flames beneath the grill, innocent smile plastered across her face. "Just cooking burgers."

"Mmm-hmm." I was suddenly very eager for this cookout to be over, and it hadn't even started.

Addie sailed by with a tray of snacks and gave the two of us a sidelong glance. I moved half a step away from Summer, because I really was standing closer than a friend would. Addie winked, making me realize we weren't fooling her. Oops. I wondered how many other people had worked it out.

"Dom." Addie set down her snacks on one of the picnic tables. "I've got a surprise for you later."

"You do? What?"

She brushed off her hands on her long summer dress and frowned at me. "Would hardly be a surprise if I told you, would it?" She wandered off to talk to Kai before I could prod her any further.

"What's that about?" I asked Summer.

She shrugged. "Probably the birthday cake she ordered. It's kinda extravagant. I think my mom likes you."

I grinned. "I'm more concerned whether her daughter does."

She raised an eyebrow. "Callie or Lennon?"

I glared at her, and she cracked up laughing. But then her gaze caught on something over my shoulder. "Is that your brother?"

I squinted in the direction she was pointing, putting a hand up over my eyes to shield it from the sun. There was a figure wandering around near the bull pen, clutching a gift bag. He had a cowboy hat pulled down on his head, and I immediately recognized it as the one Felix had worn at the honky-tonk where we'd first met. "Yeah, seems like it. I'll go grab him."

I hustled across the lawn and then down the gravel road that weaved its way around this part of the property. "Felix!"

He jolted from his spot by the bull pens, spinning around, a grin spreading across his face when he saw it was me.

"Hey. Heard it was your birthday." He gave me a one-armed hug and thrust the giftbag into my hands. "It's nothing much."

I opened it up, and inside on a bed of fluffy tissue paper, were two tickets to a baseball game in Atlanta. "This is awesome. Thank you."

He shoved a hand in his pocket, looking awkward at my gratitude. "I figured you could take Summer—"

"Or you and I could go together…"

He raised an eyebrow. "Yeah?"

"I'd like that."

"Me, too."

I pressed the tape that held the bag closed down again, so I wouldn't lose the tickets. "What are you doing all the way over here? Party is that way."

Pink stained his olive cheeks. "Yeah, sorry. I drove in along the road and it led me here. I didn't notice the party until I got out, but then I got distracted by the bulls." He pointed at Grave Digger. "He's a beauty."

Despite the fact Digger wasn't my bull, I still found a sense of pride washed over me. This place had become my home so quickly, and I'd been caring for these animals for months now. I was already a bit attached to them. Especially Grave Digger since I'd gotten the honor of taking him to his first pro rodeo. I had a soft spot for the drooly, hulking animal. "He is," I agreed with Felix. "Mean, grumpy bugger, but he's going to be a champion one day. WBRA has already called him up, and Frost had a big offer on him recently."

"Yeah?" Felix asked, eye running over him. "He selling?"

"Nah. He was offered fifty thousand, but he turned it down."

Felix's eyes widened. "Shit, fifty K? You're kidding?"

"You haven't seen him kick. And he's young. Got a lot of rides left in him yet, then years of breeding. Frost was smart to keep him if you ask me."

Felix whistled low under his breath. "Ah, to be in the position to turn down a fifty K payday, huh?"

I was a tad uncomfortable about discussing my boss's finances. I knew they weren't rich by any stretch of the imagination, but that was confidential information. Not something I was going to share with Felix. So thinking about the measly five hundred in my own account, I laughed it off. "Tell me about it."

Felix raised a hand and waved, and I realized he was waving at Summer, who was motioning us over.

"Food must be ready. You coming?" I was eager to get back to my girl.

"I'm about ready to gnaw my own arm off. Hell yes, I'm coming."

Felix followed me over to the party, the two of us walking side by side.

Frost glanced up from the bowl of chips he was picking from. "Who's your friend, Dom?" He put a hand out for Felix to shake. "Kai Hunt."

Felix shook his hand with a strong grip. "No introduction needed, sir. I know who you are. You won five WBRA titles. You're a legend."

Kai's cheeks flushed pink. "I think it was only four, but thank you. And you are...?"

Now it was Felix's turn to go awkward. "Oh, sorry. Felix Kaur. I'm Dom's—"

He froze and waited for me.

I cleared my throat. "He's my...brother."

Kai's eyebrows shot sky-high and his gaze darted between the two of us like he was at a tennis match while he put two and two together. "Well, holy shit." He focused on me. "I didn't know you were in contact with your biological family."

I shook my head. "I'm not, really. Just Felix. He only lives a few hours away in Masonville. We've only just met."

Frost's face morphed into one of his rare smiles. "That's awesome. I'm real happy for you. Good to have you here, Felix. Make sure you get some food, okay? And there's drinks in the tub over there."

Summer and her mom had disappeared, but I towed Felix around, introducing him to the twins, and Preston and the other cowboys. Apparently, Felix and Preston had ridden together in a couple of local rodeos a few years back, and the two of them fell deep into conversation about a mutual friend. But I was only half listening, wondering where Summer had disappeared to.

I wandered inside and found Addie with a set of keys in her hand, her purse slung over her shoulder.

"Escaping the party already?" I joked.

She shook her head. "Just need to pick, uh, something up. I'll be back soon."

"Sure. Have you seen Summer, though? She's disappeared."

She jerked her head toward the stairs that led up to the second story of their home. "She got oil spatter on her shirt. I think she's just getting changed."

"Oh, okay. Well, I'll just wait for her outside then, I guess."

Addie cocked her head to one side with a laugh. "Or you could just go on up there, because I know that's exactly what you're going to do the moment I leave."

Well, shit. That was awkward.

"What?" I croaked feebly, wishing the ground would swallow me up whole. Because she was right. That was exactly what I'd been thinking about doing. I felt like a little kid who'd just been caught sticking his hand in the cookie jar.

She rolled her eyes. "You think I haven't noticed that my daughter has been barely home for the last week? You think I haven't noticed her sneaking back from the cabins every morning?"

"Errr." We'd been more careful after that first time we'd spent the whole night together. I'd set an early alarm, and Summer had been leaving before the sunrise to go back to the main house.

Addie patted me on the arm. "Stop being so worried. You

think I'm not thrilled about this finally happening for the two of you?"

"Finally?"

"Do you remember the night you came to visit, and Summer was going to her prom?"

How could I forget? I still had the image of Summer in that dress ingrained into my memory.

Addie smiled knowingly. "I watched you fall in love with her in that moment."

I shook my head. "I wasn't—"

But we both knew I was. I had fallen for her in a single instant. Then I'd kept it to myself for years because I knew I wasn't what she wanted.

But I was now.

"I'm going to go upstairs," I told Addie.

She smiled. "About time. You're good for her, Dom. I hope it works for the two of you. And tell her to quit coming home in the mornings and just take some clothes to your place, will you? She's about as discreet as a bull in a china shop, and I'm sick of her waking me up before dawn."

"Yes, ma'am," I agreed. "I'll tell her."

Summer would die of embarrassment. But I'd get to keep her that little bit longer each morning, so I was sure she'd get over it pretty quickly.

23

A knock at my door had me clutching my stained shirt over my bra. "Getting changed!"

"Why do you think I'm here?"

The laughter in Dom's voice was clear, even through the door. I opened it, glancing down the empty hallway, then yanked him inside. "What are you doing up here?"

He shrugged, pulling my shirt from my hands and dropping it on the floor. His dark-brown gaze rolled over me, resting on the swell of my cleavage, then dipping lower to the tiny pair of shorts I was wearing. "You disappeared, so I came searching."

I shoved my hands on my hips. "This is your party. You can't just leave it."

"Says who?" He moved in slowly, stalking me from across the room like he was a panther, and I was a gazelle. But screw being a gazelle, running for its life. The glint in Dom's eyes lit me up. I wanted to be caught. His finger trailed down my arm, until his fingers circled my wrist, pressing over my pulse point which was suddenly beating faster than normal.

"Your mom knows about us by the way."

"What?" I yelped.

"Mmm-hmm," he murmured, brushing his lips over my bare shoulder. "She said to tell you to just bring some clothes to my place so you can stop coming home every morning."

I squeezed my eyes shut. "Ugh. She did not really say that to you."

He chuckled as he ran his nose up my neck. "Yeah, she did." He kissed the spot just below my ear. "So pack a bag for tonight."

His demands held all sorts of promises that made my skin pebble into goosebumps. "Yeah?"

"Yeah. No pj's, though."

I tilted my head to one side, giving him better access to my neck. His kisses turned openmouthed, sucking and nipping at my skin, shooting little arrows of pleasure through the rest of my body. "I might get cold without them."

His mouth trailed lower again, his head dipping to kiss the swell of my breasts. "I'll keep you warm."

I snorted on a laugh. "Corny."

He glanced up at me. "Corny?"

"Totally. Is that really the best you got?" I was taunting him, and I knew it.

His fingers came to my back, and he unsnapped my bra in a fraction of second. In the next, he had it off me, his mouth on my nipple.

I hissed at the warm, wet touch of him, running my fingers through his hair as he sucked me through his teeth.

"You want me to show you exactly how I'll keep you warm then?" he murmured.

I shrugged like I couldn't care less. But we both knew I really did.

His hands skated down my bare back and over my ass before he picked me up. I wrapped my legs tight around his waist and let him walk me back to the door. My back pressed into the wood, and Dom caged me in with his big body, his pelvis against my core, his chest to my chest. He cupped my face with one hand, using his body to keep me up, and found my mouth with his.

I moaned into his kiss, letting his tongue muffle the sound. Hopefully everyone was still outside anyway, and nobody had noticed we'd gone. Because I couldn't get enough of him. He'd been holding out on me all week, stopping us every time we got close to having sex, and instead swapping positions so he could make me come with his mouth or his hand.

If I hadn't already seen it in its hard, perfect splendor, I would have assumed he was hiding a tiny mushroom dick or that it had some sort of weird shape to it that he was ashamed of.

He ground on me now, reminding me there was nothing he needed to hide. His dick was fucking perfect, and all I wanted was for him to finally use it on me. I'd had more orgasms in the last week than I'd had in the last year. But Dom seemed hell-bent on slowing us down, every time I wanted to speed things up.

"I want you," I whispered, and he groaned in response.

He kissed me hard, like he always did, trying to distract me, but I wasn't having it. Not this time. I put my feet down on the floor so I could create a little space between us, and pulled the drawstring on his shorts, loosening them enough that I could slip my hand inside and stroke his erection.

He bit down on my shoulder, not hard enough to hurt,

but hard enough that it sent pleasure rocketing straight to my core. Precum beaded on the tip of him, and I stroked it down his shaft, aching for him to be inside me.

I jerked him until his hips moved, and he lost himself to the moment, yanking his shorts down the entire way and thrusting into my hand.

"Want you, too," he finally murmured. "Fuck, Summer. I want you so bad."

That was all it took for the two of us to go scrambling for my shorts, me popping the button and yanking at the zipper while he tried to shove the fabric down my legs.

"Hurry," I moaned. "Dom, please."

My core ached so bad, and I was desperate for the sort of relief only he could give me.

Both of us ignored the loud rumble of my mother's four-wheel-drive returning, kissing hard, a clash of lips and tongues and wandering hands. He pinched my clit, and I cried out at the sensation, needing him to do that, and so much more, all over again.

The door slammed downstairs, and a new round of excited chatter started up, but neither of us stopped. I yanked his shirt up, desperate to see him and not wanting our first time to be anything but skin to skin. I sucked one of his nipples, rolling my tongue over it as his dick slid between my legs, gliding through my arousal and brushing over my clit. He nudged at my entrance with his thick, blunt head, and I clutched him harder, sinking my fingernails into the firm muscles of his shoulders.

"God, Dom. Please!" I could tell by the full body tremble that he wanted this as badly as I did. I was sure neither of us had the willpower to stop this time.

"Condom?" Dom asked.

I froze and stared up at him in horror. "You don't have one?"

"Not on me. Don't you have one in here somewhere?"

I panted out a breath, my core clenching over nothing, mourning the fact it wasn't filled with his amazing-looking dick. "I saw the gigantic box in your bathroom and assumed we were good. I wasn't expecting..." I gestured around the room. "My sister's bedrooms are right across the hall. I wasn't planning on doing this here." I dropped my head to his chest, breathing hard. "Kill me now."

He chuckled, though I knew from the throbbing of his dick still hard between my legs, that he was in as much pain as I was.

"I'd rather make you come than kill you," he laughed. Then he gripped my face and tilted it up.

He took in my disappointment, and then he leaned in and kissed me more softly than he ever had. "Hey. I need you to know something."

"What?" I grumped, hating myself for not being prepared. Served me right for leaving birth control up to him. It wasn't his responsibility alone.

"We are going to have sex, Summer. Not right now, because I respect you too much to do that without protection." His lips drifted from mine, to my ear. "But I am going to fuck you. I'm going to fuck you all over my cabin, all over this ranch, and probably a million other spots. There's no rush when it comes to you and me. I'm not going anywhere. You hear that?"

I heard it. And my stupid overinflated heart gave a gigantic thump of approval.

"Okay?" he asked, peering into my eyes.

"Okay," I whispered, not trusting myself to say anymore,

for fear all the feelings swirling around me might come spewing out.

"Now can I make you come?"

I grinned. "I thought you'd never ask."

He dropped to his knees, and his mouth was mere inches from where I wanted him most, when footsteps echoed on the stairs.

Both of us froze when they stopped outside my door. I widened my eyes and held one finger to my lips. Which was stupid really because what did I think Dom was going to do? Yell out, "Hey, go away, I'm about to go down on Summer's pussy like it's an ice cream melting in the sunshine!" I stifled a laugh at the thought, and Dom gave me a confused look.

I just shook my head.

"Summer?" my mother asked through the closed door.

"Uh, yes?"

There was laughter in her voice. "Do you think you could come down? Dom's surprise just arrived."

"Yes, sure. I'll be right down."

Awkward, I mouthed to Dom, pulling him up off the floor. The orgasm would have to wait.

"Oh, and Dom?"

I clapped a hand over my mouth, trying to stop the mortified laughter from pouring out.

"Yes, Mrs. Hunt?"

I slapped his chest, but he just shrugged.

"I'm really glad you're keeping my daughter happy, but these walls are really thin, and neither of you are as quiet as you think you are."

Oh. My. God.

"Duly noted, ma'am."

Mom's footsteps mixed with her laughter as she walked away.

Dom and I both sniggered while we got dressed again, and we walked down the stairs together, holding hands. At the back door, he went to let go, but that feeling I'd had up in my bedroom, the one of my heart cracking open just that little bit more still stayed with me. I pulled his hand back and linked his fingers between mine.

He glanced down in surprise. "Everyone is out there," he murmured. "We go out there like this, and there's no taking it back."

"I know."

"You sure?"

I reached up and kissed his cheek. "Never been more sure of anything."

It was like I'd handed him a Christmas gift he'd been dying for all year. We stepped outside, and a little part of me expected some sort of fanfare. For everyone to stop and look at us, and notice that we were together.

It didn't come. Everybody was too busy greeting the new arrival, who had to have come in with my mother. I peered at the middle-aged dark-haired woman talking to Felix for a moment longer than I should have, before I realized who it was. It wasn't that her face wasn't familiar. It was just that it was out of place here.

I squeezed Dom's fingers. "Oh my God, Dom. Your mom!"

He peered in the direction I was pointing and did a double take, his grin widening. "Holy shit!" Dragging me along with him, he made a beeline for her, pushing through the crowd. We reached her just in time to hear her ask Felix how he knew Dominic.

We both stopped dead as Felix replied with a huge smile, "He's my brother."

24

Dominic

The shock that punched across Mom's face was twofold. Once from the bomb Felix dropped. And then again, a split second later, when she spotted me.

I let go of Summer's hand to pull my mother into a hug. "I'm sorry," I whispered.

She hugged me, but when she pulled back, her gaze bounced from me to Felix and back again.

I cleared my throat. "Felix, this is my mom."

He smiled at her but quickly turned to me. "Sorry, man. I had no idea."

"You found your birth family?" Mom asked quietly.

Felix shoved his hands in his pockets. "Uh, sorry. Should I go?"

But my mother snapped herself out of it and shook her head. "Of course not. I'm sorry, I'm being so rude. I just wasn't expecting... I didn't know..."

Guilt swamped me like a dark, damp blanket. All the good feelings that had been coursing through my body disappeared into the steamy afternoon air. "Mom..."

She blinked a few times and plastered a smile on her

face. Then she hugged me again. "It's okay. You just caught me by surprise."

Felix and Summer were both awkward as fuck, and I made eyes at Summer, who seemed to know exactly what I needed without me saying a word. She linked her arm through Felix's and announced that she needed a drink and he was coming with her.

He seemed relieved to make his escape, though he shot me another apologetic look over his shoulder.

It wasn't his fault. Hell, I'd introduced him to Frost as my brother, so of course he'd just assumed that it was okay to introduce himself that way. I wanted to call him my brother. I wanted to tell everyone about him, including my family. I just hadn't gotten there yet.

It was me I was angry at. I could see the hurt in my mother's expression, even though she tried to hide it. She had to have known this day would come eventually. She'd told me many a time that I was always free to search for my birth family.

But I'd always known deep in my heart that it would hurt her to do so. Here was the proof. I'd found them, and even though I'd tried to keep my two worlds separate, I should have always known they'd collide.

"Do you want to go somewhere and talk?" I asked her.

"I'd like that."

I put my arm around her shoulders, steering her toward my cabin. I made idle conversation along the way, pointing out the bull training rings, and the barn, even though she'd been coming out to the Hunts' ranch since before I was even born. She probably knew this place better than I did, and yet she smiled and nodded and asked a question or two as we walked, like she'd never been here before and was just visiting her son at work for the first time.

"Where's Dad? He didn't come?"

She shook her head. "He really wanted to. But he hasn't been feeling well lately.

"Is he okay?"

She faltered for a second. "He's just a bit tired. I left your brothers at home to make sure he rests. He keeps trying to get outside to work. I've practically had to chain him to the couch and force him to take a break."

I sighed. "That's my fault for just up and leaving you guys in the lurch."

"It's nothing to do with you, Dom. It's just a case of bad luck. The ranch work will still be there when your father is feeling better. Nothing is so urgent that the man can't take a few days off. Not that he listens when I tell him that." She sounded annoyed, but it was with the same soft smile she always wore when she spoke about my father. The two of them had such a perfect marriage. They argued from time to time, but never about anything important. At the end of the day, they were each other's biggest supporters. Their relationship was one to be envied.

When we got to my cabin, instinctively, we both sat on the wooden steps, side by side.

"Do you remember where we were, when we told you you were adopted?" she asked, shifting her weight on the hard wood.

I looked down at the steps beneath my boots. "Same position, but at home. I'd just come back from school. I must have been about seven."

"Eight. It had seemed like the perfect age in my head. You weren't a baby anymore, but you weren't old enough that you could really get up and run away or leave in a teenage funk. Your dad and I had debated over it for years. He wanted to wait until you were older, but all I could think about was if we told you when you were big enough to drive, or operate machinery, that you'd run off, and we might never see you again."

I shook my head. "I wouldn't have done that."

She patted my knee. "No, I know. You were always such a sensible, smart kid. You took the news like a champion, and it would have been the same no matter how old you were, I'm sure of it. You were like that with everything. Always more mature than you should have been. Always more responsible."

"Eldest child thing, I guess. Someone has to be the responsible one when you've got Theo and Spencer around."

She smiled at that. "Isn't that the truth? But I was always grateful for how mature you were. I think maybe I took it for granted. So when you acted like you didn't need to know your birth family, I let myself believe it was true. That's on me, Dom. I'm sorry."

"You're sorry? I'm the one who went behind your back like a coward. Then ran across the other side of the country when it didn't work out the way it had in my little boy dreams. Hardly mature at all." I kicked the dirt with the toe of my boot.

"Ah. Well, that explains some things. Your father and I thought there must have been a woman involved."

I bit my lip, hiding a smile. "Well, there is now. But there wasn't then. I came here to lick my wounds."

Mom's eyes sparkled. "And you met someone?"

I chuckled. "Actually, I met her a long time ago." I nodded across the way to where Summer was standing at the very edge of the party, watching us while she pretended to eat.

"Summer?"

I grinned at her. "Yeah, Summer."

"Addie told me she got rid of that horrible boyfriend of hers, but I never in a million years thought that the two of you…" She squealed and hugged me again. "I'm so happy. When you and your brothers were younger, and we'd bring you here while you were all still in diapers, Addie and I would watch her girls with my boys, and we'd plan which of you would get married. I always sort of thought it would be Lennon and Theo."

I shrugged. "Still time for that, I guess."

"I'm really happy it's you and Summer. Not that I'm saying you two are getting married…"

I didn't say anything.

Her eyes widened. "Dominic Aaron West. Why do you look so smug when I mention you and Summer and married in the same sentence?"

I chuckled and shushed her. "Stop. I'm not marrying anyone just yet. But…"

"Holy hell, there's a but. Wait till I tell Addie."

I elbowed her. "I was just going to say, but I wouldn't rule it out. I like her, Mom. A lot."

My mom's expression softened into a smile. "There's a lot about her to like."

"I like it here, too," I admitted. "I'm sorry for the way I left, but…" I hated that I was about to hurt her. "I don't think I'm coming back."

She bit her lip and nodded, gazing out across the field at Summer. "You love her."

I raised one shoulder. "I don't know. But I do know that I *could* love her. In time."

"Does she love you back? She was with that other boy for a long time, Dom. I love Summer and her sisters like my own daughters. But you're my son. I don't want to see your heart broken."

I shook my head. "I don't know what she feels exactly. But I can wait. I've waited five years. I can wait that long again if I have to."

Mom smiled softly. "That girl hasn't stopped staring over here since we sat down."

"She's worried about me."

"Or she loves you, too, even if she hasn't come right out and said it."

The corner of my mouth lifted at that thought. But it was something I wanted to tuck away for myself and consider when I was alone. "Sorry to spring Felix on you."

Mom waved her hand around, dismissing my concerns. "I know you think you can't talk to me about your birth family. But I've always known you would look them up one day. It's only natural that you want to know where you came from. Tell me about him."

Man, I loved her. She was such an amazing woman. I was so bloody lucky to have been chosen by her. "He lives a couple of hours from here. Works on a ranch, too."

She raised an eyebrow. "So you've got things in common then?"

"Lots."

She smiled. "I'm happy for you. What about the rest of your family?"

I shook my head. "Don't want to know me. Or him by the sounds of it."

A mixture of emotions crossed her face, but the one that settled was anger. "They don't know what they're missing out on."

I grinned. "You have to say that. You're my mom."

She nodded fiercely. "And I've never been prouder of

anything than that. You know, I still remember the first time you called me mommy—"

I groaned. "I know it's my birthday and all, but do we really need to go down memory lane? There is kind of a party going on over there that we're missing."

"Fine, I'll save my reminiscing for Addie or your father. Let's get you back to your party. And your brother. And your girlfriend."

I looked at Summer across the yard. She was still watching intently, poised as if she would run across the field to be by my side in an instant if I needed her to be.

Girlfriend.

I liked the sound of that.

25

Dominic's birthday cookout wore on into the evening, the trainees the last to leave. My dad eventually kicked them out, sending them back to their own cabins with a stern warning that they'd be crucified if any of them showed up even remotely hungover for training on Monday morning.

Dominic and I curled up on the couch together, his arm around my shoulders, and my hand pressed to his chest, while he filled both our moms in on everything that had been going on with his search for his birth family. The two of them watched us with small smiles on their faces, and the occasional grin shared between them like Dom and I getting together had been all their doing. My sisters sat on the floor, listening in, too, though Callie's phone kept buzzing with text messages that made her light up every time she opened one. Lennon turned a little greener with each one she read over her twin's shoulder.

It was hard to watch my sweet younger sister live through a case of unrequited love, and not be able to tell the person closest to her about it. Callie was off in a world of her own, where only she and Preston seemed to exist. And Lennon was on the outside, just like I had been with them our entire lives. But I was well used to it and had made my peace with it. Lennon wasn't there yet. The cord that held the two of them together was slowly fraying.

It was nearing midnight as I made my way upstairs and packed a small bag of clothes and toiletries to take to Dom's cabin. When I came back down, everyone turned to me, gazes drawn to the bag I was carrying.

"Where are you off to?" Dad asked.

I gave my mother a look that was a clear cry for help.

She laughed and pulled my dad to his feet. "Come upstairs and I'll explain it all to you."

He frowned but let himself be guided to the stairs. Lennon and Callie had both disappeared to their bedrooms, leaving only Isabel.

"Do you need anything before we go?" Dom asked her.

She shook her head and waved us toward the door. "Go. I've been staying here for longer than you've been alive. I know where the guest room is. I'll be just fine." She kissed her son on the cheek and left, heading for the small spare room on the bottom level that my parents always kept for Johnny and Isabel or any other guests we might have had.

I slipped my hand into Dom's and squeezed it.

He squeezed right back. "Bag, huh?"

"Bag," I agreed.

He took it from me, hefting it up and down a few times, testing the weight. "Seems kind of light."

"I forgot to pack pajamas."

He towed me toward the door so fast I had to run to keep up. Out across the night we ran, two stupid kids desperate to be alone after being among a crowd all night. We both knew what was going to happen the minute we got behind closed doors.

There was no short supply of condoms in his cabin.

He didn't disappoint me. He threw the door open, dumping the bag on the floor. We both knew I wouldn't need it before morning. And morning was still very far away.

"Longest party ever." Dom closed the door and pulled me into his arms. "Next year, we completely ignore everyone for my birthday. All I want is to stay locked in a cabin with you for an entire weekend. Deal?" He swooped in for a kiss, pressing his mouth to mine, and sinking his tongue deep inside.

I basked in the idea that he thought the two of us would still be together in a year. So I clutched him tight and kissed him back. Like it did every time he kissed me, my head spun with how much I wanted him. "Totally agree," I murmured in between hot presses of his mouth. "Parties are stupid. Far too many people. Never again."

I threw my arms around his neck, noting the tiny spasm of pain at lifting my bad arm but ignoring it in favor of getting my lips back on his. He hoisted me into his arms but then turned in a circle, first to the left and then to the right, like he couldn't decide which way to go.

"Very small cabin, Dom. Only one bed, and it's right there." I jerked a thumb over my shoulder.

"But I also promised to bend you over a kitchen counter...and then there's the bathroom. So many options. I'm struck down by sex indecision."

We both snorted on our laughter, but I loved when he was goofy. My experience with sex had never been fun or playful. I liked that he was so different. I liked laughing with him. I liked just being with him in general, no matter what his mood.

I just wanted to be with him.

And there went my stupid heart again, getting all big and mushy.

"Bed," I decided for him, laughter fading from my lips in place of something more serious. "Fuck me later, whenever or wherever you want, but right now, I don't want to just screw."

His expression changed in an instant, matching mine, and he kissed me tenderly. Instead of throwing me onto the bed like he had in the past, he laid me down gently, slowly stripped me of my clothes, then stood back to do the same to his own.

I lay there watching him. He fisted the back of his shirt and dragged it over his head. His tattoos curved over his broad shoulders and down the side of his ribs, following the flow of his body. The V lines that ran either side of his hips dipped below the waistband of his shorts, and I followed them with my gaze while he dragged them off, taking his boxer briefs with him. His phone fell from his pocket, clattering to the floorboards.

He picked it up and went to place it on the bedside table but froze halfway.

I sat up at the expression on his face. "What's wrong?"

He hit a button on the phone and paused a moment while he read whatever was on the screen. "It's my brother."

"Felix?"

"No, Theo. He's asking if Mom told me about Dad's heart attack."

"What?"

Dom shook his head, already calling his brother, phone pressed to his ear.

I wrapped a sheet around myself, but there was little else I could do while Dom paced the length of the little cabin.

Theo answered quickly, and he and Dom had a short back-and-forth conversation that I couldn't follow by only hearing Dom's side of it. Finally, he swore low under his breath and sank down on the bed beside me. "I'll talk to you tomorrow."

I moved in close to Dom's side, and he put an arm around me and dropped a kiss to my hair.

"Is everything okay?" I asked quietly.

He let out a long, slow breath. "I don't know. Theo said he had a small heart attack last week. Apparently he's fine, just has to rest for a while. But Theo said he's been off his game for weeks. They didn't want to worry me, since there was nothing I could do from all the way over here anyway." He ran his hand through his hair. "I can't believe they didn't even tell me!"

I put my arms around his middle and placed a kiss on his chest. "Do you want to go talk to your mom about it?"

He shook his head. "It's late. We can talk in the morning." He turned his focus back to me, his gaze running over my bare shoulders and the sheet that was slipping off my breasts. He drew it all the way down, exposing my nipples and stomach, the sheet pooling around my waist.

"You're so beautiful," he said quietly.

I studied his handsome face, the sharp cut of his jawline, and his dark brown eyes that I could just drown in. "I was just about to say the same thing to you."

He reached across to his bedside table and grabbed a condom from the box he kept there. "I'm prepared this time."

"You still want to?"

"Yeah, Sum. I still want to. There's nothing I can do from

here but make you feel good." He kissed me softly. "I don't know what I've been waiting for. The perfect moment, or for you to forget Austin ever existed, maybe. I'm an idiot."

"No, you're sweet and kind, and the best man I know." I kissed his lips and then the corner of his mouth. "Your face is giving away how guilty you feel right now."

He squeezed his eyes tight. "If I'd been there… If I hadn't run off to the other side of the country…"

I silenced him with another kiss. "Stop."

"I can't. It's all I can think of. If I'd still been there, he wouldn't have been so stressed. I left him and my brothers with all of my work and without any sort of notice. Hell, I've barely even called them since I left because I've been too gutless to tell them about my birth family. I haven't had a proper conversation that wasn't just about the weather, or the bulls, with any of them in months."

"You're allowed to have a life," I assured him. "They want that for you."

He dropped his head, staring down at his lap.

I hated that he was hurting. And that he was placing the blame for something that was completely out of his control on his own shoulders. I shifted off the bed to kneel in front of him so he'd be forced to look at me.

He turned miserable, sad eyes in my direction, and my heart clenched. I cupped the sides of his face and kissed him hard, because it was all I could do. I couldn't take the blame he was putting on himself. All I could do was help him forget it for a little while.

He seemed to have the same idea I did. He took barely a moment to respond, and when he did, it was with everything he had. He gripped the sides of my face, mirroring my position, his fingers tight in my hair. He guided me to my feet, the sheet falling away completely when I stood.

He lay back on the mattress, and I crawled over his body, taking his lips again in a plunging kiss. Our bodies pressed together, his erection thickening between us while we made out.

His hands skimmed down my back and over my ass, squeezing my cheeks as he rocked his hips up from below. In one swift move, he flipped our positions, rolling me onto my back so he loomed over me.

The sadness in his gaze had been replaced with a searing heat, and he wasted no time in placing featherlight kisses all over my jaw, then lower to my collarbone, and over the swell of my breasts.

My nipples beaded for him, aching for his mouth, and I was rewarded when his tongue shot out to taste one.

"I've been thinking about this all afternoon," he murmured.

"Me, too." I dragged his hand between us, guiding it between my legs.

"Fuck, Summer," he groaned. "Have you been like this all day?" His fingers slipped through the arousal between my thighs, gliding up inside me without resistance.

I nodded. I had been. He'd had me so close to orgasm this afternoon in my bedroom that I'd been on edge ever since. Two quick pumps of his fingers, each one hitting my G-spot, had me right back there, trembling with need.

"Fuck. I should have taken care of this earlier." He worked his fingers in and out of my core and rubbed my clit with his thumb. "You're so wet."

I reached between us and fisted his cock, jerking the already rock-solid length. His hips rolled in time with the rhythm I set, both of us working closer and closer to the orgasms we'd been denied earlier in the day.

But it wasn't enough. For once, his fingers inside me, and

his mouth on my lips, and my neck, it wasn't enough. I wanted more. I wanted him.

I wanted his heart, and his soul, and a connection just getting off didn't bring.

I found the condom he'd tossed onto the bed and ripped the top off the packaging with my teeth. The lubed condom slipped in my fingers, and Dom held still just long enough to watch me roll it down his thick length.

Our gazes clashed as he settled between my legs once more.

All I saw was him.

I knew who he was. He was the sort of man who waited five years. He was the sort of man, who respected me enough to give me time. He was the sort of man who pushed me to achieve the dreams I'd all but given up on.

He was the sort of man my heart could so easily love, if only I let it.

I wanted to let it.

But then his mouth lowered to mine, and he kissed me. It was softer and sweeter than he'd ever kissed me before. It was full of words that neither of us had voiced. Full of a connection that had started as kids and had finally grown into what it was always supposed to be.

"You're mine, Summer," he whispered, brown eyes locked on mine.

"I know." It was all I had to say. Because I was his. And he was mine. He always had been. Everything inside me knew it in that moment. He was why things would have never worked with any other guy, no matter how hard I might have tried to fight it. He was why my heart had cracked so wide open in just a matter of weeks.

He was easy to love. Because of the way he loved me.

Neither of us voiced it, but it was there, as loud as if we were screaming.

His cock moved between my legs, and I opened them wide, lifting my hips so he nudged at my entrance. I ached for him, but he entered me inch by inch, his gaze locked firmly on mine, watching my expression, his concern evident in every movement.

"Kiss me," I whispered.

He lowered his body right down on top of mine and kissed me deeply. His dick slid all the way home and then stilled, giving me time to adjust to the thickness and length of him. We kissed like we had all the time in the world. Deep, drugging kisses that I'd feel long after and remember for eternity. We moved our hips in unison, both of us needing more. He kept the rhythm slow, watching my orgasm build. He reached down, fingers on my clit while he worked himself in and out of my core.

"Want to feel you come," he whispered.

He'd get his wish. He picked up the pace, working me faster, until spirals of pleasure danced behind my eyes and a tsunami of feeling built at the base of my spine.

"Yes," I moaned. Each touch of him, each thrust had me closer and closer, the intense pleasure bordering the spot between ecstasy and agony.

"Dom," I yelled. "Please!"

That was all he needed. My permission to send me flying over the edge. His hips slammed home, pounding against my pubic bone and clit, his dick filling me so fully it was a wonder I could take him at all. The pleasure spiraled out of control, and my pussy spasmed hard, clamping down around his dick.

"Oh!" We both cried out in unison.

I fell over the edge and into a chasm of pleasure, while

Dom dropped his head to my neck, finding his own release in shuddering tremors that racked his shoulders, flexed his abs, and clenched his thighs and ass.

"Fuck, you feel amazing," he groaned into my ear.

I couldn't even answer him. I was too far gone and floating on a cloud somewhere outside my body.

I don't even know how long it took me to come back down to earth. Long enough for him to roll off me and gather my naked, sweaty body to his side. Long enough for him to wrap me in his arms and murmur sweet words in my ear.

I finally looked up and focused on him. "I don't know how we got here," I murmured, trying to memorize every line and plane of his face. "I don't know why we didn't get here sooner."

He kissed me softly. "We're here now."

I held him tight. We were here now. And that was what I wanted to hold on to.

Not the tiny voice in the back of my head that questioned whether his father's illness might mean we wouldn't be here like this forever.

26

Dominic

When I woke up the next morning, Summer was making coffee in my kitchenette, her long brown legs bare beneath the T-shirt I'd worn yesterday.

"You slept in," she accused, adding milk to the two mugs.

I stretched my arms up above my head, not missing the way she paused to let her gaze run all over my body. We'd both slept completely naked, in a tangle of arms and legs. I eyed hers now, wondering if she was still bare beneath that T-shirt. "It's Sunday."

She closed the milk carton and put it back in the refrigerator. "You want sugar?"

I did, but not the sort she was thinking of. I got off the bed and padded naked into the kitchen, circling my arms around her from behind and kissing her neck. She faltered with the teaspoon midway to our mugs, little granules of sugar spilling onto the countertop.

"I don't want coffee," I whispered in her ear. My palm flattened on the back of her thigh and rolled up her leg, taking the hem of my T-shirt with it. I moved my hand over the rounded curve of her ass, my dick stiffening when I found that she was indeed, very naked beneath my clothes. I squeezed her ass, fingers lingering lower, as if I might dip them between her thighs at any moment.

Her teaspoon clattered to the countertop. "Dom," she murmured.

"Yeah?" I pushed the T-shirt right up and leaned back so I could take in the entirety of her rounded ass, as she bent slightly over the counter.

"You promised you were going to take me like this." Her words were barely more than a breathy moan.

Fuck, she was hot when she talked like that, telling me what she wanted. I moved in closer, letting her feel my erection against her skin. "Then spread your legs so I can."

This time her moan was loud enough to wake the neighbors. I grabbed a condom and shoved it over my dick, while she moved the mugs of coffee aside.

"Hands on the other side of the countertop," I commanded. "Right over."

She did exactly what I'd told her to do, but I pushed her down farther until her head rested on it, too, her tits dangling, her perfect fucking ass on display. She'd widened her stance, showing me everything she had, and I swiped the head of my cock through her folds, testing her, making sure she was ready for me.

She was. Her pussy glistened in the early morning light, and her legs trembled with anticipation.

I gripped her hip, lining myself up at her entrance. "Hold on tight, Summer. Gonna do this hard and fast."

Her groan of impatience had me thrusting inside her in one full stroke.

"Oh!" Her fingers curled over the edge of the countertop, gripping it hard while I pulled out, then slammed home.

She pushed back again, encouraging me, the little noises

of pleasure telling me this position turned her on as much as it did me.

She felt so good. I fucked her fast and hard, the complete opposite of how I'd had her last night, but that was what we'd needed then. What we needed now was something entirely different. I reached around and low between her legs to touch her clit, and she went off like a firecracker. She slammed her ass back against me, taking me deeper than she had last night, and moaning my name as I filled her.

"Dom! Don't stop."

There was no way that I could, even if I wanted to. I drove into her, over and over, holding her hip with one hand and tickling her clit with the other. My palm itched to slap her ass, knowing it would send her over the edge.

"Dom," she panted. "More."

Fuck. I had no idea which way to take her. Not wanting to slap her without at least a discussion, I changed routes. I took my fingers from her clit, still slick with her arousal, and let my fingers drift back to her ass. I glanced them over the star of her rear end and waited for her reaction.

The sound she made was deep and guttural, as if I'd hit a switch inside her that took her to the next level. She panted out her breath, so I did it again, pressing at this new button.

"Dom!" she screamed out.

Her orgasm came so quick and hard it almost took me by surprise. Her walls clamped down on me, sending me spinning into my orgasm. She was so tight. So hot. And her core pulsed around me, drawing out every last drop of my pleasure.

She slumped down over the countertop, and we both

stayed like that for a long moment, both of us reeling from the aftereffects of mind-blowing sex.

We might have stayed like that for hours, just content with how thoroughly we'd made each other come.

But the pounding on my front door brought an abrupt end to all good feelings.

"Quit screwing like porn stars and get out here," Preston's voice yelled through the door. "We've got a massive fucking problem."

"What do you mean the bulls are all gone?" Frost roared, voice full of anger.

It was so unlike him that I actually took a step back in surprise.

Summer stepped in front of me and put her hands up, trying to placate her father. "We mean exactly what Dom just said. When Preston got up this morning, the gates were all open, and the bulls were gone. He came and got us. Now I'm telling you. I've already called the sheriff."

I couldn't blame the guy for being upset. It wasn't even eight on a Sunday morning, and the man had been enjoying a coffee in his living room, still dressed in the sweatpants and T-shirt he must have worn to bed.

Frost strode to the front door where his boots were and shoved one on his foot. "How the hell can they all just be gone? We would have heard trucks!"

I answered that one. "My guess is they came in on foot and let them out into the back pastures and took them from there. We haven't checked the fences yet, but I'll bet you anything they used that little access road out by the south pasture."

“Motherfuckers! What did the sheriff say?”

Summer cringed. “That they’ll be out tomorrow.”

“Tomorrow? Whoever the hell has my bulls will be long gone by tomorrow.”

I grimaced. I’d already come to the same conclusion.

Summer tried to be the voice of calm, concise explanation. “You know the sheriff’s department here is tiny, Dad. There was a hit-and-run last night—”

“Was anyone hurt? Is it connected?”

She shook her head. “I don’t know the details. But they’re tied up with that. Theft is low on their priority list right now.”

Frost finally got his other boot on, and Summer and I followed him outside. He looked exactly like we had twenty minutes earlier. All the bull pens were open, not an animal in sight.

Hundreds of thousands of dollars’ worth of animals gone like they’d evaporated into thin air.

The trainees had all wandered out with the commotion, as had my mom and Addie. Frost swore low under his breath, stormed into the office only to return a moment later with every set of keys from the pegboard inside.

“Dad.” Summer frowned. “What are you doing?”

He tossed a set of keys to me. “Going to find my damn bulls. Addie, you’re with me. Summer, you go with Dom. Isabel, can you stay here and keep an eye on the place? If the sheriff shows up, call me?”

My mom nodded. Her gaze met mine. I still needed to talk to her about keeping my father’s illness from me, but now wasn’t the time.

“I’ll help,” Preston chimed in.

The other trainees who lived on site all immediately put

their hands up and said they'd give up their Sunday to search, too.

Frost threw each of them keys, pairing everybody up and sending them in different directions. "Ask the neighbors. Stop in the town. Look for track marks. Fuck, I don't care what sort of detective work you need to pull, do whatever you can think of. I can't lose those animals. I've literally got nothing without them."

Addie chewed a thumbnail nervously, and Summer's lips were drawn into a tight, thin line.

I'd seen enough of the books to know why they were so worried. Despite the fact they'd turned down a pretty hefty payday when they'd been offered money for Grave Digger, the Hunts were not rolling in cash. All ranches took loss of stock into consideration. But not a loss like this. Not every animal they owned. This wasn't the sort of thing that a business could come back from.

It was the sort of thing that sent them straight into bankruptcy.

Summer and I got in the truck I'd been driving and followed the convoy out onto the road. At the top of the driveway, we split into two directions, and then farther down we split again, until it was just me and Summer, alone on the road. She stared out the window silently while I drove with my foot down hard on the accelerator.

"The Murphys have cameras," I assured her.

"We're completely screwed if we don't get those bulls back, Dom," she said quietly, as if she hadn't even heard me. "Even if we go through insurance, who knows how long it would take for that money to come through, and how much longer it would take again to buy new stock. It's hard to find good buckers. We'd lose all the business we have booked for the next few months at a minimum. We'd have to let go of staff..." She shot a worried glance at me.

I already knew it would be my job on the line if there was no business here to pay my wages. "I know."

She slammed the side of her fist into the padded part of her door. "Dammit! How the hell didn't we hear anything? Were we so busy screwing that we didn't notice people on the property? Fuck, they could have been right outside our door!"

I reached across the center console and took her hand. "Hey, stop. My cabin isn't exactly right on top of the training pens. None of the cabins are. Yeah, we might have heard a truck, but even if we'd been completely still and listening for a disturbance, we probably wouldn't have heard men coming in on foot. And hell, Summer. If I heard footsteps outside my cabin, I would have just assumed it was one of the other guys. I would have never in a million years assumed there was someone outside trying to steal the bulls."

She leaned forward, as if urging the car to go faster as we drove past the sign on the Murphy's fence. "This is my fault. I should have made Dad install cameras. And upgrade security."

"It's not your fault."

She whipped her head around to stare at me. "You have security at your place, don't you?"

I almost didn't want to answer her, but she already knew the answer. "Well, yeah, but our bulls are high-profile. Yours aren't. Until this year, your dad hasn't even put them in the local rodeos. They've purely been bred for the training school."

She shook her head. "Grave Digger is worth money,

though. Good money. I should have thought of this. I'm the ranch manager! Dad relies on me."

"I didn't think of it either, Sum. We're in the middle of nowhere. You know every person in this town. The people around here trust each other with their lives. Trusting that they won't steal their livelihoods is just a given." I pulled to a stop out the front of the Murphys' house and shot a worried glance at her. "This *isn't* your fault." I could see her piling all the blame on her own shoulders, the weight of it dragging her down.

She sighed as we both got out of the truck, doors slamming behind us. "Did you believe me last night when I told you your dad's heart attack wasn't your fault?"

I took her hand and squeezed it. "No," I admitted. That guilt sat firmly on my shoulders. And it was completely different to what was going on here.

She squeezed my hand back. "Yeah, well, guess that's just one more thing we have in common."

Mrs. Murphy came outside as we approached her door and ushered us inside. "Your mama already called me, Summer. I was just going to the office to get the footage from last night when you arrived. Come on in."

We followed her through the house, bypassing a living room full of framed photos of Mrs. Murphy's three small kids. An abandoned game of Monopoly sat in the middle of the floor, the money and cards strewn haphazardly across the board. I wondered where the kids were, then realized that like most country kids, they were probably outside somewhere, helping their father. Weekends were often nonexistent if there was work to be done. The woman led us to a small room in the back that was mostly taken up by a large desk, covered in piles of paperwork. Mrs. Murphy moved some things to one side and then turned on her laptop.

Summer tapped her thigh impatiently as we waited for it to boot up. I took her hand to get her to stop. I knew she wasn't trying to be rude, she was just worried, but I didn't want Mrs. Murphy to refuse to help us because of Summer's impatience.

Mrs. Murphy double-clicked a folder on her desktop, and then a few more, before she found the CCTV footage from last night. It was that awful dark grainy kind, slightly tinged green by the night vision.

"There's four cameras." Mrs. Murphy pointed to the four-way split screen. "Home paddock, house, and two on the boundary fences. You're probably most interested in this one." She touched the bottom left-hand image. "It's the camera on the fence on Dixons Road."

Summer leaned in, peering at the screen. "Our theory is someone took them out through the fence on our south boundary pasture, so yes, please. If your cameras caught anything on that road last night, that would be helpful."

Mrs. Murphy nodded. "I'll start at dusk then."

"We were outside until midnight, and all bulls were accounted for then. Can you skip forward? It had to have happened sometime between midnight and six this morning."

Mrs. Murphy hit a key on her laptop, and the video footage zoomed up to three times the pace. It flew past the 12 a.m. timestamp and kept going. But the screen didn't change. For the longest time, all it showed was a long stretch of fences, the Murphys' pasture on one side of the road, and the Hunts' on the other.

The timer rolled on through one and 2 a.m. with

nothing to show. When it hit three, I started thinking that this was a waste of time. It wasn't going to show anything.

"There!" Summer yelled. "Stop."

Mrs. Murphy hit the 'play' button, slowing the footage down to regular pace. The screen looked completely normal.

"I don't see anything," I told Summer.

But she had an eagle-eyed gaze on the screen. "Wait...there!"

A black shadow crossed the screen. All three of us moved closer. In the next second, the black shadow was back moving around, and then there were more. A white truck lit up the screen as it rolled silently down the road.

"Three guys," I said, pointing out the obvious.

"Three guys and all my damn bulls," Summer ground out.

It was impossible to make out any distinguishing features of the men. They wore black, or at least dark clothes, it was hard to tell. The grainy footage and the darkness of the night made it nearly impossible to see facial details. They herded the animals onto the back of the waiting truck, and when the last one was loaded, they hauled the ramp up and shut the back end.

"Pause." I indicated to the screen when Mrs. Murphy stopped the footage. "Plate number."

Summer grabbed a pen from the holder and started writing it down on a piece of scrap paper.

"It might be fake or stolen," Mrs. Murphy cautioned her.

Summer's pen flew over the paper, her messy scrawl getting down the number and letter combination. "I know. Or they might be that dumb. Either way, we need to give this to the sheriff so they can search it up and see who that truck is registered to."

"Don't bother." I pulled out my phone and brought up Julian's number. "I got it."

She peered over at me. "You calling the sheriff?"

"No, my friend Julian. You said yourself, this isn't a priority to the sheriff right now. Julian is a whiz with computers. He's the one who found my birth family for me."

"He can find out who the truck is registered to?"

I shrugged as the dial tone rang in my ear, waiting for Julian to pick up. "No idea, but if he can, it's going to be a whole lot quicker than waiting for the sheriff."

Mrs. Murphy's eyes widened, and I was sure she was suddenly wondering what sort of guy I was to know someone who could hack into secure databases and did so just for the fun of it. It would probably be all over town by tomorrow that I ran with criminal masterminds. The gossip hotline around here did love to pick up any tiny tidbit of information and turn it into a viral sensation.

Julian finally answered, his voice full of sleep. "Dom? What the fuck, man, it's the middle of the night? You better be close to dying and ringing to tell me your last goodbyes. It's frigging Sunday."

I'd forgotten it was two hours earlier in Wyoming. Shit. "Sorry, but listen, man. I need a favor. I have a license plate number and I need to know who owns it. Can you do that?"

"Does a bear shit in the woods?"

"I guess that's a yes then?"

Summer raised an eyebrow at me, and I nodded, confirming he could do it. I put the phone on speaker so both of us could hear the sounds of Julian stumbling out of bed and cursing as he tripped over things in the dark. His bedroom was always a complete disaster zone of computer cords and monitors and spare parts he never seemed to use, but swore he needed. I could totally picture him falling out of bed and having to pick his way to his desk.

"Ow!" he yelped. "Fuck, Dom. Next time, can you pick a more reasonable hour. I can't even see straight at this time of day."

Mrs. Murphy seemed turned off by the use of language and quietly stood to leave the room. "I'll give you some privacy," she told Summer, and the two of us thanked her profusely. She closed the door behind her.

"Who's that with you?" Julian asked.

"It's Summer."

"Who's that?"

"She's my, ah..." I shot a glance at her. I could have just explained her away as my coworker. Or my friend. But her hair was still disheveled from the sex we'd had all night. We'd only bothered to pull on clothes when Preston had started banging on the door. Neither of us had bothered to brush our teeth or even grab a hat. Her brow furrowed from staring so hard at my phone, as if she could somehow see Julian working away at his computer if she looked at it hard enough.

Even in the middle of all of this, with a grimace etched on her face, she was still the most beautiful woman I'd ever seen.

I tucked a stray strand of hair behind her ear. "She's my girlfriend?" My voice changed pitch at the end of the sentence, turning it into a question.

Summer's head snapped up, and her gaze met mine.

I raised an eyebrow.

"You don't sound real sure about that." Julian chuckled amongst the clatter of his fingers racing over a keyboard.

But a slow smile crept across Summer's face, and though this wasn't at all how I'd planned on asking her to be my partner, I was glad I'd given her something to smile about in the middle of a shitstorm.

Say yes, I mouthed at her, wanting the two of us to have something private, even if Julian was still on the line. *Please.*

It only took her a second to nod happily.

My heart soared, and I grabbed the back of her neck, hauling her in for a kiss.

"What is that noise? Are you two making out right now?"

Summer and I pulled apart with a laugh that dissipated some of the tension in the air around us.

"Yeah, sorry, J. But if she was your girlfriend, you'd want to kiss her all the time, too." I linked my fingers between hers, desperate to keep a physical connection between us.

"Good for you, bro. I'm happy for you. But I'm in the database, so you want to give me that plate number before anyone realizes I'm in here and sends national security to my door?"

Summer quickly rattled the plate ID off, and Julian plugged it into his computer.

"And done," he announced a second later. "White truck, registered to Frank Alvarez at 1003 Grays Lane, Masonville, Georgia."

I grabbed the keys and my phone from the desk, and Summer and I took off for the front door. "That helps a lot. Thanks, bro. Talk soon, okay?"

"Anytime. Bring that girlfriend of yours home soon. I want to meet her. She got a sister?"

I chuckled. "She does, but that's a whole different can of worms that you are not gonna be opening, my friend. Talk later."

Summer called out to Mrs. Murphy as we strode past the kitchen, thanking her for her help, and then we were back in the truck, staring at each other.

"What do we do now?" she asked.

I grinned at her. "I don't know about you, but I wanna go get your bulls back."

She leaned in and kissed me on the mouth. "I knew I liked you for a reason. Let's go."

27

It was weird to drive all the way to Masonville with two completely different feelings battering away inside me, bouncing around my body, and competing for my attention. One ball of feeling was all wrapped up in a shiny glowing package made of happiness and positivity and excitement for the future. A future where I was Dominic's and he was mine. But then there was the other ball of feeling, that was more like a storm cloud, chasing around my little ball of happiness and trying to dump a typhoon of rain on it. That cloud of unhappiness swirled with stress and anger, and the awareness that if we didn't sort this bull situation out, the life I'd always known could cease to exist. What the hell would I even do without the ranch? Without training, and the rookies, and now that I had riding back in my life, I didn't want to lose that again either. It sent me spiraling back to when I'd been with Austin, about to move to the city and ruin my life.

It had been one thing to do that for someone I thought I loved.

It was an entirely different thing to have it stolen by some scumbags who thought they could just waltz in and take what my father and I had spent so many years building. This didn't just affect me. It affected my family. Dom. Preston. Hallie. All the people I cared about most.

"Do you think we should call your dad? Maybe Preston? We need a game plan."

But I shook my head. "I sent Dad a text and gave him the license plate number. But if we call them all out here, and there's nobody at this property, then we'll be even further behind. For all we know they drove that truck straight out of town, so Dad checking the cameras on other properties, and Preston asking around town is a better use of time for now. Once we've checked this place out, we can reassess."

Dom's fingers gripped the wheel a little tighter. "Shouldn't be much farther now anyway, and we'll know more."

Butterflies rioted around my belly in a nervous swarm. This was insane. These guys were probably armed. Most people around here were. There were at least three of them, so Dom and I already knew we were outnumbered.

But I wasn't the sort of person to just sit at home and wring my hands either. "We aren't storming this place," I assured myself, as much as I was saying it to him. "We're just checking it out from a distance."

He shot a glance at me, a wry grin lifting the corner of his mouth. "You aren't going in guns blazing, kicking the door down like you're in a *Bad Boys* movie?"

I sniggered. "I like to think I'm a little smarter than that."

He reached across the seat and put his hand on my thigh, his thumb smoothing over my bare leg absently while he kept his eyes on the road. "Good. Because I don't want this to be the shortest relationship in the history of Milper River. Imagine the gossips? Oh, Dominic asked Summer to be his girlfriend, then hours later the two of them were taken out by cattle rustlers."

I cracked up laughing and added to his story in a high-pitched voice. I did a half decent imitation of Mrs. Bundin, one of the older ladies who liked to sit on the main street with her gray-haired friends and commentate on the entire town's comings and goings. "Oh, such a tragedy. As sad as *Romeo and Juliet*."

My phone rang, cutting through my laughter. I picked it up, expecting it to be my dad or Preston checking in with an update, but the number flashing on the screen wasn't familiar to me at all.

I answered it anyway.

"Summer?" the deep male voice on the other end asked. "Brad Pruitt, from the WBRA."

I blinked. "Uh, hi, Brad."

Dom's head whipped in my direction, and he murmured "Pruitt," a question in his tone.

I nodded.

Dom squinted but turned back to the road.

Brad kept talking in my ear. "I heard you're riding again. One-armed and all."

I frowned at the way he'd worded it. "Well, not exactly one-armed. I still have two."

Brad laughed. "You know what I mean. Rumor is, you've been riding with your bad arm strapped to your chest."

Apparently, the rumor mill in the rodeo was just as bad as the one in Milper River.

"Anyway, I just wanted to let you know that you'll meet no resistance from me or anyone else here, if you want to get yourself into the qualifying rounds for next year's WBRA tour. In fact, that's why I'm calling. To encourage you to do just that. The first round is next weekend. Are you registered?"

I swallowed. "No, sir. I'm still not sure if I'm really ready. I've had a long time off, and the way I'm riding now is like starting all over again. I'm having to retrain my entire body to—"

Brad made a 'pfft' noise, completely cutting me off and dismissing my concerns. "Summer, you were one of the best up-and-coming riders I've ever seen. You would have qualified last year if your injury hadn't taken you down."

I cringed at the unwanted reminder. I didn't need anyone to tell me how close I'd been. I knew. I'd been a handful of good rides away, and now I was right back to the beginning.

"Register for the qualifiers, Summer. I'm coming out there myself for the first round. You ride well, people will know your name by the next day. I'll see to that."

That shouldn't have spurred me on as much as it did. Except I knew, deep within myself, I did want people to remember my name. I wanted to be the first woman to qualify for the WBRA. And now, I wanted to show people what I was truly made of. I'd been down and out for too long. I wanted to show them that I had it in me to come back from a permanent injury. I wanted to show them I wasn't the girl who gave up and left everything she loved to lick her wounds in private.

I'd been her for too long, but I wasn't her anymore.

"I'll register," I told Brad. "And I'll see you next weekend."

The address Dominic's friend, Julian, had given us wasn't all that far from the fairgrounds that had housed the rodeo where I was injured. The properties weren't quite as big out here as they were at home, but the houses were still a few miles apart. We slowed, checking the numbers on fences, until we were sure the next property along would be the one registered to the truck owners.

Dom pointed it out as it came into view. An older-style farmhouse, with rusted machinery and car shells littered around the place. A dog wandered down the dirt road track, but we didn't turn in. Instead I craned my neck, trying to look for any signs of our animals.

"I need some frigging binoculars," I complained. "I can't see from this far away."

"Me neither, but I'm not about to drive any closer." Dom drove straight past the entrance to the property without slowing.

"Okay, so what are we going to do?"

He tapped his fingers on the steering wheel, thinking it over. "Park a mile or two away and walk back in on foot."

"In the middle of the day when anyone can see us?" I bit my bottom lip. "Not sure that's a good idea."

"We could wait until it gets dark, like they did."

I cast a sidelong glance at him. "You're not that patient."

He sniggered. "I think you mean you're not."

He had a point. There was no way I could sit there all day just waiting for darkness to fall. It was July. It would be hours before it got even remotely dark.

Dom stopped at the far end of the property, turned the truck around, and parked it beneath some trees that cast shade onto the side of the road. From here, we could see the ranch's driveway at the top of a hill, but it was a way off in the distance. We'd notice a car or truck leave, but we sure as hell weren't going to know what they were up to on the property.

My impatience multiplied, doubling, then tripling until I opened my door. "Come on. We can cut through their pastures. I haven't seen any cameras, have you?"

"No, but you can't see them at the Murphys' house either."

He had a point. Fence line cameras weren't always great hulking things that advertised their presence, but more often than not they were. I was willing to take my chances.

Dom looked doubtful, but he followed me through the fence, and the two of us took off in the direction of the main house and outbuildings we'd seen as we'd driven past.

"Your father is going to have my head if you get shot, you know," Dom grumbled. "I won't even get the chance to tell him you're going to try to qualify for the pros again."

I detoured around a small dam, sticking to the cover of the trees as much as possible. The detour through the field had us approaching the buildings on the property from the rear. "I don't know if I want to tell him. I don't want to get his hopes up. Maybe I should just—"

Dom suddenly yanked my arm, pulling me to the ground, and clapped a hand over my mouth.

I widened my eyes at him, and he slowly peeled his fingers from my lips. He pointed into the next field, and I finally noticed what he had.

There was movement in the pens between the main house and a huge barn behind it. A few men walked around, moving cattle between them.

The two of us shut right up, crouching low. I hoped the

knee-length grass that had been itching my legs for the entire walk would now come in handy and help hide us from view.

We waited for a moment, until the men walked out of view again without noticing us. I breathed out a breath I hadn't realized I'd been holding. "Let's go up there, to where that copse of trees is. We'll have a better view."

Dom squinted in the direction I'd pointed. "Yeah, and they'll have a better shot. Summer, seriously, are you trying to get us killed?"

I wasn't, but I was also determined to see if our bulls were there. I grabbed his hand, and the two of us sprinted to the cover of the trees. We both gunned for the thickest trunk, sliding down its rough bark when we reached it. We slumped in the dirt, trying to keep our breathing quiet. I was half expecting the crack of a rifle and a bullet whizzing by, but the reality was much less interesting.

Nothing happened.

Then even less happened for hours and hours. Dom dozed off at one point, which really proved how low the threat level felt. There was literally no one around that we could see. I hadn't seen a car or truck leave the property, though, so I assumed the men were all inside the house, but had they taken a siesta or what? There was a cool breeze, and if I'd had a blanket and a nice selection of cheese and crackers, it wouldn't have been the worst place in the world for a picnic.

Thirst was beginning to get to me, though, and I was just contemplating sending Dom into town for stakeout supplies when a truck rolled down the main road and made a swinging in turn into the property.

I dug my fingernails into Dom's arm. "Look familiar?"

I dug out the piece of paper I'd scrawled the license plate on and smoothed it out to check they matched, even though I was already ninety-nine percent sure they would.

I wasn't disappointed. "Same truck."

The men were all calling to each other, and one dropped the ramp, the other banging a metal pole along the sides of the truck to get the animals inside to move.

A few came out willingly, none that I recognized, but one animal kicked and carried on, his hooves cracking off the sides of the trailer. From our closer vantage point, we could hear the men swearing and complaining about the beast inside, one daring the other to get in there and get him out. The first guy told him he was crazy.

He was right to be wary. The entire back end of the truck rocked side to side with the force of the animal's kicks, and eventually, they shoved an electric cattle prod through the bars.

I ground my teeth. "It's Grave Digger. It's gotta be." I didn't know any other bull who hated trucks the way Digger did. He ran from the truck with his head down, horns ready to take out anyone who was stupid enough to get in his way. He slammed his big body against the fence, bellowing out his frustrations.

I knew how he felt. I wanted to kill these guys myself. How fucking dare they touch my animal with an electric prod?

With the job done, the men closed the gates and leaned on the fence, watching the cranky bulls pace in their pens. A couple of the guys high-fived each other, but one stood off to the side, his hat pulled low, just staring out at the animals.

"Who's gonna have a ride before we move them on?" one guy called out.

The small group all laughed, shoving and taunting, daring each other to have a ride.

There was a chorus of "Fuck off," and "In your dreams."

"Come on, that's a fifty-thousand-dollar bull right there! When are you going to get the chance to ride one as fine as him again?"

"I hope they do," Dom muttered, pure venom in his voice. "I'd love to see Grave Digger take one of them down."

I was in full agreement with him, my fists clenched at my sides, and everything tense in an attempt not to run straight out there and confront these guys head-on.

That would not be smart. One of them still wielded that electric prod like a weapon. I had no idea what they'd do if confronted, and I didn't want to find out.

"What about you, Lucky?"

The single guy that had moved aside from the others shook his head. "No."

The main ringleader of the group, a shorter, burly-looking man, thickened with age, didn't let up. He strode across to where Lucky stood and nudged him with the handle of the prod. "Go on. Isn't there a reason they call you Lucky?"

"It's the meaning of my name, dumbass. I'm not stupid enough to try to ride that bull."

The shorter man didn't seem to appreciate the taunt. "Fucking smart-ass kids." With the back of his hand, he knocked Lucky's hat off his head, sending it into the dirt and chuckling as he walked away.

"Well, that was mature," Dom whispered to me.

Lucky turned to pick his hat up off the ground, but when he straightened, my reply died on my lips.

Without his hat pulled low on his head, shadowing his

face, Lucky's features stood out in the mid-afternoon sunlight. "Is that...?"

I knew who it was. I just didn't want to say it.

A muscle ticked in Dom's jaw. "It's Felix."

28

Dominic

"Maybe we don't have to call the police." Summer pulled at the sleeve of her T-shirt. "Maybe he isn't involved, and this is just a coincidence. We can do this another way…"

I loved her for saying that.

But there was no denying what my brother had done. Not when the evidence was right there in front of us. "No, he's involved." I slumped back against the tree trunk and scrubbed a hand over my face. "This is all my fault."

Summer turned her back on my brother and his thieving friends to sit beside me. She tucked her knees up to her chest and wrapped her arms around them. "You like putting blame on yourself when there is none, don't you?"

But she didn't know the full story. Maybe my dad's condition wasn't my fault, but this one was. "I told him about the offer you had on Grave Digger. He knows what he's worth. Fuck, I should have kept my big mouth shut. I didn't even think for a minute…"

I squeezed my eyes shut. The disappointment was overwhelming. It slammed through my body like a freight train, destroying everything in its path until it was all I could feel.

I'd so badly wanted my birth family to accept me. I'd wanted to know my biological brother. I'd blindly trusted that he was a good person, because I was, and because we shared DNA.

Summer smoothed a hand down my arm, but I pulled away.

I didn't deserve her comfort. I was supposed to be the one comforting her, not the other way around. "We should go back to the car. There's no point us being this close anymore. We know Digger is here, and the others probably are, too. Or at the very least, these guys know where they are. We need to call the local sheriff."

Summer didn't argue. Just gazed up at me with sad eyes that I couldn't bear to face. We waited until the men moved out of sight, then stole back to the car, the same way we'd come. Summer's stomach growled so loud I could hear it over our footsteps. I was starving, too, and even more thirsty. But the sheriff's department needed to be called first. We got inside the car, and Summer took that job. I blanked out, missing most of the conversation while I stared at the driveway of Felix's ranch and berated myself over and over.

Summer put the phone down on the dashboard, the noise of the plastic against plastic startling in the sudden quiet of the truck. "They aren't coming."

I whipped my head around to face her. "Seriously? You told them we saw Digger?"

She nodded. "The earliest they can get here is first thing in the morning."

"Unfuckingbelievable!"

She reached over and squeezed my hand. "Let's just go

to a hotel for the night. We can come back in the morning when the sheriff will be here."

I realized we'd somehow switched places. Earlier today, she'd been the one flying off the handle and punching things in frustration. But ever since we'd recognized Felix, the fire had gone out of her. Replaced by a concern for me that I didn't deserve.

I needed to fix this.

I tossed her the keys. "I'm not leaving. There's no way I'll be able to sleep tonight, knowing they might be moving those bulls again while I'm tucked up in a hotel bed."

Summer frowned. "So, what? You're just going to stay here all night, watching?"

I nodded. "I don't know what else to do, do you?"

She shook her head. "Well, I'm staying with you."

"No, you should go. Get a proper night's sleep."

"And leave you out here on the side of the road for the entire night?"

"Not that big a deal, Sum. Country boy. Wouldn't be the first time I've spent a night under the stars."

She rolled her eyes. "And what do you think I am? I'm just as capable as you are of camping out for a night, Dom."

She was cute when she was annoyed. She was also the most stubborn woman I'd ever met, and I already knew better than to try to change her mind. "Fine. We'll both be uncomfortable for the night. Deal?"

She smiled. "Deal."

"Go into town and get some water and food, though, okay? They aren't going anywhere in the next thirty minutes. It'd take them at least that long to get Digger back onto a truck."

She looked as if she were going to argue for a minute,

but then her stomach growled so loud they probably heard it up at the house. "Yeah, okay. I'll go."

We both got out of the truck, and she took the driver's side, settling herself behind the wheel. I leaned on the doorframe and kissed her through the open window.

"Are you going to be okay?" she asked.

"Sure."

"I'll be quick."

I kissed her again, letting my lips linger on hers for a moment too long. "Go."

"Call me if anything happens."

"Of course."

She pulled away, leaving me on the side of road.

I sat in the shade, picking at grass and tossing pebbles into a ditch. When my phone rang, I scrambled to silence it, even though the odds of anyone noticing me out here, well out of hearing distance from the farmhouse, was slim.

"Mom? You okay?" I asked when I answered the phone.

"Fine. Just worried about you. Summer rang Kai and filled him in on what the two of you were doing."

I cringed. "So you know about Felix then?"

She sighed. "Yes." Her voice was so full of regret and sadness, it almost rivaled my own disappointment. "I'm so sorry, sweetheart. I can't even imagine how betrayed you're feeling right now."

"For more reasons than one." The words slipped out, a little harder and harsher than I'd meant them to.

My mother was no fool. She knew me well. She didn't miss the tone. "What exactly does that mean?"

Now it was my turn to sigh. This wasn't the way I'd planned on having this out with her, but it had to happen at some time, and maybe now was as good a time as any. "Why didn't you tell me how sick Dad really was?"

"He's not! He just needs to rest."

Irritation trickled through my disappointment shroud. I had no idea if she was trying to shield me from upset, like I was still the baby she'd adopted years ago. Or if she honestly believed it. "Mom, he had a heart attack! And you didn't tell me. I had to hear it from Theo."

A tiny, shocked sound escaped her. "He shouldn't have told you that."

"Why, Mom? Should he have downplayed it to exhaustion, like you did? Dammit. You lied to me."

She paused, and I knew exactly what she was doing. She'd be running her knuckles across her thigh, almost like they were a scrub brush. It was a habit she always had when she was stressed or upset about something. The more stressed she was, the harder she'd rub her knuckles across her leg. I still remembered the day she'd told me I was adopted. She rubbed her leg so hard that her knuckles had turned a distressed shade of red, and the next day, she'd been sporting a bruised thigh.

"Dom, it was a small heart attack. He didn't need surgery. He was in and out of the hospital in two days."

"And you didn't think you should call me over that?" I was trying hard to reel in my anger over being left out of the loop. I knew it wasn't all entirely stemming from my mother's lack of communication, but also the fear over my dad's condition, and the rejection from my birth mother, and of course, Felix.

Shit. I was taking it all out on her. That wasn't any fairer than what she'd done to me. I sucked in a deep breath, right as Summer came rolling over the hill in the truck. "I gotta go, Mom. We'll talk about this later, okay?"

"Okay. Dom?"

"Yeah?"

"I love you."

A little of the tension and anger fell off me. "Love you, too. But we're talking about this more. Don't go home before I can get back to the Hunts' place, okay?"

"Of course not."

Summer pulled the truck up in the same spot I'd parked it earlier today, and I grabbed the passenger side door handle, letting myself in. "Bye, Mom."

"Bye, Dom. Be careful."

"Always."

29

As the evening turned into night, Dom grew more and more quiet with each passing minute, withdrawing further into himself, while focusing his sole attention on the house we were staking out.

"I bought chocolate." I offered him the unopened bar. "Your favorite. The one with the nuts."

He shook his head. "No, thanks."

"Beer?"

He declined again. "Probably not a good idea. I want to be sharp enough to drive if we need to."

It was a fair point, and the exact same reason I wasn't planning to touch the alcohol I'd bought while I was in town getting supplies for the night. But I was worried about this funk that seemed to be settling over Dominic. It wasn't him, and it concerned me.

"I bought some crosswords, too. And there's an adult coloring book." I started pulling things out of the bag of supplies and passing them over. "A set of cards..."

That finally got his attention. He dragged his gaze away

from the property and leaned across to peer in the bag. "You really went all out, huh?"

"Well, I figured our phone batteries will probably die at some point, and there's only so much Instagram scrolling one can do anyway. We've got a whole night to kill."

"What else have you got in there?"

There was only one thing left. I lifted it out and shook the box at him with a smile.

He snorted on a laugh. "Condoms? Really? You wanna do it in the truck?"

It was the first time he'd smiled since we'd realized Felix was in on the theft. It filled me with relief. I'd barely recognized the quiet sullen man sitting beside me for the last few hours. Seeing the Dom I knew and loved shine through made me want him to hang around.

Loved.

Maybe that thought should have scared me. I'd thought I loved Austin, too, and look how that had turned out. But instinctively, something deep within me knew this thing with Dominic was different. *I* was different when I was with him. I wasn't the girl who gave up on her dreams and shut down when they were hard to achieve. So the realization didn't scare me. It did the complete opposite. It kindled a tiny fire inside me that sent pleasant warmth right through my entire body. I'd been falling steadily since the very day he'd arrived. I knew that now. Being with Austin had given Dom and I the time to build on the friendship we'd started as kids. I'd loved him as my friend, then fallen for him steadily, day by day, hour by hour ever since. The fact he was here with me, fighting for my family's ranch, just made me love him all the more.

None of this was his fault.

"Staying up all night with you has never been a problem when we've had an adequate supply of condoms."

He raised an eyebrow. "Yeah, but we're in a pretty public place right now."

I cast an eye over the pitch-black, empty road. "It's been at least two hours since a car even drove by. But hey, if you'd rather fill the time with the crossword puzzles..."

Dom plucked the crossword puzzle book from my lap and tossed it into the back seat.

I laughed and pulled him in for a kiss. His lips met mine, both of us smiling, pressing quick kisses to each other's mouths and playing around. I slid my hand down his chest and straight below the waistband of his jeans to cup him. He laid his head back against the headrest and closed his eyes. "Crossword puzzles are for people who don't have smoking-hot girlfriends."

I couldn't help but chuckle at that. "No slacking on the job. You're supposed to be watching that driveway."

His eyelashes fluttered open, and he squinted at me. "I'm male, Sum. I can't multitask."

I rolled my eyes and then moved my lips close to his ear. "You seemed to be able to multitask just fine when your tongue is on my clit and your fingers are deep inside me."

Heat flared in his eyes. "You gonna let me do that to you out here, in this truck?"

I shrugged as innocently as possible. "In the truck. Or maybe up against it..."

He groaned low. "I'll keep my eyes on the driveway if you keep talking like that."

I tugged his jeans, encouraging him to lift his ass so I could free his swelling erection. "Good, because I can't watch it if I'm sucking your dick."

He speared a hand into my hair and hauled me in, his

tongue invading my mouth in a deep, soul-drenching kiss that had me desperate to do more.

I wouldn't let myself have as much of him as I wanted. Not yet. I shifted away and fit my mouth over the head of his cock. Soft skin covered the steel hardness beneath, and I ran my tongue over the tip of him, tasting his arousal. His hips jerked up ever so slightly, thrusting shallowly into my mouth.

"Watch the driveway, Dom," I warned without looking up at him.

His only response was a tighter grip on my hair and a low moan.

I wanted to hear more of it. I wanted to make him feel as good as he made me. I wanted to show this man I loved him, even if I couldn't quite find the words to tell him yet. It had been a shit day, but having him by my side had made it easier. Now I wanted to be there for him. I wanted to distract him from the guilt I knew he'd placed on his shoulders

I took him deep into my throat, rolling my tongue up and down his length, with one hand moving in time to cover the bottom half of his shaft. I cupped his balls with my free hand, squeezing and stroking them, and enjoying the way he somehow stiffened further beneath my touch. His fingers tangled around the lengths of my hair, tugging and releasing as I bobbed over his lap.

"Still watching?" I asked, pulling off his dick only long enough to mumble the words. Shooting tingles started up between my thighs, just from the way his breathing changed, the longer I worked him.

His gaze clashed with mine. "I'm watching," he assured me.

We both knew he didn't mean the driveway.

I reached for a condom and stretched it down over his

cock. Once he was suited up, I undid my own shorts and shimmied out of them, taking my panties with them. Then I climbed across the center console, settling my knees either side of his thighs, and hovered over his straining dick.

He gripped my arm tight. "I haven't even started with you."

I shook my head. I knew what he meant, but I didn't need it. I was wet just from sucking his cock, and probably a little from the excitement of being in a public place, even if it did feel incredibly private, shrouded in darkness and half hidden beneath the low-hanging branches of the tree. I just wanted to feel him inside me, and to wrap my arms around his neck and kiss him while I rode him, making him forget all about the shit things that had happened today.

"I need you." That realization hit me hard. But it was easier to voice than an I love you.

"I don't want to hurt you."

"You won't."

I reached between us and guided his dick to my entrance. He watched me silently, his gaze steady on my face while I eased myself down onto him.

It was only when he was fully sheathed inside me that he finally relaxed enough to move. His fingers gripped my ass, and I rocked my hips over him, rising and falling, riding him in the darkness, our breaths and little noises of pleasure the only sounds in the quiet night. He lifted one hand to my breast and pinched my nipple through my T-shirt and bra, but neither of us was game enough to get fully naked out here. I already had no idea where my panties and shorts were, and if someone drove past, they'd cop a glaring eyeful.

But nobody was driving past, and Dom felt too good to stop. I rode him harder and faster, while he stretched me deliciously and kissed my mouth until my head spun.

"Wanna make you come," he groaned, thrusting up into me with a jerk of his hips. He yanked the lever on the side of his seat, and the backrest went flying down, taking Dom and me with it.

I squealed, completely unprepared, and ending up lying completely on top of him.

"Don't stop," he demanded.

I found my rhythm again, kissing him hard while rolling my hips, taking him deep inside me, only to pull out then do it all over again.

His fingers squeezed my ass cheeks, then wandered in between.

My eyes rolled back.

"I love how much you love that," he whispered. "It's hot."

If anyone else had said it to me, I probably would have been embarrassed. But Dom's gaze and the deep rumble of his voice left no doubt in my mind that he meant every word.

His tongue slid up my neck and over my ear, sending shivers down my spine.

"I want to take you here," he whispered, a dirty little secret just for the two of us. "Not now. But one day, when you're ready." He pressed his finger just a tiny bit inside my ass.

Sparks went off behind my eyes.

"Don't stop, Summer," he encouraged, lifting his hips to meet mine.

I kept my rhythm while my internal walls clenched down around his cock and his finger. I rode him harder and faster, my orgasm demanding it.

Dom worked me just as intensely, that finger rimming my entrance, his other hand guiding the movement of my hips. He thrust up, over and over, until the entire truck was rocking, but neither of us cared.

"Oh my God," I moaned, orgasm overtaking me again, blinding me with its intensity.

"Fuck," he groaned. With a final piston of his hips he clutched me tighter, muffling his shouts by clamping his mouth down on my shoulder.

My head spun in dizzying circles, my pussy continuing to clench and release around him, the aftereffects of my orgasm still holding on to his. But the two of us stilled, me sticky and sweaty on top of him, the windows fogged with our heavy breathing.

He pressed a slow kiss to my neck. "Summer?"

"Mmm?" I said groggily, the orgasm relaxing me so much that I felt like I could take a nap.

"I...um..."

I lifted my head to peer at him. "What?"

He swallowed hard, his Adam's apple bobbing. Indecision flickered all over his face.

My heart picked up the pace, shouting hopeful little exclamations that he was going to tell me he loved me.

"I need to use the bathroom."

The hopeful exclamations disintegrated. But I picked myself back up quickly. We had all the time in the world. We didn't need to rush it. It wasn't like I was saying it either.

But I would. I already knew the feeling in my heart was soon going to be too big to contain.

But I kind of wanted him to say it first. I could wait.

I climbed off Dom and went back to the driver's seat, finding my panties and shorts and pulling them back on as Dom did the same with his own clothes.

"Shit, we really fogged the car up," he laughed, wiping a

hand over his window. “This is some next-level, Titanic-style fog. I can’t see shit outside.” He opened his door.

My bladder gave a gentle nudge that using a bathroom might not be the worst idea, even if out here the bathroom was the side of the road. “Wait for me. I’m coming, too.”

I stepped out and circled around to his side of the car. “I guess this will make us a real couple, huh? Peeing on the side of the road, side by side? How romantic.” I reached for his hand, not wanting to fall down an embankment in the dark.

A flashlight lit up the night.

Dom and I both froze and spun around, raising arms to block the glare and blinking rapidly to clear it from our eyes.

The deep male voice cutting through the darkness was completely unfamiliar. “Want to tell me what the two of you are doing out here on my property in the middle of the night?”

30

Dominic

On instinct, I pulled Summer behind me. The light lowered to my chest level, and I was finally able to see through the darkness beyond.

I didn't recognize the man who held the flashlight. But I did recognize the gun he held. A single-barreled shotgun, pointed right at us.

"Car broke down," I explained. "We're just camping out for the night until our friends can come get us in the morning."

The man cocked his head to one side. "That so?" He circled us, never dropping his gun, and went to the driver's side door. With one eyebrow raised, he opened it, and turned the key Summer had left in the ignition.

The engine started perfectly.

Fuck. I cursed myself for not loosening the battery or something.

"Doesn't sound very broken down to me."

Neither Summer nor I said anything. There was no point in denying it.

"Why don't the two of you come up to the house? It's getting chilly out here. I'll make you a cup of tea."

"No, thank you." I held Summer's arm a little tighter.

The older man raised his bushy eyebrow again. "No? You're refusing my hospitality? Where's your manners, young man? Is that any way for you to speak to your relative?"

"Relative?" I blinked in confusion. But then took in the man's olive skin, noticeable even in the darkness. His dark-brown eyes, almost black in the low light cast by the flash-light. I suddenly remembered Felix saying he worked for his grandmother's brother. This had to be him.

"You're Maria's boy."

I shook my head. "I'm Johnny and Isabel's boy, if I'm anyone's," I corrected.

The man huffed at that. "You're a Kaur. Through and through. Lucky told me all about you. Refused to invite you around, though, but that kid ain't got no manners either. Not like me. Which is why I expect you'll come on up to the house. And maybe while we're there, you can tell me what the fuck you're doing out here, watching my property." The gun inched closer to me.

"We should go," Summer said quietly.

The man took a step closer. "I wasn't asking. Move."

He wasn't playing.

I took Summer's hand, holding it tightly in mine, and tugged her toward the road. "Just do what he says," I muttered to her.

I kept my body between her and the gun, and with a tiny bit of nudging from me, I got her moving. A tremble rolled through her body, and I squeezed her hand.

"It'll be fine," I assured her. Though I really had no idea if it would be.

It took some time for us to walk up to the house, neither Summer nor I moving particularly quickly. I was in no rush to be surrounded by a group of men who had already proven to have no morals.

And I sure as hell was in no rush to confront my brother. With every step, I blamed him for this. He'd played me. Like a complete fool, desperate to know his own flesh and blood, I'd fallen for it. Had that night at the bar been all a hoax? Had he already known by then that the Hunts had bulls of worth and that I was an easy ticket in? Or had it been more of a crime of opportunity? He'd seen Grave Digger at my birthday party, and I'd opened my big mouth and confided in his dollar value. Had he then called up his friends and got them to bring a truck down?

They were the questions that had plagued me all day, only quieting when Summer was in my arms. At the door to the farmhouse, I stopped and looked to the older man.

"Well, go on in."

I pushed at the door, but it didn't budge.

"Give it a bit, you pansy. It sticks."

I ground my teeth. Was this who I was related to? One man who had played me for a fool and taken advantage of me, and another who thought nothing of stealing and holding a gun on people. I gave the door a harder push, stumbling a step or two when it gave and crashed back against the wall.

Summer jumped at the sudden crack of noise.

The man just sniggered.

"What the fuck is going on?" A new guy hammered down the stairs, rubbing sleep from his eyes. He was bare-chested, a beer gut hanging over a pair of sleep shorts.

I recognized him as the guy who'd held the cattle prod that afternoon. The one who'd flicked off Felix's hat and given him a hard time about not wanting to ride Grave Digger.

More bodies thundered down the stairs at the commotion, and eventually, Felix's dark head appeared. He stretched his arms over his head, casually walking down the stairs, until his gaze clashed with mine.

His eyes widened, and he pushed his way to the front of the group. "Dominic?" His gaze darted to the left. "Summer? What the fuck?"

I didn't answer him. I couldn't. Not without spewing out the hate that had been building in me all day.

"Found my great-nephew out on the road, watching the place." The older guy turned to Felix. "What we going to do about that, kid?"

Felix's gaze darted to the older man's gun. "How about you start by lowering that fucking gun? Jesus, Frank! What are you doing?"

The older man tapped the barrel on the scuffed-up floor. "What am I doing? I'm making sure you'll have a paycheck this week!"

Felix ran a hand through his hair and turned to me. "Dom, I swear, I had nothing to do with this."

I choked on a laugh. "Wow. I'll just add 'bad liar' to your list of qualities then, will I?"

The pudgy guy thumped a fist into the wall. "Shut the fuck up! Has anyone realized that these two would have called the sheriff? Instead of standing here while you all have a family fucking reunion, do you think maybe we should be moving the stock?"

The older man peered at Summer and me. "That true? You call the sheriff?"

I shook my head. "No."

The pudgy guy laughed. "Bullshit. What the hell were you doing outside then?"

"We were just looking for an opportunity to take our cattle back," Summer spoke up. "We've been out there all day. Don't you think the sheriff would be here by now if we'd called them? We don't want any trouble. We just want what's ours. Give us back our bulls, and we'll go on like nothing ever happened."

The older man stooped so he was eye to eye with Summer and leered at her. "So pretty. But so stupid." He nodded to Beer Belly. "Go get the animals down to the back pasture. That'll buy us some time."

Beer Belly nodded, and the other guys followed him outside.

Felix didn't move. "Now what, Frank? You going to let Summer and Dominic go?"

Frank tossed Felix the gun. "Nah, you can fix your own mess. Watch them until I get back. If the cops show up, get rid of them."

My eyes widened.

So did Felix's as he caught the gun. "What? How?"

"You're the one with the gun and the hostages. Work it out." With a final glare, he stormed after his men. The door slammed shut behind him.

Felix slumped back against the wall, then slowly slid down it until he was sitting. He put the gun on the dusty floorboards, but he didn't look up.

"What now, Felix?" I asked finally. "You gonna shoot us if we try to leave?"

He dragged his gaze up to meet mine. It was full of regret. "No. You guys can go. Just wait ten minutes, and they'll have moved down over the hill, so they won't see you."

"They're going to notice when they get back and we're gone," Summer pointed out.

He shrugged, voice heavy and full of defeat. "That's not your problem."

I went to the window and peered out from behind a grubby set of curtains. He was right. The men were herding the animals over the crest of the hill. Their shapes were already disappearing into the blackness of the night. A muscle in my jaw ticked. Priority number one was getting Summer out of here, and I was itching to rip the door open and storm out of here with her tucked safe against my chest. But I couldn't walk out of here without knowing one thing.

"Why?" I asked Felix.

"Why what?"

"Why would you do this? Are you desperate for money?"

He shook his head. "Dom, I swear. This wasn't my idea."

I laughed, the sound hard and bitter. "So you just happened to find out that Grave Digger was worth big money, and coincidentally, he was stolen the same night?"

He shot to his feet, ripping at his hair. "I'm an idiot, okay? I fuck everything up! You have no idea, Dom. Your family is amazing. Your mom? I talked to her for ages. She asked me a million questions about who I was and what I liked. And you know, the whole time, she smiled at me with this motherly expression, like I was important, because I was your brother. You think anybody ever looked at me with that sort of interest before?"

I blinked. "Our grandmother raised you."

He threw his hand up in the air. "Raised me? I was lucky if there was even food in the house. You think she ever really cared about where I was or what I was doing? As soon as I did one wrong thing, she sent me out here, washed her hands of me. She never bothered sitting down with me to find out who I was. I was just a government check. She'd didn't raise me. I raised myself. You should thank your lucky stars she let you go."

"But you said she regretted it..."

"She did! She regretted that you could have been an additional hundred bucks on her paycheck each week."

It was like being slapped in the face with a cold, dead fish. "You didn't tell me..."

"Of course I didn't tell you. I've been working for years to put all that behind me. You think I wanted to meet my brother, the only person in the entire fucking world who seemed actually interested in knowing me, just to tell him that our grandmother was as bad as our birth mother? Hell, she's worse really. At least Maria knew she couldn't be a mother."

Felix got up and paced the length of the room, his shoulders hunched, his fingers clenched into fists. "I came home from your party happy, Dom. I just wanted to tell someone. The guys here, they aren't all bad. A couple of them have been real interested in how I met you. So I was telling them all about it. About you. And Summer. And the amazing place you owned. I didn't think..."

My teeth sank into my bottom lip before letting it go, grazing the soft skin as it went. I barely noticed the sting. "You didn't think they'd see a fifty-thousand-dollar payday?"

Felix didn't say anything.

"This isn't the first time they've stolen, is it?"

Felix sighed. "I had no proof. I'm not part of Frank's inner circle. Sometimes I wake up in the mornings and we have new stock. I asked once, when I first got here, and got a backhand across the face for my trouble. Then he threatened to send me back to Wyoming. So I stopped asking. Today is the first day I've known for sure." He turned to

Summer. "I'm so sorry. I honestly never meant for this to happen."

Her gaze wavered. She crossed the room and took my hand again, looking up at me as if I had the answers.

I didn't. I had nothing. Felix talked the talk, but I had no idea whether I believed him or not. And my heart hurt too much to even try to work it out.

"We're going," Summer told him. But then her gaze softened a little. "The sheriff will be here by dawn. Maybe you shouldn't be."

She pulled me toward the door, yanking it open.

I glanced back over my shoulder at my brother.

Then followed my girl, leaving Felix behind.

31

Dominic

Summer and I hustled down the long drive and the road back to the truck. She got behind the wheel, and I jumped in the passenger side, closing it behind me. She immediately reached over and hit the central-locking button that slammed all the locks down.

"What do you want to do?" I asked her.

"Get the fuck out of here?" She started up the engine. "I don't want to call the others out here to try to get the animals back. Not when these guys have guns. Call the sheriff again. Tell them where they're moving the cattle." She bit her lip, pulling out onto the road, her reluctance clear as day. "Then I guess we just hope like hell they're still there in the morning. I'm not hanging around anymore, waiting to get shot. No bull is worth that."

But I wasn't entirely sure she believed that. She looked like she wanted to drive the truck straight through the property and yell for Digger and the other bulls to just jump on the back. If they'd been capable of doing that, I think she might have tried. Giving up wasn't in her nature, and this was killing her, I could see it.

But she was right. We couldn't keep hanging around, not after what had happened. I patted my pockets, but they were empty. A quick rummage of the center console left me empty-handed as well, so I fumbled around the floor, searching for my phone. I finally found it, kicked beneath the seat. I sat back up, brushing it off. It must have fallen out of my pocket when Summer and I had been having sex.

God, that felt like a whole lifetime ago now.

I hit the 'home' button on my phone, and the screen lit up. "Whoa."

Summer took her eyes off the road just long enough to glance over at me. "What?"

"I have about twenty missed calls from my mom, and more from your parents' home line." I pressed the 'call' button beside a little photo of my mom and put the phone up to my ear. "I thought they would have gone to bed hours ago."

"Dom?" Mom spluttered into the phone when she answered. "Oh, thank God."

The pure fear in her voice startled me. All my guards went up instantly. "What's wrong? Didn't Frost tell you we were camping out for the night? I'm fine."

"No, no. It's not that. I need you to come back."

I frowned. "We're on our way. But why?"

"It's your father. We need to go back to Wyoming. Dom, he had another heart attack."

Fear sliced through me, deep and cutting. It loosened my fingers, and I had to catch myself to keep my phone from sliding through my grasp. "What?" I croaked.

"I don't know how bad it is yet. Spencer was just on the phone. He and Theo called an ambulance, and they took him straight to Jackson Hole for surgery. I need to get back there. Please come home. I need you to come with me. If he... If he dies—" A quiet sob echoed down the line.

I nodded, even though she couldn't see me. My mother was one of the toughest women I knew. She'd moved halfway around the world, from Australia to Wyoming, in order to be with my father. There were countless stories of her watching my father start his bull riding career and then taking over the ranch. She'd had to learn how to deal with snow, and cattle, and living in a small town. And she'd done it all with a smile on her face because she loved my dad more than life itself.

I didn't know that she would survive it if something happened to him now. They were only in their fifties. This couldn't be happening. Not yet. Not now, when they still had all their best years to live out together.

"Of course I'm coming," I told her. I glanced over at Summer, and my heart cracked. I didn't want to leave her. Not when she was in the middle of a family crisis of her own.

"Dom? What is it?" she asked quietly.

"My father had another heart attack."

Her shocked intake of breath made her chest rise sharply. But then she refocused on the road and put her foot down a little harder. "Tell your mom to book your flights. We'll meet them at the airport."

I relayed the message to my mother. But as I hung up, Summer and I lapsed into silence. Neither of us even bothered to put the radio on. The only sounds for the next couple of hours were the constant drone of the truck's engine and roaring of my thoughts.

I couldn't lose my father. Not now. Not like this. Not when I'd just up and run across the country without even a proper goodbye. That couldn't be the last time I'd see him.

So at the airport, I pulled my beautiful girlfriend into my arms and held her tight. She stared up at me with those gorgeous deep brown eyes, tears glistening behind them.

"I'll come as soon as I can," she promised.

But I shook my head. "You can't. You need to stay and train for the first round of qualifying."

She started to argue, but I wasn't going to hear it. I just stared at her, and she knew. She knew I wasn't going to be Austin. I would have loved for her to come with me to Wyoming. Fuck, I wanted it so bad it was eating me up inside. There was nothing more I needed than to have her hand in mine when I got to that hospital and had to face the fact that the man I'd called Dad for the past twenty-five years might not be with us anymore.

She was the only thing that made the thought of even walking through those hospital doors bearable.

But I needed her to chase her dreams more.

I cupped her face and tilted it up to look at me.

One tear spilled down her cheek, and I brushed it away with my thumb. "You're Summer Hunt. When you go out there next weekend, you're going to remember that. You're going to show every person who ever doubted you exactly how good you are."

She nodded reluctantly.

Through the overhead speakers, they called my flight for boarding.

I wasn't done. I'd never be done with this woman, and I needed her to know it. "I need you to remember something else."

She nodded.

I stared deep in her eyes, so she'd know it with everything I had. "I love you. I love you so fucking much, Sum. You're going to be amazing."

She let out a sob and launched herself into my arms, clinging on so tight I wasn't sure she'd ever let me go.

I didn't want her to.

But we both knew I had to go. And she had to stay.

"I love you, too." She gripped the sides of my face and repeated it fiercely, "I love you."

My heart soared at her words, and at the love that shone in her tear-filled eyes. I slammed my mouth down on hers, kissing her hard, gathering her to me, filling myself with as much of her as I could.

I kissed her with everything I had. I gave her enough to last until I could come back. I took as much as she could give, knowing I'd need it to get me through until I had her in my arms once more.

"This isn't goodbye, Sum," I assured her. "You're it for me. So even if I'm in Wyoming, and you're here, you're always my girl."

"Always," she promised.

I enveloped her in one last hug.

Then I walked onto a plane. Leaving my heart behind me.

32

Dominic

The minute we touched down in Wyoming, Mom called my brothers for an update on Dad's condition. I held her hand while she talked, leading the way around the groups of people welcoming loved ones home, and got us to the taxi line. I hadn't brought anything with me except my wallet and phone. Mom only had carry-on, so we weren't slowed down by stopping at baggage claim.

"Well?" I asked when she hung up.

She got into the back seat of the taxi, scooting over to make room for me beside her. "He's still in surgery."

"Shit." I'd Googled the surgery times after having a heart attack, and it had said three to six hours. I just assumed that the worse the heart attack was, the longer the surgery would take. It had already been over three hours. So this wasn't minor like the first one had been. Even without talking to a doctor, that seemed to be evident.

My mom had cried off and on for the entire flight, but now she was dry-eyed, her gaze calm and focused as the buildings whizzed by outside. I wasn't sure if that was a better or worse reaction than her tears.

"You okay?" I asked her softly.

She nodded. "I'm a bit embarrassed, actually. Sorry you had to see me like that."

"Your husband just had a heart attack, and you were stuck across the other side of the country, not knowing if he's going to even make it through. Of course you're going to be upset."

She patted my arm absently. "I know. You aren't a little boy anymore. But it's still hard for me to flip that switch sometimes, from being your mom, who you needed constantly, to..." She smiled. "Whatever we are now. More of a friend, I guess."

I put my arm around her and kissed the top of her head. "I'm not your friend. And I still need you. You're always my mom. But that doesn't mean you can't cry in front of me."

She sniffled back a little laugh. "Okay. I'll try to remember that."

The trip to the hospital at Jackson Hole was thankfully short. Nerves racked me as we walked through the automatic glass doors and into the air-conditioning. Mom spoke to the woman behind the desk, nodded a few times, and then led us to the surgery waiting rooms.

Theo and Spencer both glanced up from their phones when we entered. Theo's face flushed with relief, and he stood, grabbing Mom and wrapping her smaller frame in a bear hug. Spencer grabbed me, and his embrace was tighter than I remembered it.

"Thank fuck you're home," he murmured. His voice cracked.

It was only then that I realized how much strain the two of them had been under, being the only ones here when it had all happened. I was their elder brother. They were used to me being the one to take on any responsibility that needed shouldering.

I hadn't been here.

I thumped him on the back and held him that little bit closer. "You're good. I got this."

He nodded into my shoulder and sniffed.

The four of us sat down, and Mom and I quizzed the two of them endlessly, on everything from what he'd looked like when he went into surgery, to what the doctors had said when they'd come to update them.

The answer at the end of the day was that there was nothing to be done but to sit and wait. Theo and Spencer went back to aimlessly scrolling on their phones. Mom stared at the wall, lost in a world of her own. I fished out my phone, charged up on the plane, and texted Summer to let her know I was here. I asked for an update on the bulls, but there wasn't one. So I unfurled the crossword puzzle book that Summer had bought during our stakeout and pretended like I was doing it. When really, I just read the same line over and over, too tired to even read the clues properly. The sun rose outside the hospital windows, and still, there was no news about my dad.

Just after seven, when I was slumped uncomfortably in a hard, plastic chair, sleep about to pull me under, a doctor pushed through the set of double doors and cast an eye over an exhausted West clan.

His gaze landed on my mother. "Mrs. West?"

She'd been dozing, but at her name, she jumped up, smoothing back her hair. "Yes? How is he?"

The doctor gave her a nod. "There were some complications."

I reached over and took my mother's hand. "What sort of complications? He'll be okay, though?"

Theo sucked in a sharp breath at my question. I knew how he felt. It was as if the air had suddenly punched from the room and I was having trouble breathing.

The doctor didn't smile, but he did give a curt nod. "Yes, we expect he'll make a full recovery."

Mom burst into tears.

Those tears wiped out any feeling I might have had on my own. Theo, Spencer, and I all swooped in on her, crowding her into the middle of a group hug, the four of us laughing through our tears of relief.

"I knew he'd be fine," Spencer said. "Never a doubt in my mind."

I shoved his shoulder, and he grinned at me.

Theo clipped him across the back of the head. "You cried like a baby."

"Shut up, dickhead. He looked dead when I found him. You would have cried, too, if you hadn't been locked in your bedroom with Jessica Aruid."

"Okay, okay, that's enough," Mom said, disentangling herself from her pack. She turned back to the doctor. "I'm sorry."

He shook his head. "Don't be. It's nice to see a family as connected as yours is."

I swallowed hard. I wondered if he'd still think the same if he knew I'd only just returned after completely bailing on them months ago.

"We're going to have him in intensive care for a little bit, so I suggest all but one of you goes home and gets some rest. He can only have one visitor up there. Once he's moved to the cardiac floor, in a day or two, he can see you all."

"Mom, you stay," I said immediately. "If you aren't too tired, that is."

Theo and Spencer nodded.

Mom kissed my cheek. “Thank you. I couldn’t sleep without seeing him anyway.”

“One more thing,” the doctor interrupted. “This was a very serious heart attack for a man his age. I suspect there is a genetic component, and it might be worth you boys getting tested.”

My gut twisted. I already knew that wouldn’t apply to me.

“He’s also going to need to take it easy for a while. No driving, no heavy lifting. Light exercise and rest is what he needs for the next few months.”

My eyes widened. “Months?”

The doctor nodded. “It will probably be at least six months before he’s even close to where he was.”

Mom nodded and shook the doctor’s hand. “Of course. That’s fine. We’ll get him back on his feet. Can I see him now?”

The doctor agreed.

Mom gathered up her bag before hugging each of us goodbye. “I’ll call you as soon as he can have visitors.”

I hugged her tight, then followed my brothers out to Theo’s car. The two of them chatted happily in the front seats the whole way home, their laughter and jokes fueled by lack of sleep and pure relief. But I was quiet. I rested my head on the window, my body begging to just switch off and let sleep take me, but my brain wouldn’t allow it. It whirred a million miles an hour, desperately trying to sort through everything that had happened in the last two days.

When we turned into the long driveway of the home I’d grown up in, I sat up a little straighter. I put one hand to the window and peered out. “What the fuck, guys?”

Theo bristled with annoyance. “I knew you were going to be like this.”

I snapped my head around and stared at the back of his head, wishing he weren't driving so I could see his face. "What does that mean?"

Spencer sighed. "We see what you see, you know, Dom."

"Oh good, because I see a ranch that's full of jobs that need doing. There's a whole section of fence down over there. And that herd should have been moved down to the back pasture at least a week ago."

"One of the four-wheelers is also broken," Theo added in a monotone drone. "And nobody ordered hay at the start of the month so we're down to our last bale. Yeah, we get it, Dom. It's all good for you, running off to another state. But you left us shorthanded. When Dad got sick, it left the lot on me and Spencer. Two men, for four men's jobs, means shit doesn't get done. We've been trying, but I can't magically make there be more hours in the day. Dad wouldn't let us hire anyone. He kept hoping you were coming back."

I stared at my middle brother, my observations about the things that needed doing dying on my tongue. I scrubbed a hand over my face. "Fuck, Theo. Sorry. I'm tired and being an ass. I know you've been doing your best. I just had no idea what was going on."

He gave a curt nod and pulled the truck up outside the main house. When we got out, and he twisted to face me, it was like another kick in the gut. All I'd really noticed at the hospital was his worry. But on closer inspection, there were dark circles under his eyes, and he'd lost weight since I'd seen him last. His cheeks verged on gaunt. The guy wasn't just tired from the last twenty-four hours. He was tired because of the load he'd taken on.

It was too much. I could see that now. And the part of me that still saw Theo as my baby brother kicked in. I slung an arm around his shoulders. "I'll fix this," I promised him.

Theo focused down at the ground. "I never wanted this job, Dom. I don't live and breathe ranch life like you do. Getting up at four every morning and getting snorted on by asshole bulls doesn't do anything for me. This is a paycheck. But I don't want to run this place. I'm shit at it—"

"You're not, you just got thrown in the deep end."

But Theo held a hand up. "No, I'm not looking for a pep talk. This isn't my passion. Fuck, man. I don't even know if I want to work here. Not in the long run. There are other things I want to do and try. I don't want to get stuck managing this place and never get to do any of them."

This was all news to me. "And you?" I asked Spencer.

He shrugged. "I'm doing online college classes. There's more to life than bulls and rodeo, Dom."

"You are? Shit. That's awesome." I nodded slowly, really seeing my brothers for the first time. I'd always just thought they were lazy and slightly spoiled.

Now I saw their late starts and low enthusiasm for what they really were.

Ranching wasn't in their soul the way it was in our dad's. The way it was in mine. For me, bulls and rodeo *were* all that were important. Bulls, rodeo, and Summer.

I toed at the dirt. "Well, this is eye-opening. And kinda fucked up."

Theo grimaced. "I didn't mean to just dump it all on you the minute you got home. I was going to tell Dad, but then he got sick, and well, then that escalated into where we are now."

"Yeah, I get it. Don't worry, I'll work something out."

He eyed me. "You gonna stay?"

I bit my lip. I had no idea.

33

Summer

My heartache was the only thing that kept me awake on the drive home from the airport. Every mile that rolled past took me farther and farther away from the man I loved. I missed him already. We'd lived in each other's pockets for weeks, so not having him in the passenger seat beside me just felt wrong. Everything about being here without him felt wrong. I wanted to turn around, go back to the airport, and put myself on a plane. I wanted to be there in the hospital with him. I didn't want him to do this alone.

But I also knew if I did that, he'd put me on a plane and send me right back home. Sure, there were bulls at his place that I could have practiced on. But his ranch was set up for breeding, not for riding. As much as I wanted to think I knew everything there was to know about bull riding, I couldn't pull my own gates, and act as my own spotter, and coach myself. I needed my dad for that. And the crew at our ranch, who were all trained in those areas. Dom would be busy with his dad and his family. He couldn't be trying to coach me on top of all that. It was too much.

I deserved this shot at the pros. And Dom needed to be with his family. It sucked that those things were on opposite sides of the country, but I consoled myself with the knowledge that he loved me. We'd make this work long distance, for as long as we had to, if that's what it came down to.

When I finally drove beneath the heavy wooden Hunts' Bull Riding School sign, indecision stopped me in the middle of the driveway. I'd slept in Dom's cabin every night since we'd been together. The thought of going back to my little bedroom in the main house was completely unappealing. I just couldn't do it. I was tired and sad.

I'd ask his permission later, whenever he called to update me on his dad, but for now, I dragged my weary body up the stairs of Dom's cabin, pushed open the door, and collapsed onto his bed, not even bothering to take off my clothes. I pressed my face into his pillow, inhaling the familiar scent of him. And let sleep take me hard.

When I woke up, it was to the banging of someone's fist on the cabin door.

"Summer! You dead?"

I blinked sleep from my eyes, groggily sitting up. Peering through the window, I realized it was dark outside. What the hell? I stumbled to the door and yanked it open. Hallie was on the other side, huge grin on her face. "Oh good, not dead. You were asleep so long I wasn't entirely sure."

"What time is it?"

"Past the time that I'm employed to work, but your dad asked me to stick around and help with the bulls."

Was she making no sense or was I still half asleep? "The bulls we no longer have?"

Hallie grabbed my boots from the front porch and tossed them at me. "The bulls you got back. The truck just pulled in. Come on, we got work to do. It's all hands on deck."

That shocked me back into action. I hopped on one foot, trying to shove my boot over my sock. "We got them back? When? How?"

"The sheriff called not all that long after you got back from the airport, but we didn't want to wake you. They found all the bulls in the back pasture, just like you'd reported. It took a few hours to get trucks out there to bring them home."

A wide grin spread across my face. "All of them? They're okay?" I got my other boot on finally, and Hallie and I took off on foot, down the road that led to the bull pens and the training arena.

"See for yourself."

The truck was backing up, and everyone had come out to see the bulls safely returned. Preston and the other guys cheered as the first bull ran down the ramp.

Hallie put her arm around my shoulder and grinned. "Good to see them home."

Grave Digger thumped the back of the truck with his hooves before he ran out, making everyone laugh.

I shook my head. "I see someone's mood hasn't improved any for his little adventure."

My dad closed the back end of the truck, letting it slam shut with a bang. "He just needs a good ride. An outlet for all that aggression. You up for it, Sum?"

I blinked. "What, now? What time is it?"

Dad shrugged. "You missed a whole day of training. And you have a lot of work to do in a very small amount of time if you're going to nail your ride next weekend."

I folded my arms across my chest. "Who told you about that?"

In a rare display, my dad cracked a massive smile. His relief at having his bulls back was evident in his almost jovial mood. It was very un-Frost-like. "I don't know if you recall, but I won several WBRA titles."

Preston sniggered. "Like, thirty years ago."

Dad shot him a look. "I still know people there." He turned back to me. "Brad called me. He said he'd spoken to you."

"He did."

"This is pretty big, him giving you the green light. You up for it?" He already knew what my answer would be. If I wasn't up for it, I would have been in Wyoming right now with Dom. If I wasn't up for it, I would have taken any excuse to get out of this rodeo. The pride in my father's eyes made me remember that this was his dream, too. We'd been a team, ever since I could remember. And I wanted to win for him, almost as much as I wanted to win for myself.

Almost. But just a little bit more for myself. The old man did have his own titles after all.

I pressed up on my toes and kissed his cheek. "I'm up for it. Get me a bull."

I rode for hours that night. Then got up the next morning and did it all again. Dad took over the trainees, giving me Preston and Hallie to work with. And work we did. The three of us were filthy, covered in dirt and sweat, and every muscle in my body ached by the time a beat-up white truck rolled down the driveway. I didn't pay it much attention, too busy preparing for another ride.

"Who's that?" Preston called, gate rope wrapped around his hand. He shielded his eyes from the midday sun and squinted at the truck kicking up a dust storm around its tires.

"No idea. Pay attention," I griped at him.

He mock saluted me, and I flipped him the bird.

He sniggered but put both hands on the ropes. When I nodded, he yanked it hard, releasing Grave Digger into the ring with me on his back.

When the eight-second buzzer rang, I jumped off, excitement flushing through my body.

Preston let out a whoop of excitement. "Nice ride!"

I opened my mouth to answer him when clapping from across the ring drew my attention. I frowned when I realized who it was. "Take five," I told Hallie and Preston. "Get a drink or something. I need a minute."

They both took off for the office and the mini refrigerator we kept inside, while I shoved my hands deep into my pockets and walked across the ring to stand in front of Felix.

I eyed him, taking in his jeans, T-shirt, and baseball cap. "You're a surprise. Thought you would have fled the country by now."

A tiny smile curved the corner of his mouth, but then it fell away. "Got arrested."

I raised an eyebrow. "Not much of a thief, are you? I warned you."

"I know. But it just didn't feel right. When the sheriff got there, I turned myself in. Told them everything I knew."

"And you didn't get put away?"

He lifted a shoulder. "Frank and the others did. There was video footage of them stealing your bulls, and I suspect they'll find more, once they put cases together from other counties."

"But you're not on them?"

"No, ma'am. I'm not. What I told you out there the other

night is the truth. I suspected. But I never knew for sure. I'm going to testify when their cases go to trial."

I blew out a long breath. "Shit, Felix. Against your grandmother's brother?"

He snorted. "Especially against him. That bastard held a gun on my brother. And on you. Actually, that's why I'm here."

I cocked my head to one side. "You didn't just come to admire my bull riding?"

He smiled at that. "No. But wow, I had no idea you could ride like that. You're amazing. I'm gonna be watching you on the WBRA next year, no doubt about that."

I flapped a hand around, brushing off the compliment. "Don't try to distract me with your flattery. Why are you here?"

He sobered. "To say I'm sorry. And I guess to tell you the sheriff let me go. I kind of hoped that might mean you would believe me."

I studied his deep brown eyes. They were so like Dom's. The emotion behind them seemed genuine.

Ugh. I was such a sucker. I shook my head. "Call me gullible, but I believe you."

Relief flooded his face, and he reached his arms out as if to hug me but then dropped them by his sides, settling for a "Thanks," instead.

I gave a curt nod and then turned to walk away.

"Wait, Summer?"

I swiveled on my heel. "Yeah?"

"Can I see Dom? I wanted to try to explain...fix things between us...maybe." He was like a little kid, asking his parent for a chocolate and praying they'd say yes.

"He's not here."

"I can wait."

I shook my head. "His dad got sick. He's gone back to Wyoming."

"Oh. Shit. I'm sorry to hear that."

I swallowed hard, fighting down a wave of emotion. "Yeah, me, too."

Felix headed for his truck, but something inside forced me to call out to him. "Did you mean any of it? The excitement over being Dom's brother, I mean?"

Felix leaned back on the side of his truck and focused serious eyes on me. "Every word."

Well, that was something. "What are you going to do now?"

Felix chuckled. "Honestly? I've no idea. I've got no job. No home. Everything I own is in the back of my truck. I haven't even thought past coming to apologize to you and Dom."

Dammit. I couldn't just let him walk away. "We probably have a spare cabin, if you need a bed. For a little bit."

But he shook his head. "Thank you, but no. I think this is something I kind of need a bit of time to work out. I need to work out what I really want."

He tossed his keys in the air and caught them easily. "See you around, huh?"

"See you around."

I watched him leave, wondering if that was the last time I'd see Dom's brother.

34

Dominic

The next week ticked by agonizingly slowly. Each day blended into the next as I went through the motions. Dad was allowed visitors two days after I arrived, and once that happened, we did a lot of traveling back and forth to the hospital. When I was at the ranch, though, I was working my ass off, trying to help Spencer and Theo get it back into working order.

They were right. There really was too much work for the two of them alone. The more tasks I completed, the more I found extra things that needed doing. I didn't think anyone had touched the paperwork since I'd left. I trawled through my father's office, frowning at the ridiculous price of feed, and vowed to find a new supplier. A quick check of his calendar showed a meeting with the bank about a loan for that very afternoon. "Shit," I muttered. "Theo! Did you know about this bank meeting?"

Theo stuck his head around the doorjamb. "What bank meeting?"

I slumped my head down on the nearest pile of paperwork. "I've no idea. But it's in an hour. So I guess I'll find out."

"Good luck with that."

"Thanks. Super helpful."

He and Spencer had reverted right back to their annoying younger brother statuses now that I was here to run the place. But I'd also watched Spencer spend an entire afternoon studying for an exam, and every night Theo idly flipped through a job listing site when he thought I wasn't paying attention. I didn't really think either of them was going anywhere in the short term, but they were both clearly relieved to be free of the responsibility of running this place.

More and more, I realized that this was why my dad had wanted to pass this place down to me and not one of his biological sons.

Neither of them was here for the long run.

But I didn't think I was either.

I wanted to go back to Georgia. Summer filled my thoughts night and day, and FaceTiming or talking on the phone weren't even close to satisfying the need I had to hold her. I'd watched her fall asleep on my phone screen last night, and all I'd felt was frustration that I wasn't there to brush the hair back off her face or kiss her goodnight.

The two sides of me warred night and day. One side, the side that was the dutiful son, tugged me to stay in Wyoming. While the other side, the one that was so stupidly in love with the girl, yelled to get my ass back on a plane before she realized she could do better.

"You're gonna miss that meeting," Theo said, sticking his head in again. "Better get moving."

I threw a pen at him, but then I dragged my ass out of my father's chair, went back to my cabin for some clean clothes, and the drove myself into town. I made it to the bank with two minutes to spare, and after giving my name to a woman behind the desk, I sat in the waiting area.

I didn't mind the delay. It gave me time to daydream about Summer and what we could be doing right now, if only we weren't in different states.

"Dominic West," a woman called a few minutes later, startling me out of my trance.

She smiled patiently while I gathered the handful of papers I'd thrown together that I thought might be needed, and I followed her down a hall of offices. At the end, she rapped her knuckles across an open glass door and stuck her head inside. "Maria? Your next appointment is here."

The woman walked away, leaving me face-to-face with my biological mother.

Her eyes widened as she recognized me from the single other time we'd met. She glanced down at her paperwork, shuffling through it frantically, mumbling my name like perhaps I'd gotten the wrong office.

I swallowed hard. "You know what? Never mind. I think I've changed my mind."

I strode down the hall, back in the direction I'd come. Fucking hell. This was the last thing I needed. I'd only just put my birth mother's rejection behind me, and now I had to have it shoved in my face again?

"Dominic, wait."

I froze at the sound of her voice saying my name. I didn't want to turn around. I wanted to walk away, just like she had. I wanted her to feel even an ounce of what it had felt like when she'd walked away from me.

But that wasn't who I was.

I turned around and waited for her to say something.

Her fingers trembled, still clutched around the paperwork. The pages shook like a summertime breeze had just rolled through the building. "Could you... Would you come back, please? I'd like to speak with you."

"If it's about the loan, forget it. We'll go somewhere else."

She dropped her hands to her side. "No, not about the loan. I can set you up with another loan officer. I...I can't be involved in your loan process now, since we're..."

I laughed, but it was cold and bitter-sounding. "Related? We might share genetics, but we aren't family."

She motioned to her office. "Please. Will you come inside?"

I moved stiffly toward her, and she stepped out of the way, giving me a wide berth like I was a stray dog that might suddenly snap at her. I ignored it and went inside her office, taking one of the chairs across the desk from hers.

To my surprise, when she walked in, she didn't take the spot behind the computer. Instead she took the seat next to me, the one intended for her clients.

I let out a slow breath, and my gaze wandered over her face. There were similarities in coloring, but I was more like Felix than I was her. "We don't look alike," I said bluntly.

A tiny smile lifted the corner of her mouth. "You're like your uncle. My brother. He died, not long before you were born, but there's definitely a resemblance. Felix does, too. So maybe the two of you are a bit like me."

"What about our father?"

Maria's eyes dropped. "He's not a man you'd want to know. I don't know where he is anymore. But I can give you his name if you want to find out for yourself. Though I don't recommend it. I know you're a grown man, but he'll bring you nothing but pain."

I had enough manners not to say that she'd brought me nothing but pain as well.

She bit her bottom lip. "I'm sorry about how I reacted the day you came to my house. You caught me off guard, and I had to think about my family."

"It's fine, I get it. Felix and I are your dirty little secrets."

She shook her head. "It's not you that I'm ashamed of. It's me." She clasped her hands together, her fingernails digging into her skin. "I'm not the same woman I was. I've thought of you often. Felix has been easy to check in on. But you...you were always something that I couldn't quite grasp. All I knew was that you'd been adopted by a local family. Did you...have they treated you well?"

That at least, was easy to answer. "They're amazing."

The tilt of her lips bloomed into a full-fledged smile. "Good, good. I'm very relieved to hear that. I wish now that I'd been able to give that sort of life to Felix. If I hadn't left him with my mother, things might have been different."

I didn't comment. I really had nothing to say and wondered if I should just get up and leave. Absolving her of her guilt wasn't my job.

But Maria seemed to notice my gaze flicking to the door and rushed to fill the silence. "Felix is back, you know? Staying at my mother's place again." She frowned at that. "She told me what happened. With you and him."

"It is what it is."

She deflated a little. "He's not a bad person, Dominic. You're lucky. You were raised by good people, who obviously cared about you. I researched the property your family owns, in preparation for this meeting. I should have realized who it was, but West is such a common name, it didn't even trigger. But the point is, you've grown up with a privilege that Felix never had. My mother was no more a mother to Felix than she was to me. And look what happened there. At least Felix didn't abandon two babies before he turned twenty."

"No, instead he turned into a thief."

"I don't believe that," Maria said softly. "The sheriff let him go."

"I know." I was well aware of everything that had happened. Summer had filled me in on her conversation with my brother.

"I can't offer either of you a family, Dominic. My husband is religious, and he would never understand. He thinks Felix is my younger brother."

"I have a family," I assured her. "I don't need one that includes you. That wasn't why I sought you out."

She smiled stiffly. "I know you do. But Felix doesn't."

I stood stiffly. "I think it's probably time for me to leave."

Maria nodded, staring up at me as I moved toward the door. I didn't say goodbye, but I'd heard her words. They churned over and over in my brain on my drive home, chipping away at the armor I'd built up ever since Felix's betrayal. And by the time I got home, I knew what I had to do.

35

"Nervous?" Dom's eyes twinkled with amusement even via the video linkup.

Nerves tossed around my gut like a cement mixer, but I shook my head, putting on a brave face. "Nope. I'm fine. Ready to crush it."

"Hell yeah, you are." He squinted at the screen. "Where are you?"

I panned my phone around to show him the completely empty locker room. "Just hanging out here with all my friends." I tried to laugh, but the nerves were getting to me. This was the worst part of being the only female rider at most competitions. The guys would all be in their locker room right now, talking about their rides, and cracking jokes, and giving each other a hard time. There was a sense of camaraderie between them that I was always on the outside of.

Locker rooms were lonely when you were all alone, with too much time to think. It gave the nerves the chance to get the better of you, and that was the last thing I needed tonight. Tonight was my first chance to show everybody I was back. That I still had it. I didn't have to get a big score to continue on with the qualifying rounds, but I wanted to. I wanted to start the season with a ride that knocked the judges' socks off.

I wanted my name at the top of the leaderboard. And I wanted it to still be there in the last round when the top competitors would get to move on to the WBRA tour. Chills danced over my skin at the very thought.

I wanted it so bad I could almost taste it. It was delicious after ignoring it for so long.

I squinted at the screen again. "Where are you? You going to be watching on YouTube? Or I can give Hallie my phone, and you can watch it live."

Dom's mouth lifted at the corners, showing just a hint of the dimple in his cheek. He had the cameras so close to his face that he completely filled the screen. "I'll be watching—"

The video disappeared, reverting back to my home screen. "Dammit." I tapped at the button again, trying to reconnect the call.

A phone rang behind me. I glanced over my shoulder to see who had come into the women's locker room and dropped my phone right out of my hand. It cracked on the cement floor.

Dom folded his arms across his chest and leaned on the cinderblock wall. "Lucky I'm here because I think you just smashed your phone. Ain't nobody going to be watching anything on that screen."

Smashed phone screen forgotten, I launched myself at him with a yell of delight echoing in the quiet room. I threw myself into his arms, wrapping my legs around his waist and my arms behind his neck. "You're here! You said you couldn't come!"

He held me up, his hands beneath my ass, making a seat for me. "And you believed me? You really think I'm going to miss my girl's first rodeo back?"

My heart thumped erratically, and tears pricked the backs of my eyes, but I wasn't going to let them spill over. I ran my fingers through the short lengths of his hair, staring into the eyes I'd missed so much. I hadn't dared to tell him how much I wanted him here. How much I needed him in my corner tonight. I'd played it down during every phone call, knowing his family needed him more than I did. "I didn't want to ask. I was trying not to be selfish."

He brushed a kiss over my lips. "That's not a word I'd use to describe you, Summer Hunt. Smart. Beautiful. Brilliant. Competitive. The love of my life... They're the words I'd use."

A lump clogged my throat, and I tugged him closer. "I love you so much. Thank you."

"Right back at ya. I wouldn't have missed it for the world."

His lips found mine as my feet slowly slid back to the floor, and I pulled his face down, kissing him until all my nerves disappeared. All that was left was the confidence that even if everything went to shit tonight, I had him. Always. Even though we were living apart right now, we were still together.

When we finally stepped apart, though, I frowned. "How's your dad?"

"He wasn't allowed to fly here for your rodeo, much to his disgust, but he's getting there. At least he's out of the hospital now, so it's not as much work for Mom, going back and forth."

"That's great. How long are you here for? Please tell me you aren't jumping straight back on a flight?" I cringed. "I'm getting legless drunk after this, either in a victory celebration, or as a way of commiserating my epic failure. Would be nice to have my boyfriend to buy me drinks at the bar once I get cut off."

He chuckled, brushing a stray hair back off my face. "I'd be honored to be the one who gets to hold your hair back while you puke. I'm here for the night—"

I brushed my lips over his again. "Only one night? Maybe I won't get drunk after all. There's other things I'd rather do with you if I only get you for twenty-four hours."

He kissed me back, but a smile kept curving his lips, making it hard to kiss him properly. Eventually, I gave up and pulled back. "What?"

"You cut me off. What I was going to say was, I'm here for the night. And every night."

My heart stopped. "What?"

"I'm back. For good."

"How, though? Your dad..."

"Is doing well. And I'll definitely be flying home for visits while he's recuperating, or he'll drive my mother insane. But this is my home now. I don't want to be apart from you, Summer."

There was no stopping the tears this time. Happiness burst through me like fireworks, and I wrapped my arms around him again.

He pressed his lips to my forehead and hugged me back.

But niggling doubt and worry crept in. "What about all the work that needs to be done at the ranch, though?" I sucked in a deep breath, already in disbelief at what I knew I was going to say. God dammit. I wanted to be selfish and keep him, but I just couldn't. "I can wait," I promised him. "I can wait for you, as long as you need. I'll do my thing here, and you'll do yours there, and we'll see each other when we can. Maybe when your dad is stronger."

He shut me up by putting his finger to my lips. "I love you for saying that. I know you'd wait. But I already waited years for you. I don't want to wait anymore. Dad will get back on his feet slowly. And Theo and Spencer still want their jobs, at least for now. They just don't want to run the place. But I found someone who does."

"You hired a manager? How did your dad feel about that? You've only ever had family work there."

He brushed a stray tear off my cheek. "Family still is the only ones working there. I hired Felix."

My eyes widened. "No way?"

He nodded. "He was back in Wyoming, staying with his grandmother while he tried to work out what to do. I ran into someone who kind of gave me the idea that Felix needs family even more than I do. I think that's why he stayed working for Frank, you know, even though he knew the man was dodgy. He was just looking for any sort of bond."

I picked up Dom's hand and squeezed it. "So you offered him a job?"

Dom grinned. "Yeah. But I also offered him my cabin. So this thing between you and me?" He gestured back and forth between us. "It better work out, or I'll be the one who's homeless."

Happiness like I'd never known wrapped itself around my heart. I lifted up on my toes and kissed the man I loved once more. "We work, Dom. I've never been more sure of anything in my life."

Dom's answering smile was heart-melting. But then he jerked his head toward the door. "You know what I'm sure of?"

"That I'm going to miss my ride if I don't get my ass out there?"

He slung an arm around my neck, and we walked side by side into the backstage hustle and bustle. He touched his lips to my temple. "I'm sure you're going to go put your name at the top of the leaderboard. And I can't wait to watch you do it."

"Good to have you back, Summer."

I nodded to the guy who'd spoken, vaguely recognizing his face and appreciating his encouragement, but the pit of snakes writhing in my belly snatched the ability to reply.

The man gripped the back of my safety vest, the one all riders were required to wear, and the thing that would hopefully protect me from a horn through my heart.

"I gotcha. You're good to go."

I slapped my palms against my jeans and climbed over the top of the bucking chute. The bull beneath me gave a snort of annoyance, kicking out at the gate and lurching forward, trying to free himself. I had no choice but to get lurched along with him, and my spotter grabbed my vest tighter, making sure I wasn't going to slip off the bull's side and end up beneath his hooves.

"Take it easy," I muttered, as much to myself as the bull. His name was Spin Kick, and I hoped he'd live up to it. He just needed to wait until we got out of the gates.

"You okay?" One of the guys passed me the ropes with a frown of concern.

I couldn't answer him. I was too busy reminding myself that I *was* okay. The last time I had ridden in an arena like this, I'd come off so injured I'd never fully recover. But it had been a turning point in my life that had led me here.

My attention flickered, and for the tiniest moment, I looked up from the ropes and found Dom standing off to the side.

You got this, he mouthed.

Damn straight, I did. This wasn't last time. This wasn't going to end with me crumpled and hurt, lying on the dirt, bleeding.

This was going to end with a winner's buckle on my belt.

Determination roared through me, obliterating everything else. I grinned at Dom and got myself set on the back of the bull, wrapping the rope around my glove, and locking my bad arm in against my chest. My fingers wrapped around my vest.

Eight seconds to glory. That's all I needed.

The gate burst open, and Spin Kick went with it, shooting out into the arena, dirt kicking up beneath his hooves.

I preempted it, moving with him, compensating for my bad arm with the new strength I'd gained in my legs and core. All those months of physical therapy paid off. My heart hammered behind my rib cage, sending adrenaline soaring through my body, but I welcomed it. It focused me, propelled me on, fed my determination until I knew, deep within my gut, there was no way I was falling off.

This bull could buck and kick and throw himself around. But I wasn't getting off until that buzzer sounded.

No way. No how.

Spin Kick launched into his second attack, changing directions, and kicking his back legs so high I was sure he was almost completely vertical.

Yet I hung on.

I hung on until the buzzer sounded, and the crowd around me all leapt to their feet, stamping and cheering and screaming my name. I held on while the green eight-second qualifying ride signal flashed up on a screen. I held on while the bullfighters ran out, circling me and Spin Kick, waiting for me to dismount so they could get him out of the arena.

I waited until it sank in that I'd done it.

"Yes!" I screamed, letting out a war cry that was swallowed up by the crowd. I got my hand free of the ropes, and on Spin Kick's next buck, I got myself off him.

My boots hit the dirt, and muscle memory kicked in. I ran for the fence and hauled myself to the top, twisting back around to stare up at the scoreboard.

The announcer's excited voice pumped through the speakers. "We all knew what she was capable of, and she's done us proud. Summer Hunt with a ninety-two-point-four!"

I blinked, not really sure I'd heard him properly. But a split second later, the score flashed up on the screen. I pumped my good arm into the air, and the crowd around me lit up again.

And then my gaze landed on the man behind the fence. The one standing there in a cowboy hat, cheering that I was his girl. I climbed down the other side of the fence, and he caught me easily, his arms wrapping around me.

"You're back," he said with a grin.

"And so are you."

He ducked his head, gripped the sides of my face, and kissed me long, slow, and hard. I was back in the ring. He was back on my ranch. We were back on track. Together.

EPILOGUE

One Year Later...

Madison Square Garden was like no other stadium I'd ever ridden in before. The crowd screamed a little louder. The pyrotechnics lit up a little brighter. The anticipation in the air thickened in a way I'd never experienced.

Or maybe it was just me, and my full-body reaction to riding in the opening night of the WBRA pro tour.

In the wings of the stadium, surrounded by the other guys I'd be competing against as we traveled the country for the next year, I finally felt like I was where I was supposed to be.

In just a few minutes, I'd be introduced as a professional bull rider for the very first time. My photo would go up on the big screen, my stats displayed beneath it, while the announcer called my name.

My phone buzzed in my hands with an incoming message. I glanced down at it and frowned when Austin's name was displayed on the screen. I hadn't heard from him since the night we'd broken up.

Always knew you could do it. So proud of you, baby. Can we talk when you get home?

Ugh. I deleted the text and blocked his number. But there was no way I was going to let Austin rain on my parade. Not tonight. Not any night. He was no longer my problem. There'd be no talks. He was a chapter of my life that had well and truly closed, and one I had no interest in ever reopening.

The announcer started calling riders out in alphabetical order, and I shuffled forward, nervously waiting for my turn. At the mouth of the tunnel, I looked up into the friends and family section and spotted everyone I loved. My parents. Sisters. Preston, Hallie, and Nate. Felix, Johnny, Isabel, and Dom's other brothers were all here, too.

And Dominic. He wasn't up in the stands. Grave Digger was competing tonight as well. And had been booked for every round of the competition, so Dom was somewhere backstage, making sure he was well cared for and ready to do his job.

But I knew he'd be watching me.

My dad had assigned Dom to be Grave Digger's handler for the entirety of the tour. So this was truly the first night of our new lives. Traveling around the country, just the two of us, a busload of cowboys and a convoy of trucks filled with prize-winning bulls.

All my dreams come true.

I grinned up at the sky, thanking my lucky stars for the life I'd found.

And the man I loved.

"Number seventeen, first woman to ever qualify for the WBRA tour, Summer Hunt!"

The crowd roared my name, and with my heart pounding, I stepped out from the darkness of the tunnels and into the arena. I took off my hat and waved it at the crowd simultaneously trying to find the X marked on the ground in the middle of the arena. That was where I'd been told to stand, so the pyrotechnics didn't set me on fire.

The crowd screamed my name like I was a rock star, and I gazed out at all the proud, smiling faces, focusing in on one little girl who jumped and waved from behind the barrier of the front row. Her cheeks still held the chubbiness of childhood, two pigtails falling from beneath her wide-brimmed hat. I waved right at her, watching as her eyes lit up in excitement.

I hit my mark, and the pyrotechnics lit up the arena in a dazzling display of fire. The orange-yellow flames flew high into the air in huge bursts before the stadium plunged into complete darkness.

I jerked at the sudden, and total lack of light, waiting for the lights to come back on.

They didn't.

Seconds ticked by, and nothing happened.

Something had to be wrong. They shouldn't have taken this long to turn back on. I didn't dare move, though, for fear the pyrotechnics would go off again.

A murmur rippled through the crowd. I sensed people moving around me, but I couldn't see a thing.

The lights suddenly flooded the arena once more, and the crowd let out a relieved breath as one.

Then they saw what I saw.

A shocked gasp ripped through the stadium, slowly turning into a cheer.

Dom grinned up at me from down on one knee, a ring box in his hand. "Surprise?"

My fingers started up a tremble like none I'd ever experienced. "What are you doing?"

"I think you know." He winked at me, like he wasn't even aware there were thousands of people cheering around us right now.

He opened the box, and I gasped at the gorgeous diamond ring inside. It wasn't big or flashy. The diamonds were set into the band, and I knew instantly he'd chosen it because it wouldn't get caught on things while I was riding or working.

It was the sort of ring I could wear every day, a constant reminder of the man who had given it to me. It was as if the crowd disappeared. All I heard, all I saw, all I could think of, was him.

"I love you, Summer. I've loved you long before I ever told you, and I'll love you long after the last time I get to say it. But I want there to be a million times in between. I want to be by your side for all the moments. The bull riding. The teaching. The traveling. Family. Babies. I want to watch you chase your dreams and then conquer them. I want you to watch me achieve mine. Then I want to make new ones together. For the rest of our lives."

He sucked in a breath, like he was suddenly nervous. "Summer? Will you marry me?"

I didn't need to think about it. Not for a single second. "Yes!" I dropped down into the dirt with him, kneeling, not even caring about the ring. All I wanted was him. His lips on mine.

He kissed me soft and slow, arms wrapping around me and holding me tight.

I knew the crowd cheered. I knew somewhere in the stands, our moms would be crying, and our fathers would be shaking hands, and grinning with pride.

But all I saw was him. Our dreams. And a beautiful future where all of them came true.

THE END

The next book in the Dirty Cowboy world is now available! Get **Can't Bucking Wait** here. Or read on for a sneak peek!

Want to know when the next book in the series is available? Join my newsletter to stay up to date with sales, new releases and for free bonus scenes from your favorite cowboy books.

CAN'T BUCKING WAIT PREVIEW

It was kind of ironic that becoming a doctor would be the thing that killed me.

Pain radiated down the back of my neck, a byproduct of hunching over my laptop and the half a dozen phonebook-thick textbooks spread out on the desk around me. I'd lost track of how many hours I'd been here for. Four? Five? And that was on top of a full morning of classes and an afternoon of shadowing a doctor at the hospital.

Amongst the study materials was the evidence of the poor diet I'd been living on. A half-empty Chinese takeout, chopsticks discarded for a fork because I had to get it down quickly in between papers on pathology and microbiology. Candy bar wrappers that had become the main way I stayed awake because there were only so many coffees and energy drinks one could consume before your racing pulse and fluttering heart became a cause for concern.

The words swam across the screen, blurring into one big mess, and not for the first time—that day or that year— I wondered what the hell I was even doing here. My session at the hospital this afternoon hadn't helped that feeling. I couldn't remove the image of a mother crying over her sick child, while explaining to us that she hadn't sought help because they had no insurance and couldn't afford the bill that would likely bankrupt them.

My roommate, Zach, stretched out on the couch behind me, his long legs propped up on the armrest while he watched a zombie apocalypse movie with a huge bowl of popcorn resting on his flat stomach.

His head swiveled in my direction when he noticed me looking his way, his lips moving.

I pulled an AirPod from my ear. "What was that?"

"I said, you could join me, you know? All that moaning and groaning coming from your direction is making me think it's you who needs a doctor. I'm not trained for anything other than making cocktails."

"Sorry," I muttered. I hadn't realized I'd been making any sorts of noises. The fact Zach had picked up on my frustration levels meant I was in a pretty bad state. He wasn't exactly the most observant of roommates, and we didn't really do feelings. "I probably just need a break."

"This chick is about to get eaten, and not in the fun, sexy way. If you know what I mean."

Heat flushed my cheeks at the implication of oral sex, and I busied myself by picking up my phone so I didn't have to answer him. I let my long dark hair fall around my face so Zach wouldn't see the pink in my cheeks.

I scrolled through my phone messages, though there wasn't much to see. My mom and my older sister, Summer, were the top two entries. Zach the third, his message chat filled with one-sentence replies to my questions on whether we had any milk or reminders that his half of the rent was due. A girl from one of my classes who I studied with once a month rounded out the top four.

Somewhere below that was my other sister, my twin, Callie. But there may as well have been tumbleweed emojis surrounding her name. That's how long it had been since she'd messaged me.

Or vice versa. I hadn't messaged her either.

I tapped the top entry, my mother's, and smiled at the love that poured through her past texts. She messaged me most days, but only ever once, just to check in and make sure I was still alive. She'd told me many a time that she didn't want to cramp my style now that I was living in another state, even though I'd reassured her that I wanted to hear what was going on at home. Unlike most twentysomethings, who actively avoided their parents' calls in favor of parties and friends, I wished mine called more.

Despite already checking in with her this morning, I tapped out a question.

How's the bridesmaids' fittings going? Is there anything I can do to help?

The little dots that indicated she was replying popped up immediately, and I opened another candy bar while I waited. The sugary goodness hit my tongue, delivering instant satisfaction, and probably adding an extra curve to my hips, but I munched on anyway. I still had hours of study left before I could collapse into bed. I needed something to get me through. I didn't smoke or drink or do drugs. I needed at least one vice.

Everything is going great. Wait until you see your dress. You're going to love it.

Both my mother and Summer had refused to send me a photo of the bridesmaids' dresses, Summer insistent that I needed to see it in person to appreciate its beauty.

I wasn't concerned about not liking it. Neither me nor my older sister were much into clothes, especially not dresses, but Callie was. She wouldn't have been shy about voicing her distaste for a dress if she hadn't liked it.

I would happily wear a brown paper sack to Summer and Dominic's wedding. I just wanted to be there, standing next to her when she married the love of her life.

A spear of jealousy shot through me, disintegrating quickly in my happiness for her. But a familiar throb of homesickness replaced it.

What if mine doesn't fit? I could come home this weekend. Try it on...

The idea took hold so swiftly it knocked the tension right out of my shoulders. A quick trip home wouldn't really hurt...I had finals coming up, and a lot of studying to do, but I could do that on the plane. Zach would definitely appreciate having the apartment to himself for a while. I'd walked out of my room at two this morning for a glass of water and had found him dry humping one of the waitresses from his work against a wall. I'd just been grateful he hadn't been naked.

No need. We have Callie's measurements.

I bit my lip. I hadn't been home in over six months. I hadn't seen Callie in longer, because she'd gone skiing with a friend at Christmas instead of coming home. I'd been back at school by the time she'd returned. I was pretty sure that had been a deliberate move on her part, but it meant I had no idea if we were even still the same size. The candy bar wrapper crinkled in my fingers.

I can't wait to see you at the wedding, baby, but I know you have a lot of study to do so I won't keep you. Talk in the morning. Three weeks to go!

I sighed and looked over at said study. Three weeks felt like a lifetime when you wanted to be anywhere else.

Not ready to drop that link to my home and family, I

dialed Summer's number, grinning when she answered with a squeal that was most unlike her.

"What are you doing calling me? Aren't you in the middle of studying for finals?"

A trickle of guilt rolled down my spine at the reminder. "I am. I'm just...taking a break. I wanted to see how the wedding prep is going? It's only a few weeks away."

She groaned. "Don't remind me. Dom is being the biggest bridezilla. He and Callie have organized some sort of flower arch that I really don't know about..."

I laughed. "What's wrong with a flower arch? That sounds beautiful."

I could practically hear the scrunch of Summer's nose. "Bit over the top, don't you think?"

"I think you'd get married in boots and cow shit if Dom let you."

"What's wrong with that?"

The funny thing was, she wasn't even joking. My older sister lived for her cowboy lifestyle. She rode bulls on the pro circuit, Dominic traveling with her as a handler for the bulls we had on tour. In the middle of our family ranch, surrounded by animals and dirt and sweat was where she was happiest.

It was no surprise they'd chosen to get married on the ranch. Summer wouldn't have had it any other way.

But a pretty flower arch never hurt anyone.

I tried again to offer my services. "I could come home and help with the decorations? Sounds like someone needs to keep Dom under control."

Summer's cute laugh tinkled in my ear and set off another pang of longing. I missed her.

"Don't be silly. Mom said you have finals two days before

the wedding. It's such bad timing for you, I know. I'm sorry. You know I would have made it later if I could."

I shook my head, even though she couldn't see it. "You guys don't get long off from the tour. I understand. It's no problem at all."

"Even less than we thought, actually. Brad Pruitt called yesterday. We're back on the road two days after the wedding." She chuckled. "Our honeymoon is going to be spent with an eight-hundred-pound bull and a bus filled with cowboys who don't shower as often as they should. How romantic."

My heart squeezed. "You're gone that quickly?"

"Mom didn't tell you? I thought she would have said something in her daily 'is my baby still alive' texts to you. We all had dinner last night, and I told them then."

She hadn't. I couldn't help the disappointment that coursed through me. And the irrational hurt that they'd all been together without me. I'd thought I'd have at least a couple of weeks of the summer to hang out with my family after the wedding. Now it seemed all the quality time was happening before it.

I was missing it all.

"Summer, get off the phone. I need your opinion on the bouquets. You still haven't told me whether you want all neutrals or a splash of color..."

The voice somewhere in Summer's background was as familiar to me as my own. "Is that Callie?"

I already knew it was.

"Yeah, she's here to torture me with more flower decisions. Do you want to talk to her?"

I opened my mouth to say I did but then closed it when Summer said, "Oh, wait a minute..."

Callie's voice was a low hiss. "Is that Lennon?"

Summer must have nodded in the affirmative.

There was a noise, and I suspected Summer had pressed the phone to her body while she argued with Callie. Their muffled voices carried through to me, but I couldn't make out the individual words.

By the time Summer spoke to me again, I already knew what she was going to say. "Callie didn't want to talk to me, did she?"

"She had to run back to the main house for something..."

I wondered if the excuse felt as weak on Summer's tongue as it did to my ears.

That same old familiar hurt sprang up. It was easy to ignore it here, surrounded by classmates, and teachers, and practical rotations at the hospital. But all of this only widened the gap between me and my twin.

We'd always been our own people, so different it was hard to believe we'd actually shared a womb at one time. But this rift that existed between us now...this was deeper and wider than any differences we'd had in the past. A crack had marred the foundation of our relationship when we'd both fallen for the same guy and had erupted the night I'd found her in his bed.

It was easy to say never let a man come between friends.

It was a lot harder when the woman was the sister you'd long felt inferior to.

And when you were truly, stupidly in love with the man.

Even if he hadn't known it.

There had been no argument. No drawn-out yelling match where we spewed hurt and jealous feelings at each other. I'd just quietly left for college.

But the damage had been done anyway. It bled in the silence of my phone and the calls that neither of us made. It was there in the way she avoided coming home when she knew I'd be there.

Something had broken between me and Callie that night. Something we hadn't been able to fix in the two years since.

I said goodbye to Summer and dropped my head down onto my hands.

"You good, Len?"

I jumped at Zach's voice. I'd almost forgotten he was there. I plastered on a fake smile before I glanced over my shoulder at him. "Sure. Fine. Just a bit stressed."

"Family will do that to you. That's why I don't talk to mine." He stood and crossed the space between us, putting his hand to the back of my neck and digging his fingers into the tight muscles there. "Jesus Christ, woman. Your neck is like a rock. You need to chill out."

I laughed, letting him knead out the tension in my muscles. We didn't do physical touch. We were friends, but that was it. He wasn't a hugger. Well, not unless he was dick deep in someone, and he'd certainly never been there with me. But I craved affection. I hadn't had so much as a hug since the last time I'd seen my mother, and that felt like a very long time ago. So Zach's warm palm on my neck was welcome.

All too quickly, though, he stopped, patting me on the neck like I was a good dog.

He pulled a joint from his pocket. "You want to smoke some weed? It's better than any massage."

I shook my head. "No thanks." I'd never tried pot and had no desire to start. I doubted getting baked would help my studying any. "I've got my candy. That'll have to do." I held it up then took another bite to emphasize my point.

He shrugged. "Sex?"

I choked on the huge chunk of chocolate in my mouth. "Sex?"

He chuckled at me. "Oh, that's right. I forgot. You don't do that. Neither for fun nor stress relief." He lit up the joint around his grin. "You know you're seriously missing out, right?"

Heat flushed my cheeks again, and not for the first time, embarrassment rose over my complete and utter lack of sexual experience. "Oh, I've heard everything I'm missing out on through our bedroom walls. They aren't that thick, you know."

He took a drag on his joint, slowly blowing out the smoke in my direction.

I waved it away with the back of my hand.

"Anytime you want to join me in there, you know you're welcome."

From anyone else, that might have sounded sleazy. But I was comfortable with him after sharing four walls with the man for all this time. I was well aware that to him, sex was no big deal. He wasn't pressuring me. He was simply offering a stress-relief service.

One that would probably be quite enjoyable, if the moans and screams of pleasure that filtered through our walls most nights were anything to go by.

"Not gonna happen, but as always, thank you for the offer."

He kissed the top of my head in a brotherly fashion and went back to his zombie movie.

I tried to refocus my efforts on the paper I was supposed to be writing, but it was a losing battle. The talk of sex and thoughts of home swirled miserably in my brain until I gave up for the night and shut down my computer. I didn't bother turning on the light in my bedroom. I stripped to my underwear and crawled beneath the sheets.

There was only one person I'd ever thought about having sex with. And he was a thousand miles away, on a ranch in Georgia.

Homesick to my core, I fell asleep missing the open fields, the clean fresh air, and the man who had never wanted to be mine.

Get Preston and Lennon's swoon worthy romance here and catch up with ALL the Dirty Cowboys, their ladies, and their kids!

ALSO BY ELLE THORPE

Dirty Cowboy series (complete)

*Talk Dirty, Cowboy (Dirty Cowboy, #1)

*Ride Dirty, Cowboy (Dirty Cowboy, #2)

*Sexy Dirty Cowboy (Dirty Cowboy, #3)

*Dirty Cowboy boxset (books 1-3)

*25 Reasons to Hate Christmas and Cowboys (a Dirty Cowboy bonus novella, set before Talk Dirty, Cowboy but can be read as a standalone, holiday romance)

Buck Cowboys series (Spin off from the Dirty Cowboy series. Ongoing.)

*Buck Cowboys (Buck Cowboys, #1)

*Buck You! (Buck Cowboys, #2)

*Can't Bucking Wait (Buck Cowboys, #3)

*Mother Bucker (Buck Cowboys, #4)

The Only You series (Contemporary romance. Complete)

*Only the Positive (Only You, #1) - Reese and Low.

*Only the Perfect (Only You, #2) - Jamison.

*Only the Truth - (Only You, bonus novella) - Bree.

*Only the Negatives (Only You, #3) - Gemma.

*Only the Beginning (Only You, #4) - Bianca and Riley.

*Only You boxset

Saint View High series (Reverse Harem, Bully Romance. Complete)

*Devious Little Liars (Saint View High, #1)

*Dangerous Little Secrets (Saint View High, #2)

*Twisted Little Truths (Saint View High, #3)

Saint View Prison series (Reverse harem, romantic suspense. Complete.)

*Locked Up Liars (Saint View Prison, #1)

*Solitary Sinners (Saint View Prison, #2)

*Fatal Felons (Saint View Prison, #3)

Saint View Psychos series (Reverse harem, romantic suspense. Complete.)

*Start a War (Saint View Psychos, #1)

*Half the Battle (Saint View Psychos, #2)

*It Ends With Violence (Saint View Psychos, #3)

Saint View Rebels (Reverse harem, romantic suspense)

*Rebel Revenge (Saint View Rebels, #1)

*Rebel Obsession (Saint View Rebels, #2)

*Rebel Heart (Saint View Rebels, #3)

Saint View Slayers Vs. Sinners (Reverse harem, romantic suspense. Complete)

*Wife Number One (Saint View Slayers Vs. Sinners, #1)

*Torn in Two (Saint View Slayers Vs. Sinners, #2)

*Three to Fall (Saint View Slayers Vs. Sinners, #3)

Saint View Murder Squad(Reverse harem, romantic suspense. Coming 2025)

* X's and O's (Saint View Murder Squad, #1)

*Whips and Chains (Saint View Murder Squad, #2)

*Reaper and Ruin (Saint View Murder Squad, #3)

Saint View Strip (Male/Female, romantic suspense standalones. Complete)

*Evil Enemy (Saint View Strip, #1)

*Unholy Sins (Saint View Strip, #2)

*Killer Kiss (Saint View Strip, #3)

*Caged Bird (Saint View Strip, #4)

Add your email address here to be the first to know when new books are available!

www.ellethorpe.com/newsletter

Join Elle Thorpe's readers group on Facebook!

www.facebook.com/groups/ellethorpesdramallamas

ACKNOWLEDGMENTS

So, do we love Dominic as much as we loved his dad, Johnny? I know I do. Johnny has been my favorite from my cowboy books for a long time, but I think Dominic might have knocked him off the top spot. Seems only fitting that Johnny's son was the one to take his crown haha.

Summer and Dominic's romance wasn't an easy one for me to write. I cursed them many a time during the writing process. Just ask my readers group, and my newsletter. They got to hear all my frustrations as I wrote. But you know what? The best stories are always the ones that push me the most. And I love how Buck You turned out. Though who is next? Callie or Lennon? Preston? Maybe one of Dominic's brothers? I don't know yet, but maybe they'll go easier on me? Doubtful haha. But do let me know if you have a preference. I love hearing from you guys.

Thank you to Jolie Vines, Zoe Ashwood, Emmy Ellis and Karen Hrdlicka who make up my stellar editing team. And an extra thanks to Jo and Zoe for being my author besties too! Thank you to Sara Massery for the chats, sprints, and graphic design advice. Thank you to Shellie, Lissanne, Kirsty, and Louise for your early feedback. A massive thank you to my promo and review team for always being there for me.

And as always, a huge thank you to my family. To Jira, Thomas, Flick, and Heidi. You four are the loves of my life and I couldn't do any of this without you.

Love, Elle x

ABOUT THE AUTHOR

Elle Thorpe lives on the sunny east coast of Australia. When she's not writing stories full of kissing, she's a wife and mummy to three tiny humans. She's also official ball thrower to one slobbery dog named Rollo. Yes, she named a female dog after a dirty hot character on Vikings. Don't judge her. Elle is a complete and utter fangirl at heart, obsessing over The Walking Dead and Outlander to an unhealthy degree. But she wouldn't change a thing.

You can find her on Facebook or Instagram(@ellethorpebooks or hit the links below!) or at her website www.ellethorpe.com. If you love Elle's work, please consider joining her Facebook fan group, Elle Thorpe's Drama Llamas or joining her newsletter here. www.ellethorpe.com/newsletter

facebook.com/ellethorpebooks
instagram.com/ellethorpebooks
goodreads.com/ellethorpe
tiktok.com/@ellethorpebooks

www.ingramcontent.com/pod-product-compliance
Lightning Source LLC
LaVergne TN
LVHW091252150826
845673LV00006B/1391

* 9 7 8 1 9 2 2 7 6 0 6 9 2 *